Veronica Sweeney
After failing f...
Tasmania, she ...
actress and ...
Emancipist, was ...
novel, *South Li...*
novel, *A Turn of ...* in 1996, was
a departure from the historical settings of her
previous books and the first of a series of novels to
be set in modern-day America. *Dark Obsession*
continues in the psychological thriller vein, but is
set in modern-day Australia. Veronica lives on the
north coast of New South Wales, but travels
extensively to research her work.

Dark Obsession

Dark Obsession

VERONICA SWEENEY

HarperCollins*Publishers*

HarperCollins*Publishers*

First published in Australia in 1997
by HarperCollins*Publishers* Pty Limited
ACN 009 913 517
A member of HarperCollins*Publishers* (Australia) Pty Limited Group
http://www.harpercollins.com.au

HarperCollins*Publishers*
25 Ryde Road, Pymble, Sydney, NSW 2073, Australia
31 View Road, Glenfield, Auckland 10, New Zealand
77–85 Fulham Palace Road, London W6 8JB, United Kingdom
Hazelton Lanes, 55 Avenue Road, Suite 2900, Toronto, Ontario M5R 3L2
and 1995 Markham Road, Scarborough, Ontario M1B 5M8, Canada
10 East 53rd Street, New York NY 10032, USA

National Library Cataloguing-in-Publication data:

Sweeney, Veronica Geoghegan.
  Dark obsession.
  ISBN 0 7322 5893 6.
  I. Title.
A823.3

Cover photograph: The Photo Library/James Randkley
Set in Sabon 10.5/14.5 by Midland Typesetters
Printed in Australia by Griffin Press on 79 gsm Bulky Paperback

5 4 3 2 1
01 00 99 98 97

This book is —
just has to be —
for Jill Hickson,
for her unfailing belief in it.

DECTORA

  Does wandering in these desolate seas
  And listening to the cry of wind and wave
  Bring madness?

FORGAEL

  Queen, I am not mad . . .
  If it be not that hearing messages
  From lasting watchers that outlive the moon,
  At the most quiet midnight is to be stricken.

DECTORA

  And did those watchers bid you take me captive?

FORGAEL

  Both you and I are taken in the net.

DECTORA

  . . . I understand you now,
  You have a Druid craft of wicked sound
  Wrung from the cold women of the sea –
  A magic that can call a demon up,
  Until my body give you kiss for kiss.

FORGAEL

  Your soul shall give the kiss.

DECTORA

  I am not afraid,
  While there's a rope to run into a noose,
  Or wave to drown. But I have done with words,
  And I would have you look into my face
  And know that it is fearless.

FORGAEL

  Do what you will,
  For neither I nor you can break a mesh
  Of the great golden net that is about us.

W. B. Yeats
The Shadowy Waters

LEO

How do you explain passion to an archbishop? The invitation into his presence lies before me, clear black type on crisp white paper, and the Archdiocesan crest at the top of the page. The same emblem graces the envelope also, and, although I had half-expected it, when an owlish Mrs O'Donnell placed it in my hand on my return from the hospital, I felt my stomach contract with apprehension.

A pupil summoned to the headmaster's office . . . And this analogy brings St Jude's so close, so very close, that I can almost smell the beloved place. Did it all begin at St Jude's? But I followed orders – I did only what I was told.

I did not follow my heart. I chose obedience over conscience.

Evil flourishes when good men do nothing.

I have led such a quiet life. A boring life, I'm sure, to most people. At best, a popular but ungifted teacher, a capable but uncharismatic priest, I have done the best I can with a character lacking in any real personality. I am a grey sort of man. Mine is not the adventurous spirit that sails forth to discover new worlds, nor even the stable, solid wharf that awaits the return of the voyagers. I am like the buffer of rubber along the quays. I am a soft man. My only gift is that I have been able, on occasion, to smooth the way for others, quietly, unobtrusively. I think, when I die, my friends will say, "What, poor old Leo gone?" And, on meditation, "He was a good man, a good worker."

Now I think about it, that would not be a bad epitaph.

What I am questioning, I suppose is – why me? I no longer sleep through the night, and, when I awake, there are voices in my head. Ghosts of the dead, and of the living. Still explaining to me. When the voices stop my own mind begins, listing and re-listing what I *should have done*. A more knowledgeable man would have seen more, a more confident man would have done more.

If I had not led such a quiet life . . .

And now the voices will never leave me. I am the recipient of others' pain. I have known so little of my own, and now, filled with the pain of others, I have no catalogue of my own, no system of file and retrieval to help me deal with this. Their pain lies entangled about my heart, and I grieve, and I grieve for them.

His Grace will want opinions, conclusions. "Surely, Father, you who knew them all so well, who knew the boy for twenty-two years – surely you have a theory?"

I must telephone him and agree to his meeting. In three days time, at two in the afternoon. Doubtless he has cancelled all his afternoon appointments. He will seat me in a comfortable armchair, and he will take another – probably by the window – and he will turn his rather heavy, kindly face towards me, and say, "This terrible business of Mark Parrish and the Harcourts – how did it come about?"

I will have to tell His Grace of the existence of the tapes. More, I must inform him that all fifty-three of them, and the nine diaries, are in my possession.

"My dear Leo," he will say, the thick grey brows lifted in disbelief and remaining there in concern, "you must take them to the police at once!"

I would, of course, (I will tell him) if I thought that anyone could be helped by the knowledge of their existence. But, could Your Grace say that, in all truth?

The thick grey brows will remain arched, for he will, at this, be asking himself if this is, indeed, Leo Calder, speaking to him in such a manner.

And I will continue speaking, with, I hope, common sense and impartiality, for His Grace and the Church are all that stand between me and the world, and I am all that stands between Geoffrey, Rosalind, Linda and Mark – and that same world that would claw and gloat and ridicule their names. And I will not have it.

The Archbishop's Dinner is the largest and most important event on the Church's social calendar. This year, as every year, I accompanied Doctor Linda Parrish. And, as every year, we had a port together afterwards, seated on either side of the fireplace in the library of that great dark house on Castle Crag Road.

The house was not as menacing as that description suggests, for there were gardens and green lawns, and the sounds of the children and dogs of wealthy young neighbours floated over the hedges on warm afternoons and weekends. Still, I wished that Linda would sell the house. For her sake, and for her son's. Mark hated it. He rarely spoke of it, but he stayed in that house for Linda's sake, nothing more.

It is like a museum, that house. Taller than it is wide, with verandahs that give it an illusion of warmth and welcome, and ancient ivy plants that break up the bulwark expanses of stone between the high and narrow windows. The verandahs are the only concession to the house being in Sydney, Australia. Take away the verandahs and the house – both the grounds without and the decor within – is pure Hampstead Heath.

The house had been built by Bill's grandfather. And there, in surroundings redolent of Parrish old money, tradition and faded memories, Linda remained. "For Mark's sake," she would murmur in that deep and beautifully modulated voice, "I must keep the house for Mark's sake." Mark, whose small feet as a boy, in their shiny, regulation St Jude's shoes, had rarely passed over the threshold. Mark who, at eighteen and a man, finally strode through the door and demanded to come home.

I must not pass judgements. I must not draw my own conclusions, nor must I run ahead of myself, nor digress. I cannot afford for His Grace to be puzzled, impatient. Yet this is difficult for me. I am not an articulate man, and the voices have spoken too loud, too long in my dreams, and old resentments are ready to fly off my tongue as if they were my own.

We drank a port or two, Linda and I, after the Archbishop's Dinner, and we spoke of friends, and of Mark, and of my work, and of Linda's psychiatric practice – but mostly we spoke of Mark.

He was our child. Good grief, I must not use that phrase in front of His Grace. But, after all that has happened, I can say this to myself, at least – for better or worse, Linda and I shared the responsibility of raising Mark. She, with his father Bill, until he was five years old, when she placed him in my care. Placed him with St Jude's, but I was in charge of the infants' school, and was thus responsible. And I remain responsible.

I hate that house on Castle Crag Road, because it's a kind of shrine. Linda would deny it, but it *is* a shrine – to Bill Parrish and those happy years she had known with him. But he left them, the beautiful, intelligent, loyal wife and the handsome, loving, sensitive little boy. So they came to me, guided into my path by an omniscient God, whom I cannot help but feel picked the wrong man for the job.

Over the port, this year, our talk was mainly of Mark, and it was worrying. "I know he ought to have friends – I'm as aware as you that he's work-oriented, impatient, perhaps a little arrogant. It's hard not to be, when one is as gifted and intelligent as Mark, and when one is involved in such a stressful field as oncology. But this friendship has been going on for six months, Leo – the woman is *married*. And, through her husband she's a sort of . . . media personality." I could hear the touch of distaste in Linda's voice.

"They're not . . . I mean, he's not having an affair?"

"No. Don't be horrified, but a brief affair, over in a few weeks, wouldn't worry me. She's older than he is, and he has no experience of women – the encounter wouldn't do him any harm." Linda lifted her firm little chin and gazed at me, defiantly. I was not horrified, but I was certainly shocked. Over the ten years since Mark came to live with her, Linda had come to depend on him more and more. She was never in any hurry for Mark to find a girlfriend, a wife – it was as if, having discovered her son, she wished to hold him to herself a little, to make up for lost time. And so much time had been lost. To hear her then, speaking like that, brought it home to me how very concerned she was.

"Rosalind Harcourt is a very wealthy woman," I said. "You introduced them yourself, didn't you, at a charity function for the psychiatric unit? Perhaps, with the Children's Hospital needing money . . ."

"He's not interested in her money." Linda turned towards the fire in the hearth. "And anyway, it's her husband's money."

"He's a very generous man, I believe. And she does so much for charity – "

"What else can she do? She was nothing when he married her, some kind of showgirl. She has no career of her own."

"A showgirl?" I reviewed my few sightings of Rosalind Harcourt, in newspapers and magazines, and, lately, at her husband's side when he was surrounded by press clamouring for questions about his besieged empire. A slender woman in her late thirties, well-groomed and expensively dressed, hair always worn back from her face – thick, dark hair, like Linda's. Now I thought about it, a manner, a shape of face, a style, very much like Linda's.

Linda, usually generous and always honest, was amending her words. "No, I was being unfair because I'm cross. She wasn't a showgirl, she was a dancer – a legitimate one – with the Australian Ballet, actually."

"She looks a little like you."

To try to explain anything to this exceptional woman that she did not want to hear was always difficult. Her head, with its coils of heavy hair, came up and around to me, and her eyes, hazel, but very dark in the faint light, gave me a look of impatience before her interest and her gaze slid away from me and all I wished to say.

"You must have noticed – the same colouring – though she's not as beautiful as you." And this was not flattery, for even at fifty-two years old, Linda Parrish was a very beautiful woman. "Perhaps, because she looks like you, Mark feels more able to relax with Rosalind . . ."

She did not think much of my theory, and cut across my words, "Leo, I want you to have a talk with Mark."

"But – "

"He'll listen to you. He respects you."

"He respects *you*. If you tell him that the relationship is causing you distress . . ." I stopped. "What is it that bothers you, Linda? If it's an innocent friendship – "

"She has a whole coterie of eligible men who dance attendance on her. Her husband's always too busy to accompany her to most social events. Oh, she's not alone in that – I know lots of women who do the same – and lots of men, mostly gay, who are only too happy to be invited into the charmed circle."

"Gay? Homosexual?"

"Don't be naive, Leo, it's been going on for centuries. The husband is too busy, the wife has to have an escort – who better than a young man whose natural predilections place him beyond suspicion?"

"But not all these men were – are – homosexuals, surely? Gigolos are heterosexual – "

"So one would hope," Linda interrupted, drily. "Do you see why I'm concerned? My son should be dating a string of vacuous young nurses, but instead he's making a fool of himself over a woman thirteen years his senior, as well as running the risk of being labelled a homosexual or a gigolo."

I considered her words, chewing my lip a little as I tried to find something positive to say. "Perhaps this woman might be able to draw Mark out of himself a little. He's always been so competitive, so work-oriented, as you say. From his friendship with Mrs Harcourt he may move on quite naturally to a young woman of his own age and interests. And a little gossip – that would be forgotten soon, surely?"

"I don't want any slurs against my son. He's surrounded by jealousies – always was. The scholarships and awards he won when he was studying, the success of his private practice. And he's so good-looking – people think it's been easy for him because of his looks, his money – only you and I know how hard he's worked, and the price he's paid, all his life. I don't want this woman making a fool of him, leading him on, taking advantage of him."

I knew, then, what made Linda afraid. That Mark would fall in love, genuinely in love, with this dangerous Mrs Harcourt. "Oh, no, Linda. Mark wouldn't allow himself to . . ."

But suddenly it *was* possible. And those possibilities fell smoothly into place like well-oiled machinery made to enmesh and turn. If any kind of woman could bring Mark's interest from his vocation – and his work was more than a profession, it *was* a vocation to him – then it would be such a woman. So like his mother, a woman of style and sophistication, but with the spontaneity and natural gregariousness of a youth spent in the theatre, with the practised ease and grace of a woman who had become a gifted hostess and a social asset to her husband's way of life.

But, of course, I did not say any of this to Linda. For the first time, I saw that perhaps it had been a bad thing for Mark to come home after matriculating from St Jude's – not just because of the house, with its memories of his oncologist father whose footsteps Mark had tried so desperately to follow. Mark loved Linda, and he needed her, but I suddenly realised how difficult it must be for him, as difficult as it was for myself, to tell this woman things that she simply did not wish to hear.

I sat there, that evening, waiting for Mark to come home. Linda went to bed, and I was left alone with the firelight and one soft lamp glowing, and the smell of cedar and old leather that came luxuriously from the high shelves and their burden of books. Perhaps it was the smell, but I had been dreaming of St Jude's when I awoke from a doze and glanced, startled, at the clock. It was twenty to three, and Mark's footsteps, swift and purposeful, despite the thick carpet of the hall, were approaching the door.

He entered the room abruptly, shutting the door after him with a controlled movement that bespoke the fact that he would have slammed it, if he had dared. The only lamp burning was that by Linda's empty chair, and Mark's angry glance took this in as he strode without pause to the drinks cabinet.

I should have spoken immediately, but could not gather my still drowsy wits in the face of his obvious agitation, the sudden snap and charge of his presence. Mark is a heavy-shouldered young man, six foot three inches tall, and now he seemed to fill the room, bringing his pain and rage with him. I felt like an interloper. He yanked at the bow-tie and collar of his evening suit, the whisky decanter chimed dangerously hard against the lip of

11

his glass, and I heard, rather than saw, the liquor spill, heard Mark's breath coming in gasps. I sat paralysed in my chair.

He turned and saw me.

"*Shit!* I mean . . . God, Leo, what are you trying to do, lurking there in the shadows?"

"I'm not lurking," I managed, "and stop your blaspheming. Pour me a whisky too, will you?"

He glared a moment longer, then turned and did as I bid him. He handed me my glass. I took it and thanked him and watched him calm himself, slowly, with difficulty, for my benefit. He was standing by the fireplace, his fair hair and the normally calm strength of his features were lit on one side by the flickering of flames, so the shadow play gave the illusion of him being half-devoured. I shivered. First the wild rage, now a quiet, unblinking stare as he gazed into a corner of the hearth, unseeing. I realised that Linda had been right to be worried.

"Something's wrong, something's very wrong," I murmured, and became aware that I had spoken aloud only when he turned to me.

"No. Not at all. What makes you say that?"

"I . . . I couldn't help but notice – you seemed so agitated when you came in. I thought – "

"Where's my mother?"

Mark did not usually interrupt me. He has kept much of his early respect for me, and I have, perhaps, become too easily gratified and flattered. I now looked at him a little coolly before informing him that his mother had felt tired and had retired early. "I fell asleep," I added. "I wanted to wait to see you – it's been a few weeks now – you never seem to be home when I call."

Mark turned away at the mention of his mother's name, and I could not judge, from his uncommunicative back, just what he was thinking. This was unlike Mark, dangerously unlike his usual controlled, courteous self.

"She wanted to leave us alone together, so you could give me a fatherly lecture on the subject of Rosalind Harcourt." And he turned to look at me, smiling a little.

I had not expected this. "I . . . It . . ."

"I don't mind." He moved away from the fireplace into the room, and switched on another light. Suddenly he was more approachable, more open. The shadows of the room, like the shadows within Mark, seemed to lift abruptly.

"I'm sorry if I seem to be acting strangely. It was a ghastly day. Young Michael Halvorson – I told you about him, didn't I? We lost him this afternoon."

"Oh, Mark – I am sorry. How old was he?"

"Nine. He was nine." Mark was gazing down into his glass, turning its contents about. He said, then, in a different voice, "I wonder if I'm in the wrong field. I didn't think . . . it's devastating. Even when expected. We were working on him for three years, you know. I knew him for three years."

"You did all you could, I'm sure."

"We all did. Everyone's gone out to get drunk tonight. It's affected us all – even Professor Stewart. She took me for coffee this afternoon – can you imagine it? The Iron Angel herself."

"Mark . . ."

"I should have gone off by myself this evening – instead I took Rosalind Harcourt to a production of *Madame Butterfly* and drank too much champagne in the intervals. *Do* you want to talk about Rosalind Harcourt?"

I did not answer immediately. Words do not come easily to me. At the seminary the most common criticism of my homilies was that they were ponderous. I pondered hard now. "Do *you* want to talk about Mrs Harcourt?"

"So you can report everything back to my mother?"

"Mark – "

"No. No, I'm sorry. Well – what's there to say to stop your dear old head from growing more grey hairs? Rosalind and I are very close friends. I've been able to speak to her about my work, about the pressures, about lots of things. She's a good listener – better than my mother. My mother has perfected the art of selective listening – have you noticed that? Perhaps all psychiatrists do. Perhaps it comes after years of people yattering nonsense at you."

"Mark – were you in love with Rosalind Harcourt?"

14

He paused, and gave what was close to his old grin. "I like the way you use the past tense. It gives me an option – I can declare that I was, but am no longer. I hope I don't disappoint you, but no, I wasn't in love with her. Nor am I now. I was one of several male friends who enjoy the same cultural pursuits as she does. We became very close, as I said, but it was always platonic."

We looked at each other for a long moment. Mark's eyes are a pale, clear blue, and rather pronounced, giving the impression that he may be short-sighted. But he is not. His gaze has always been steady, intense. At school, to less secure boys, it had often held a challenge. Until he grew to be the biggest boy in the school, until he became our best athlete and scholar, he often had to fight – but frequently he could stare down an opponent with that look. Now he stared me down.

"I'm glad," I murmured. "I'm sorry if it seemed as if I were prying."

"You have every right to." He took rather a large gulp of his drink. "Do you know," he began, suddenly, "I used to daydream, when I was a boy, that you'd leave the brotherhood and marry my mother, so you could become my father."

I stared at him. He had thought that? I was so moved, so surprised, I could not speak. But then –

"Instead, you bowed to pressure from the Archbishop and searched around beneath your love

15

of teaching, of poetry, of football, to see if you couldn't come up with a vocation. And you did. Obliging Leo. So you forewent your teaching career and became a priest, thereby becoming 'Father' anyway. Why did you do it?"

Was he drunk? Whisky, on top of champagne?

I tried to find an answer. "It was pointed out to me, quite correctly, that the Church could always find lay teachers, while priests – "

"I envy you." He spoke calmly, but his voice cut across my words and made me stop. Mark has a deep voice, as pleasant in a man, as mellifluous, as his mother's in a woman. Neither needed to shout or raise their voice at all in order to gain attention. Their voices were easy to listen to. But it was Mark's words that silenced me.

"How comforting that must be – to follow orders. Not to have to question, to search one's conscience. Yes, I envy you. You can walk through life totally blameless."

"Mark!"

It was worse than even Linda believed. Never had I heard him speak this way. Moved as I was by his saying that he wished me to be his father, I had known it, known for years, by the fondness we had for each other, the warmth and respect he showed for me.

But tonight it was gone. Lacerated himself, he was turning the cutting edge of his tongue upon me, and I, with never a hope of defence, let alone the

16

ability to attack, could only gaze at him and wonder at the change in the boy. For he was not finished with me yet.

"I've never asked you this – but now is as good a time as any – were you following orders at St Jude's, too? I refer to a discussion you had with Brother Docherty – "

"The headmaster? But he died when you were only – "

"Eight. I was eight. I remember the funeral. But he was still hale and hearty and running St Jude's with an iron fist when I was six. I was waiting for you in the corridor outside his office and, as you came out the door, I ran to meet you as I always did, to place my hand in yours . . . And you pushed me away."

I had somehow found my feet, for this was impossible.

"Oh, it was only a gentle push," Mark continued, "to arm's length. But that was the way it was to stay. From that day on you sounded just like the other brothers – 'Stop hanging back, Mark, join the other lads', 'Get your nose out of that book, young man, and get out into the sunshine'. You came out of that office and your face was *white* – and you pushed me away. Why? What did Brother Docherty say to you?"

I recovered my voice with difficulty. "You remember that? At six years old, you remembered that?"

"Did he tell you that you were spoiling me? That it wouldn't do to single me out from the other boys? That because I was the youngest, you mustn't coddle me? Did he hint – just a little – at homosexuality? Or did he tell you that the object of St Jude's was to turn out stalwart Catholic men who didn't *hug*?"

I could see him – Dominic Docherty, his face already grey with the cancer which would claim him in eighteen months time, telling me grimly that St Jude's was not a children's home, but a school. I was a teacher, not a foster father. That the young Parrish boy would not adapt to the rough and tumble of boarding school life if I allowed him to become dependent upon me.

I was twenty-five years old at the time, and ashamed to be criticised by my superior. I knew I lacked experience and was not a *practical* man. Brother Docherty was sixty-three – the difference between us was that I *cared*. But I knew so little, and believed myself so unworthy, that to use that as a defence was preposterous.

"We ..." I almost spoke about the hierarchy, about the way we ourselves – students of St Jude's who had gone on to become members of the teaching order and returned to train up new generations – were as much bound by convention and discipline as the boys. But I would, again, simply be negating responsibility for my actions, placing it elsewhere. Instead, all my inadequate brain could think of was, "You mustn't blame Brother Docherty. In those days teachers – even lay teachers – weren't trained as they are now, with great emphasis on psychology and child development. In those days it was mostly academic. The system was – "

"The system was rotten! You took a child, deprived him of his family and environment, subjected him to lectures that preyed on fear and guilt . . . the chanting of dogma . . . a discipline as rigid and repressive as a high security prison!"

He stopped, very suddenly, only then realising that he had been shouting.

How could I explain this speech to anyone who did not know the calm, devout young man that was Mark Parrish? Even His Grace – a great admirer of Linda and her work, who had met Mark many times on social occasions – would suspect that Mark could not be a devout Catholic, to cry out these words in the face of a priest who had taught him, known him for twenty-two years.

I myself was amazed, could not have been more shocked if Mark had taken to me with a knife. "You felt *that* – all these years? Captain of the school, top of the State in your matric results, respected by every boy in the school . . . We were all so proud of you – and you hated it?"

He blinked, as if coming to himself suddenly, half-turned, went to speak, but hesitated. Then, "No. No, I didn't mean that. I don't know why I said that. I'm tired – depressed by losing young Michael. Forgive me."

But it would not do. Whether it was the boy's death, the strain of Mark's work, the alcohol, or Rosalind Harcourt, I had seen, for a moment, the grey and stormy depths behind those normally tranquil blue eyes. "You're very unhappy," I said. "You've been unhappy for some time. Is it Mrs Harcourt? Has she said something tonight that – "

"No! I tell you, we're friends, that's all! It's mostly stress – I've decided to go away for a while, take a friend's cabin down at Thredbo and work on an article I've been planning for some time, for submission to the *Australian Medical Journal*. I'll need peace and quiet for a few months at least – and it's the right time to go – there'll be skiing and a good social life down there. I haven't had a holiday in more than two years."

"I envy you. Thredbo couldn't be colder than my presbytery."

He smiled at me, grateful, I think, for my attempt at levity. He is a kind boy, and was already regretting his outburst, knowing that it may have hurt my feelings.

I said, carefully, "When you come back from Thredbo, if you're still troubled, will you speak to a friend of mine?"

One of my parishioners was a GP with a degree in psychology – a level-headed, down-to-earth man. I felt Mark would have responded to him, but . . .

"Thanks, but I get all the counselling I need from my mother. No, don't worry about me, I'll come back from Thredbo a changed man."

He moved across the room to the whisky decanter and poured us each another drink, and I knew that we would talk about football, or skiing, or politics, for the little time left of my visit.

If I ever speak to him again, there is so much to say. So much to ask. Nearly a year of his emotions and actions are recorded in his diaries, and on those tiny tapes from his portable recorder. But nowhere have I been able to find an answer for what I wish to ask him.

Why didn't you tell me, Mark? Why didn't you feel that you could trust me?

CHAPTER ONE

Much of Rosalind Harcourt's charity work was concerned with hospitals, so it was inevitable that the circles in which she and Mark Parrish moved would one day enmesh. But even then, after the function at which Mark's mother had introduced them, no relationship might have developed except for David Papadimitriou.

David and Mark had been schoolboys together at St Jude's, had gained their medical degrees at Sydney University, went their separate ways to train for paediatrics and oncology and had met up again at the Children's Hospital. Both were at the charity ball to aid the North Sydney Psychiatric Unit, and though not close friends – for Mark never allowed himself close friends – the ebullient and good-natured David, never questioning the extent of their relationship, felt he knew Mark Parrish as well as anybody did. And perhaps he was right.

Certainly Mark's reserve, and sometime asperity, did not bother David, who respected Mark's work and considered his ascetic personality suited to his career. "Let's face it – oncologists, pathologists, neurosurgeons, we're a breed apart, aren't we? Or we'd go mad. Often we do," he added.

David drove a sleek, red Italian convertible and boasted of not one little black book but three. Mark listened to him tolerantly, but David couldn't persuade him to take a girl out. Work was everything.

David had hailed Mark in the hospital car park, early in January. "Look, you'll do! I was beginning to worry." He jogged up to Mark, delighted. "How'd you like to help me out this evening?"

"I'm busy."

"Don't give me that. Seriously – you like opera and ballet and all that cultural stuff. A friend of mine has two tickets and I was supposed to go with her, but there's this nurse I'm interested in who's leaving for Darwin tomorrow . . ."

Mark smiled, turned towards his car. "I don't want your rejects."

"It's not *that* sort of date – strictly platonic! Though if she was willing . . . It's Rosalind Harcourt – you know, Geoffrey Harcourt's wife? We're good friends, and she has these tickets – she always does, in the hope that Geoff can accompany her, but you know him . . ."

"No." But Mark had paused, and was remembering the woman called Rosalind Harcourt.

"I have to phone her now and tell her I can't make it – I've got the 'flu, see." David grinned.

"And then I saw you and – it'd be great if I could tell her that I have this big bronze Anzac of a mate . . ."

"Get off it."

"And he loves ballet, is guaranteed to stay awake and looks great in a tux. You do *have* a tux, don't you?"

"Yes," scowling.

"Come on, Mark – help me out! She's a lovely woman. You'll like her."

"I've met her."

"Well, then! What do you say? Can I tell her you'll pick her up at a quarter to seven?"

And it was totally out of character, Mark wrote in his first diary – some six weeks after that first visit to the ballet with Rosalind Harcourt, *but I agreed to take David's place. I was curious about the Harcourts – I suppose everyone in the country is. It should, at the very least, I thought, be an interesting experience. This is a terrible and a wonderful thing – my Rosalind, my Rosalind. She has become my best friend and it's wonderful. And if I had only that – her friendship – that would be enough. Someone to understand me, someone to listen, someone to give their time without considering what she can get in return. To be with her was a joy, but now – this evening – it was frightening. The feelings within me frightened me.*

24

She danced on ahead of me – we were crossing the corner of Hyde Park – and it had been raining but was clear now, and the lights spangled in the trees and reflected in the grass. "It looks like a set for Les Sylphides," *Rosalind said. "I danced in* Les Sylphides . . ." *And she danced for me then, just a few steps and a turn, ahead of me, across the grass that looked like jewels, in that pale blue dress – chiffon, I think, light as gossamer – and she looked fifteen as she turned to me, her face alight.*

And I loved her. I saw her as she was, and as she always will be – the child within the woman, the dancer in the light. It was this I sensed about her from the beginning – the feeling of light about her.

I loved her, God help me. What am I going to do?

And the boy was right, Father Leo Calder thought, reading that same entry in Mark's diary. It *was* wonderful. And it was terrible. More terrible than it was wonderful, for Mark and for everyone around him.

It was terrible for Leo, to read those diaries, listen to those tapes. Why had Mark kept them? Was it the scientist within him? That cool, detached individual who could look upon suffering and still find it valuable enough to record for future generations?

And why, Leo agonised, had Mark entrusted them to him?

Rosalind had been very fond of Mark. The diaries catalogued every meeting, every dress she wore, every gesture she made, every word she spoke. She was, indeed, a woman of perspicacity and a kind heart. But it was painful for Leo to see, even between Mark's lines of hopeful adoration, that there was nothing on which to base his assumption that Rosalind loved him in return.

She spoke of Geoff's plans for mining exploration in Colorado, how it will necessitate him going to the States to meet with a man called Manzone. I said he sounded like Mafia and she looked rather cool – as she does, sometimes, when I anticipate her thoughts. I have learnt to keep silent. This game she plays, that no one must know of our feelings for each other, as if even my Volvo was wired for sound, would be amusing if it wasn't for the fact that I long to hear her say, "I love you", out loud . . .

She talks of Geoff as if he is a real part of her life, but it's the fondness of two friends only, I can tell. She feels guilty that she can't give him what she gives me – these precious moments – so she speaks of him fondly, anxiously, like a mother speaks of a son who works too hard.

I held her hand as we came down those steep stairs from the Wharf Theatre. She shook it free, but smiled, in case I was hurt. I was. Barriers, all the time, between us. Sometimes I think she's laughing at me behind her eyes – but no. In the car, when we're alone, when I speak to her of my work, of the children, of the terrible problems, the overwhelming tasks we have and how close to defeat I feel – the love in her eyes is there. Sometimes she almost reaches for me, to touch my hand, my face – but it's a dancer's feint. I could shake her then, shake her and demand all her love – or take it. It's mine, and she won't allow me what's mine.

Geoff doesn't even suspect – he's a good man, a strong man – but they've been married eighteen years and it's over. I see it in their eyes when they look at each other – only the fondness for a brother or sister, the shared laughter of family. Not lovers. She doesn't look at Geoff the way she looks at me.

She had a child who died. James, they christened him, for her father, but she called him Jamey. Dead at five months old. Perhaps the love between herself and Geoff died then. The child was conceived in vitro – her only chance – and it died at five months. Sudden Infant Death Syndrome. Rosalind's mother had died only weeks before Jamey. She had

tears in her eyes when she told me of this
time – I wanted to hold her so badly – I almost
did. I wanted to tell her how I wished we
could have a child. I would give her the world
if she wanted it.

Interspersed with these descriptions, over the
months, were comments on Mark's work, and here
the writing – made worse by the technical subject
and Mark's idiosyncratic shorthand – became even
more difficult for Leo to decipher. However, one
entry in particular leapt out at him:

Melissa O'Neil again, in the hospital canteen.
I'd worked through lunch and was starving
and then my steak went cold because I had
to talk to her. She's the most difficult of
females – just saying the usual "But I don't
want to go out with you because I'm put off
by your big bum/bad skin/flat chest/bad
breath, doesn't work. She's physically quite
perfect, and so smart that she'd see through
this anyway, and laugh in my face. So I
simply avoid speaking to her, though lately
this, too, hasn't worked. Last week I even
walked off in the middle of what she was
saying, but she's a stubborn girl.

   In a way I can't blame her for thinking I'm
interested because I do like to look at her
when she hoves into sight. But women like

Melissa think that beauty is enough – she can't see that there's a certain fascination in a perfect accident of skin texture, sinew and bone structure, coming as it does with the grace of utter self-confidence. She thinks that because I went to school with her brother, and danced with her at those grotesque 'formals' between St Jude's and St Theresa's, we have a sort of 'past'. She's a damn good doctor, but goal-oriented – and I object to being a goal.

"Alright," she said, "I'm not asking for dinner and candlelight – let's dispense with all the preliminaries. One night. That's all I'm asking." *She was smiling with those perfect teeth, and all I could think of was my congealing steak and eggs.*

"I could have any number of diseases, Melissa."

"Bullshit."

"You *could* have – "

"I don't. But if you're worried, we'll use condoms."

I sighed. "What's the point of the exercise? You don't like me, and I don't like you."

She was still, but stood her ground even in the face of this. "Do you have to have a reason for everything you do, Mark? You're not a computer, no matter how much you'd like to be. But if you do need a reason – warmth,

29

affection, a few pleasurable hours indulging in some great sex."

"But I might find you to be something of a disappointment."

Her stillness had something of rigidity about it now. "You won't," with a tight, sweet smile. "And if I don't turn you on – what does?"

I grinned, knowing what was coming. "Melissa . . ."

"Are you gay? People say you're gay."

"Are you challenging me into bed? If I perform to your satisfaction, will you give me a reference?"

Melissa isn't used to not getting her own way. "I only want you to try it. Just once." Her eyes narrowed. "Have you ever *made love* to a woman, Mark?"

I held her gaze and leaned across the table a little. She half-leaned towards me, and moistened her lips with the tip of her tongue. I caught a drift of her perfume. "Melissa, you and I could bang away all night – and I still wouldn't have made love to a woman."

And she emptied the sugar bowl over my head.

I told this to Rosalind when we were playing golf this afternoon. Rosalind said I should be thankful there wasn't a teapot on the table.

That he was one of several escorts who accompanied Rosalind to social functions never seemed to be a matter of jealousy to Mark. He seemed, oddly enough, to be very sure of her affections for him. Certainly he was not, in those early days, jealous of Geoff. He liked and respected the man. And when Leo had met him, during those dark days when the newspapers were full of conjecture, and Mark and Rosalind could not be found, he had liked Geoff also.

Though he had no direct experience of marriage himself, Leo thought it possible, as the years slid by, each one bringing only imperceptible changes, to find oneself taking one's partner for granted. Geoff admitted this had happened, "without any fault of Rosalind's, without it affecting our love for each other". His broad, strong face behind its dark beard looked concerned that Leo might think disparagingly of their relationship. "She was so much a part of me. That was it. She was like an extension of myself. You don't consider your arm, your leg, every minute of the day – they're part of you, vital to you. That was the kind of closeness we had – we felt safe with each other.

"The guys who accompanied her to the theatre, the charity dinners and stuff, when I couldn't – I knew them, I liked them. They were honest blokes, not gigolos or bimbos. Rosalind could tell if a bloke was insincere, or coming on too strong. She never flirted, never went too far. She was a lady, with everybody – ask anyone and they'll tell you. She was too honest to lie to me, to anyone. And if some bloke fell in love with her, she'd break off the friendship – and she'd tell me why. I never blamed the man. But their friendship would be over.

"People say I'm bull-headed, arrogant. I've had to be, to get where I am. And I've had to be single-minded. Sure, money matters to me – and power. Rosalind understood that, and she supported me in everything I've tried to do, everything I've built up. But I carried it all too far, I know that now. When the stock market crashed I should have sold off a few companies, consolidated. Instead I went crazy for years, trying to hold on to everything. It was then that Roz used to say I was changing, that I didn't have any time for her any more . . .

"But I was running scared. Terrified to stand still, hating to lose even one share of what I'd built up. It was my own ego I was trying to shore up – when I should have been worrying about my marriage.

"Yet she never betrayed me. I don't care what the world says – she was too honest. She'd have told me."

And Geoff, too, was right.

CHAPTER TWO

Mark began to fantasise more and more, making plans, that he recorded in his diaries, for the time when he and Rosalind would be together. They would buy an apartment in the city, high above the harbour and the rest of the world, and they would rarely entertain. They would be a world in themselves. Or this dream of romantic isolation would shift settings to a farm near the coast, where they would walk their dogs along the beach. He lived these fantasies, and Leo, reading them, became heavy-hearted with grief for him.

The growing pressures of Mark's work were becoming more stressful – he was reprimanded by the Professor of Oncology for his hypercritical attitude and impatience towards the staff, and his incivility towards fellow doctors. His mother became more and more worried about him. He ignored everyone – even Rosalind, who advised him to take time off, to go overseas for a holiday. How could he? For to go would be to leave her, and he could not leave her.

He kept his feelings from her, yet his rational mind never considered that this was strange – that he and she were so much in love, yet could not express themselves. He made excuses for Rosalind's reticence, and her reticence affected his own. He would not speak of it until she was ready. The logical inference, that she never spoke of her love for him because there was no love to speak of, was unthinkable, impossible. It never occurred to him.

Rosalind should have seen. Somehow Leo could not help but wonder if she did see the signs and yet did nothing. Mark was so very handsome a young man, and he loved her. Could a woman of her sophistication and maturity *not* see what was happening?

Rosalind frequently invited Mark to play golf with her, at her exclusive North Shore club. One particular afternoon, they were playing on handicap, and Rosalind was losing. She had no idea that Mark, never a keen golfer until these fortnightly games, was now practising hard, and he was amused to see that her vanity was threatened.

"You can't expect to win all the time."

"I haven't lost yet."

"Only three holes to go."

"Stop putting me off – none of your psychological warfare." She pushed her tee vengefully into the soft turf.

"I'm not putting you off, I'm just amused that you're so competitive. I didn't think you had such a killer instinct."

"Me? Nonsense, I'm a pussycat." And she had bent her head over her club, when –

"You're not a pussycat – you're a falcon. 'My gay young hawk, my Rosalind . . .'"

The words came of their own volition, and would have sounded strange to anyone not familiar with this, one of Tennyson's lesser-known poems. Mark regretted speaking almost immediately, for Rosalind had paused, and her head came up.

"Why did you say that? 'My gay young hawk, my Rosalind'? My father used to call me that."

"It's a poem. By Tennyson." He found himself beginning to flush, turned and took his two wood out and began cleaning an invisible piece of mud from it with the cloth to hide his embarrassment. Mark was extremely well-read when it came to poetry and classical prose – he often quoted from *Rosalind* in his diaries – but he had almost given himself away, before he was ready.

But Rosalind did not simper, nor flirt, nor toy like a cat with his use of the possessive pronoun in the quotation. She was genuinely interested. "A poem by Tennyson – and I thought my father had made the words up."

She teed off, and scowled after the shot that had hooked badly into the rough after a hundred yards. "Bitch."

They took their buggies and walked down the fairway. Rosalind was thoughtful. "My father was a teacher – maths and science – but he loved poetry. When I was a little girl and couldn't sleep, I'd creep into bed between my father and mother and he'd read me poetry until I fell asleep."

Mark grinned. "What a popular little girl you must have been sometimes."

They laughed and separated, Rosalind to search about in the long grass, and Mark, confident of winning now, walking ahead to his own ball.

It was not until later, walking back to the clubhouse along the shrub-lined path, that Rosalind said, "Recite it for me – my *Rosalind* poem."

Mark, surprised, found himself reluctant. "It's a love poem."

"So? Go on. Or is it too sentimental for your clinical doctor's mind?" she teased.

"I'd never call it sentimental . . ."

"Well then . . ."

"You have to be in the mood for that sort of thing."

"But I am in the mood."

"I'm not. I can recite *Jabberwocky* for you – "

"I want *my* poem."

They had almost reached the clubhouse steps, and so intent were they in this banter that they did not see the man come down the steps from the building until he was directly in front of them.

He was about forty, not quite Mark's height, slim and well-dressed, with a quiet assurance about him.

"Rosalind . . ." He knew her well, would have reached for her, kissed her cheek – but Rosalind had taken an imperceptible step backwards, and held out her hand.

"Andrew – how good to see you."

In the politically delicate ceremony of the taking of hands, Mark, now so well-attuned to Rosalind's moods, sensed something at work here, something not right. He looked at the older man, and did not like him, wanted to get Rosalind away from him. But Andrew was smiling, and saying, "Geoff isn't playing today?" More as a statement than a question.

"No. Business, as usual," Rosalind replied, and her smile was her Reserve Polite Smile, for people whom she did not like. In the six months Mark had known her, he'd learnt that it was reserved for the hypocritical, the cunning, the malicious; it was the thinnest veneer of courtesy.

"Business as usual for everyone," was the equivocal reply. And turning to Mark quickly, "Andrew Braithwaite . . .", he held out his hand.

Mark was not used to games of any sort, and his natural good manners had him returning the handshake. "Mark Parrish."

With a fond look towards Rosalind, Braithwaite said, "Rosalind and I go back a long way. In the lost days of her youth, I, too, was one of Mary's little lambs. But be careful, Mark – "

"Andrew, you've been drinking."

But Andrew Braithwaite, his considerable charm directed at Mark, was continuing without a pause, "Rosalind's lambs don't follow her to school – like most foolish lambs, they end up in the slaughter-house, don't they, Rosalind?"

It was an ugly scene, but over very quickly, for Rosalind was already walking up the steps. A crowd of players were coming down, and in the mêlée, she had disappeared before the two men could move. They both gazed after her. When he did glance at the older man, Mark caught there the angry patches of colour on the pale face, the old hurt naked in his eyes.

Braithwaite recovered – it had taken only a second – and looked at Mark, who felt his anger towards the man draining away from him. Only pity was left, and Braithwaite seemed to know it. He smiled. "Good luck," he murmured softly, and headed off down the path towards the car park.

Mark hesitated. Rosalind was out of sight within the building. This was unlike her; it was the first time he had seen her in flight, discomfited. To gain time both for himself and for Rosalind, Mark took their golf clubs to his car and placed them in the boot, dismantling the buggies slowly, carefully, running over in his mind the scene with Braithwaite, all that it might have meant.

When he went to the clubhouse he did not find Rosalind immediately. There was a small garden off the restaurant area, with a fountain and a square patch of lawn that overlooked the putting green. Rosalind was seated on a wrought-iron bench, with a half-empty glass of whisky beside her.

"What are you doing?" He stood in front of her, surprised at the tension in his own voice.

She looked up, her eyebrows raised. "I beg your pardon?"

Mark found himself angry, had been growing progressively angrier since the scene at the front steps. "I can understand your walking out on that idiot Braithwaite, but don't walk out on me."

"I'll do what I want. You're not my keeper."

Tension between them. Between *them*. It was too sudden, too strange, but neither of them could back down. Mark scowled at the glass as she picked it up and half-drained its contents. "How many of those have you had?"

"Three."

"*Three?*"

"I drank them very quickly."

"Why?"

"I wanted to."

"Because of Andrew Braithwaite? Was he your lover?" Even saying the words made him ill, truly physically ill. But his demeanour was cool – he was too well-trained, and she would never have known.

"Don't be absurd," she said. "Of course not."

He believed her. After a moment he sat down on the bench beside her. "I felt sorry for him. He's in love with you, isn't he?"

She looked away. "I doubt it. It has nothing to do with me, anyway."

Mark must have been rigid, for in the silence she hesitated and looked at him. As if defending herself, "I didn't lead him on – he was a charming, well-educated man – a good friend of Geoff's . . ."

Mark cut across her words, "It happens fairly often, I suppose. One of your escorts falls in love with you and you drop him, end the friendship."

She finished the drink with an air of carelessness, but was still confronted with Mark's attentive face, patiently waiting for his answer. She almost hissed at him, "Not *me*. They don't fall in love with *me*. They fall in love with the third richest wife in Australia. With what they think I can do for their careers. They look at me and see money, power, influence – I'd be attractive to them if I had two heads."

Her glass was empty. The silence between them was not. Rosalind held out her glass. "Would you get me another one of those?"

"No. Is that what you think of *everyone*? That they want to use you? Is that why I'm here, now? Is that what you think of me?"

She looked at him for a long moment, and he could sense her considering, but even Mark was not prepared for her words. In a slow and deliberate voice, she said, "I think you're very pretty. Almost perfect, but not quite. Your jawline is a little too pronounced . . . But we look very well together. My friends envy me for having you in tow."

And into Mark's shocked mind came Shakespeare's words, oddly enough, and out of context – *I do believe her though I know she lies*.

"Why are you looking like that?" Rosalind scowled. "Why that superior little smile?"

"I'm wondering why you want us to quarrel. *I* wasn't ill-mannered just now – it was Andrew. Now it's you. But I seem to be taking all the blame."

She held his gaze, and the smile began in her eyes and finally curved her mouth. "Yes. I'm sorry. It's just that Andrew embarrassed me – he spoilt a lovely afternoon with his poison."

"Do you think I'd pay attention to his ravings?"

He watched her as she turned the glass about, unhappily, her eyes on the toes of her golf shoes, crossed before her. "I'm . . . I'm not used to feeling threatened," she began, with difficulty. "I know what Andrew said wasn't all that bad, but I've been protected, in a way, by Geoff's position and power in the community. I should be stronger. I have friends who could cut Andrew and people like him into ribbons with a few words."

"You do pretty well yourself, when you try," he could not stop himself from saying, and her gaze swung up towards him in surprised reproach.

"I don't know why I said that. The alcohol, perhaps." She placed the empty glass beside her on the bench as if, by putting it from her, she could as easily negate what had been said.

But Mark was not about to let the moment pass. This was contact, real contact, with the woman who, until now, had been all graceful propriety. These were instinctive emotions from the heart, and Mark was hungry for them.

He said, "Geoff's power and position isolates you and protects you. Yet, on the other hand, the people who are attracted to you are only drawn to you because of Geoff's wealth and influence. Does Rosalind appear in any of this? What part does she play?"

He had brushed too close to some truth she did not wish to confront. She looked at him with a faint underlying fear in her eyes, and he could see her struggling to be free of his logic and the paths it was leading her down. But again, probably because she felt threatened, she escaped him as surely as she had escaped from Andrew's venom.

"Rosalind merely plays golf. And after that, she has five very staid and boring members of Carringal Children's Home coming for dinner. Angelina will be beginning to panic if she's left to make preparations alone."

So they left the garden and the golf club and he drove her home.

She escapes me, always. I wished that walled garden was my walled garden and I could keep her there – make her answer me, make her face herself. For I know, now, that she never has. I would keep her there, hold her there, make her find herself – and then find me, within her eyes.

CHAPTER THREE

The third of July: the day that young Michael Halvorson died of leukaemia; the evening of the Archbishop's Dinner; the evening of a performance of *Madame Butterfly* at the Sydney Opera House; the evening Mark told Rosalind that he loved her.

Leo opened the diary to that page.

I told her, in the car on the way home from the Butterfly performance. She rejected me. She didn't want to know. When I stopped the car, finally, in the drive, I could see she was longing to be up those steps and away. I could almost taste her fear. I could kill her. She wouldn't face the truth – and what could I do? What more could I say? I was very cool, made an exit as best I could – and, oddly, at the end, when I told her I was going on holidays for a few months, I could tell she was regretting her behaviour.

What angered me most were these plans of hers to go to Queensland. I've never heard her mention Silver Palms Resort, but she says she goes there for part of every winter. She mentioned this after I told her my feelings. But I was very cool – she doesn't know what she's done to me. Though when I walked her up to the door she went to touch my face – so bloody fondly, like a sister or a mother – and I took her wrist and stopped her. For a second she was afraid of me.

I have never been so angry in my life.

Father Leo was here when I got home. I gave the poor man a really hard time – he was even more afraid of me than Rosalind was. I'd write him a note, apologise, but what excuse could I give? I'd never hear the end of it if he knew how I felt about Rosalind. She's Catholic, too, though Geoff isn't – her marriage vows would still be sacred in Leo's eyes. I couldn't bear him to know what I've become. I've stopped praying.

What sort of woman is Rosalind that she can get between me and God? Does she know the power she has?

Leo read on, his distress increasing as he found more and more evidence of Mark's tortured state of mind. He learnt how Mark could not sleep, how he went to his study and took his father's Smith and

Wesson .357 and loaded it and placed it against his temple. And then – thank the Lord, thought Leo – Mark had remembered the half-dead he had seen in the hospices, whose chosen bullets had missed their proposed trajectories and had blown away only a part of the brain, leaving them instead in a comatose peace, an embarrassment to their families and a chore to hospital staff.

Through the mouth, perhaps – if he aimed higher. Or through the heart – he could be sure of that.

But Mark did not want death. He wanted Rosalind.

Kill Geoff? But it isn't Geoff's fault. He loves her – or would say he does. Even dead, Geoff would still hold her – he has had eighteen years with her – eighteen years in which to bend her to his will, to convince her that she's part of him. For all I know, if she should disappear, Geoff may not even miss her. Yet she will cling to him – the very loyalty and strength of character I love in her is keeping us from each other. How can I break through that shared past they have, to convince her that her place is with me? If she is Tennyson's bright-eyed, wild-eyed falcon, she has been manned to another falconer, and it's to his call that she descends, not mine.

He left off there, and the next entry was the last in that diary, though there were further blank pages. It was as if he had found the need for a new book, a new beginning. The last entry in that first diary was a dreadful scrawl, Leo found some of the words indecipherable. It was written while Mark was still watching that fateful television program, Leo suspected, and he may have been drinking.

This must be Fate – or perhaps it's God – for something like this must be _____, for it was all there, perfectly (presented?) before me.

I don't know what the documentary is called – it's made in Tasmania – I had no idea that the sport of falconry still existed – it's incredible – a kind of behavioural modification programming – brainwashing if you like – of this sleek little killer into a tractable pet – for one man.

It was there, all the time, like a voice telling me what to do – it spoke through Tennyson's words, and now through this bearded Tasmanian falconer. He walks exhausted, all through the night, moving about his house, out into the farmyard and field, back to the house – and talks to the female hawk upon his wrist. She has a hood over her eyes, a cunning _____ of leather topped with feathers, and sometimes he tests her by removing it, gently, training her to the

sensation of being with him, "manning" her,
they call it – and all the time keeping her
awake. She must not sleep, for only through
exhaustion will her wild spirit bend to his.

My God, the planning, the expense – I
would have to give my life to this.

But what is my life unless I do it? Will I be
doing anything worse than Geoff has done,
society has done, insidiously to her, over the
years? Cruel, yes, I may be cruel – but my
motive is the best possible motive. I will make
her happy.

It's a terrifying experiment – for Rosalind
and for myself. How I wish I could take
Mother's books with me – I must begin a
library of my own.

There, in his room at St Anne's presbytery, Leo read
the diaries for the first time. And there it was that
he heard the tapes, tiny, one by two inch tapes filled
with Mark's mellow voice, Mark's tainted thoughts,
that had Leo with his head upon his hands,
weeping. What had happened to that boy, he asked
himself, that child? *My* child.

Leo did not see Mark again, after that night of July
third, when Mark had unleashed his pent-up rage
upon him. He was hurt by Mark's words. He knew
Mark would be leaving soon for Thredbo, but did
not call. He hoped that Mark might telephone in

his turn, but no call came. When Leo rang Linda, three days later, it was to find that Mark had left for Thredbo the day after their heated conversation.

Linda was not pleased that Mark had decided to stay at a friend's remote cabin, instead of one of the large chalets. Thinking back, Leo suspected that perhaps Linda had sensed something was wrong, that Mark was disturbed, but so well did he hide his emotions that even she, who was closest to him, did not suspect the truth.

Or perhaps she did, and could not face it.

When Leo arrived for dinner the Saturday following Mark's departure, Linda reported that Mark had seemed agitated, preoccupied, intent on going away immediately, without any forewarning to the hospital or his staff at his consulting rooms. He had been fortunate in finding someone to take care of his practice for the two months he planned to be gone – a young man who had been hoping for a long time to buy into Mark's practice, but Mark, of course, always worked alone. The young doctor left his own work in disarray in the optimistic hope that Parrish had changed his mind. And, at that time, who was to know what Mark had in mind for the future. Nothing in the diaries recorded any thought of the future beyond his dark and immediate plans.

Linda and Leo did not speak of it, but both believed that this sudden flight from Sydney was caused, in some way, by Rosalind Harcourt, or, rather, by Mark's feelings for her. Leo had told

Linda of his own belief earlier on the telephone – that Mark had, perhaps, said something to Mrs Harcourt and had his suit rejected. He was a young man of great pride, inherited from his mother and his Parrish forebears – Leo would not be honest if he did not acknowledge that. It was the most serious of Mark's character faults, and led him, sometimes, to appear arrogant.

However, Leo was not worried about Mark. The idea of him snowed in at Thredbo with his medical textbooks, cogitating over an article for the *AMJ* and getting over his first, and long overdue, rejection by a woman, did not disturb him in the least. Leo thought it would be good for Mark to find there was something he could not have simply by wishing for it. He did not, however, approve of Linda's insistence on Mark taking his father's revolver with him.

"The cabin is isolated – there's not even a proper address – access is by four-wheel drive, and he's staying there alone. Who knows what bad characters are lurking about in those hills? The cabin doesn't have a phone."

"I never approved of him having that revolver – "

"Leo, pistol-shooting is a sport – Mark has a whole bureau full of trophies."

"I don't approve of it," Leo insisted stubbornly. "What if someone breaks into the cabin while Mark is buying supplies in Thredbo? That'll be one more gun in the hands of unscrupulous people."

"Well, it's too late, now," Linda said, primly. She did not like it when Leo disagreed with her. And Leo never insisted unless he was certain he was right.

It was months later before Leo realised that Mark had not given his mother a description of where the cabin was located – "up some nameless fire trail, seventeen miles from town", had been Mark's only description. Linda had accepted this, without approving of it. But Mark had said he would phone her every three days, and he was punctilious about this. For a long time.

But Mark was not in Thredbo. He had flown to Cairns, in the far north of Queensland, and had spent the first few days looking at coastal properties.

It was easier than he expected, he noted in his diary. With a brand new four-wheel drive vehicle and money to pay cash for the house, no one questioned his story of being a record producer tired of the Sydney rat race.

He found a huge, seven year old house on ten hectares at Tilga Beach, south of Cairns. He was able to move in almost immediately, and the builders began their work that day.

Even if nothing works out the way I wish it to, he reported that first night in his house, writing at his new desk in his study overlooking the Pacific, *I'm glad I came here.*

I need the peace, the solitude, of this place. Already I feel as if I'm no longer the man I was when I left Sydney. I'm filled with a certainty that when she's here, when she sees this house, everything will be alright.

Whatever happens, I can never go back. Something happened when I held that gun against my temple and faced the thought of death quite calmly. I knew then that I could more easily face death than the loss of Rosalind. There's still that option – and this is a beautiful place to die. When the time comes, I won't be afraid. I watched Nathan and Emma and Michael die with courage – how could I not do the same?

From what she told me, Geoff leaves for Los Angeles on the twentieth, and she flies to Cairns on the twenty-first. If she changes her mind about the date I can always find her at the resort. But I want to meet her plane. I want to see her face as soon as possible. I want her here as soon as possible.

The first plane from Sydney on the twenty-first arrived in Cairns at 7.15 am. Mark was there an hour early, having been unable to sleep all that night for his restless sense of anticipation. The next plane was not until 9.00 am. And during the waiting, drinking coffee in the restaurant, the first doubts began to form in his mind. What if he had made a mistake with the dates? Worse, what if Geoff did not go to Los Angeles to meet the mining magnate Harry Manzone and decided instead to accompany his wife on her holiday?

His hands began to tremble a little, and his forehead was damp, despite the cool of the air conditioning. But the thought of Geoff giving up work for weeks in order to lie beneath a palm tree in Northern Queensland made him smile, and relax a little.

No, if Rosalind came, she would come alone.

He was prepared to wait at the airport all day. He had the times of the flights written in a notebook, and if she had not arrived by the last evening flight he would phone Silver Palms and find out the date of her arrival.

And then, when Rosalind came through the gates after the 2.05 pm flight, he almost missed her. Only her bearing, her walk, gave her away, for her hair was hidden in a navy scarf and a large hat shaded those parts of her face that the large dark glasses did not conceal.

As he moved in front of her, his nerves almost betrayed him. This was reality. Here she was, and all his speeches, so well-rehearsed over the past three weeks, left him as she lifted her head, her green eyes, veiled behind the dark glasses, intent upon him.

But she was smiling, and one well-manicured hand came up and took the glasses from her face. "Mark!" she said, with surprise and pleasure.

He kissed her cheek, and they were two old friends meeting suddenly, unexpectedly – though Mark, in the intensity of relief, the joy of her touch, the scent of her, had to stop himself from enveloping her within his arms, holding her to him.

She was laughing, "What on earth are you doing here?"

"You'd told me what day you were arriving – I rang Angelina and asked the time of your flight. You don't mind?"

This could be explained later. She would be flattered, later, to find that he had arrived at 6.00 am and prowled the airport, gazing at the southern skies, praying for her.

"Of course I don't mind, but... you left for Thredbo three weeks ago."

They began to walk towards the baggage retrieval as Mark explained. "I only stayed a week, and then came up here – Brisbane first. I bought a four-wheel drive and headed bush – I had a lot of thinking to do."

There was concern behind her smile as she took in the fact that he was tanned and fit, but thinner, and seemed tense. "I know," her voice low. "Geoff and I were both worried about you. I phoned your mother after you left for Thredbo. She told me you were working well and were enjoying yourself. I was relieved to hear it – but upset to find that you'd lied to me."

He had been thinking, *of course my mother wouldn't tell me that Rosalind had been in touch with her*, but now his footsteps slowed at Rosalind's accusation. Something of his dismay must have shown in his eyes, for she slowed her own pace and faced him.

"The night of *Madame Butterfly* – the little boy with leukaemia, Michael? He died that day. I asked you how he was, and you didn't tell me the truth." Her silent question hung in the air between them.

And now it was easy to speak, far easier than he had thought. "I wasn't thinking clearly that day. Michael's loss – it made me question a lot of things. For a few days I was a little crazy – certainly, that night, it was all I could do to function at all."

He smiled a little, wryly, and hoped that she would see that his words were also an apology for his reckless declaration of that evening.

The knowledge was in her eyes, the acceptance of his answer, and the empathy that had first drawn him to her. "I understand," she said, and they fell into step once more. "And how did you end up in Cairns?"

"You'll think I'm still crazy – I found a house. I was driving out of Tilga – this little township a few hours south – and there was this forest and a sign saying: *Beach front property for sale*. I drove down to look at it – and that was it. I just had to have it – the only house on a mile and a half of white-sand beach."

"You're going to live here?" Her eyes widened with surprise.

His gaze was serious as he looked down at her, and he said, truthfully, "I'm not going back to Sydney. I've had time to see my life very clearly – where I've been, what I really want. If things work out as I wish them to, I'll go into general practice in Tilga. I'll hang up a shingle there and spend the rest of my life treating tonsillitis and coral cuts."

She was clearly delighted for him. "Doctor Mark Parrish, GP . . ."

"A wiser, and a much happier man," Mark interrupted with a grin.

They were at the baggage retrieval.

"I'll drive you to Silver Palms, if you like."

She smiled up at him, gratefully. "That would be lovely."

"Or . . . I suppose you've had lunch?"

"Only a little of the plane food."

"I haven't eaten, either. What do you think about coming to see my new house? I could make us a late lunch, show you around the place, and drive you back to Silver Palms this evening."

He looked so appealing, standing above her, leaning forward with all his attention upon her and his handsome young face alight.

"Well . . ."

"You'll be there in plenty of time."

"Alright, yes. We will. I'd love to see your new house."

There was a minor problem when one of Rosalind's expensive pieces of luggage was claimed by a prim little grey-haired woman who insisted volubly that it was hers – until an identical piece rolled out on the conveyor belt, along with the four other pieces of Rosalind's matching set. The little woman, with her English skin and neat linen suit, retired in embarrassment with the correct case.

Rosalind was amused, but Mark, nervous and eager to get away, was inwardly cursing the woman. He had been so pleased that Rosalind had been wearing the broad hat and sunglasses; few people could have recognised her, despite the media coverage of the Harcourts over recent months. But the elderly woman had studied them – the pale, shrewd eyes darting from Rosalind's face to Mark's and back again – and she had the look of a schoolteacher or librarian, the look of a woman with intelligence and a good memory.

He relaxed once the luggage was stored in the back of the car and the long-wheel-base Landcruiser was carrying them away, together, towards the house, and freedom and the future.

From that moment of setting off, Mark felt Rosalind was his. No matter what happened, he promised himself, he would never let her go again.

He chatted about the house and the Tilga area and the passing scenery, and placed a cassette of Frank Sinatra in the stereo system.

Night and day, you are the one,
Only you, beneath the moon
and under the sun ...

They sang together as they drove.

CHAPTER FOUR

W hat will the media say, Leo wondered, when the truth comes out. They, the journalists, will have the world presuming that everything that happened was due to Mark's relationship with Linda, and his childhood at St Jude's.

"I will not have Linda blamed," Leo murmured. He saw her still, as on that first day, all those years ago. Leo had been hot and exhausted, coming straight from football practice, yet went at once to Brother Docherty's office when he was summoned.

On knocking and opening the door the first person he saw, as usual, was the angular frame of Dominic Docherty behind his desk. But beside him, as if he had drawn the child closer to his chair in order to speak with him, was the handsomest small boy Leo had ever seen. Straight fair hair and an oddly mature bearing, clearly-sculpted even features and quite startling blue eyes that looked towards the door and Leo with confident curiosity. Even then, there was that sense of guarded self-control that *was* Mark Parrish.

"Ah, Brother Leo . . ." Dominic unfolded himself from his chair and looked now, not at Leo, but, as if in explanation, at his other visitor.

She did not turn immediately, a slim woman dressed in a Chanel-styled suit, black and in the height of fashion and good taste. A black straw hat, its broad brim swept up and back from an elegant pale neck and coils of heavy dark hair. And, when she turned to him, the loveliest face he had ever seen.

There is such beauty that can make one stare and stare, and Linda had that effect on everyone that met her. Leo was twenty-four years old and had never been in love, but he came close to falling in love in that moment he first saw Linda Parrish.

She was going overseas, Dominic explained. Mark was to board with them. "He'll be our youngest," with a smile that told Leo that he was sure he could manage to look after the child. Five years old! But it was not Leo's place to object. He looked at the woman. About thirty years old, she gazed back at him with a look of trust that he hoped was not misplaced.

There was about her, at that moment, in that office, such an air of – the only word is gallantry. She was so warm, so courteous, and yet, while she spoke of her son and her reasons for bringing him to St Jude's, Leo could sense her bravery, sense the hurt, the effort she was making, for their sakes and, certainly, for the child's.

Her husband had been in the United States at a medical convention, and had had a stroke. She would be very busy caring for him and did not feel that she could give Mark the attention that he would need.

Beauty and character and courage. Even Dominic was affected. He asked Leo to take the child on a tour of the school and, on the way through the kitchens, to ask Mrs Tobin for tea to be brought to his office.

Leo wished he could have stayed. There was such an air of mystery and drama about the woman that he felt sure the discussion would be interesting. Leo, who had no curiosity about the world outside St Jude's, was suddenly captivated by all that surrounded that very contained, very feminine form of the woman who had been introduced to him simply as "Doctor Parrish".

Her hand had been small and cool, her hazel eyes direct, and her voice! It sounded in his ears all that afternoon. Deep, slow and mellifluous, combined with the steady gaze and the slight pressure of her hand in his ... Leo was not the only one smitten. News had travelled fast: Dominic said at dinner that he had never had such a plethora of brothers knocking on the door of his office, nor heard such a lot of lame excuses, in all his years as a headmaster.

The small boy accompanied Leo over the school grounds. He wore a well-fitting and expensive blue suit, a white shirt and small maroon tie. His hand was placed confidently in Leo's and he looked at the panelled rooms and cloistered passages and sprawling grounds of St Jude's with calm interest.

"Most of our younger lads are a year or two older than you, but they're a nice lot, and you'll make friends very easily. I'll introduce you to David Papadimitriou, he's a friendly boy. I suppose the buildings look very large to you."

They were nearing the football field. Mark was looking back at the large main edifice, which Brother Gerard, the art teacher, once described as Versailles Gothic.

"Yes," Mark said, calmly, "but we live in a very large house, so I'm used to that." Leo was thinking that the Parrish family must be wealthy indeed, when the boy added, "I like big old buildings – there are lots of places to hide."

"Oh? When you play hide-and-seek with your friends?"

Mark looked at Leo, not puzzled, but almost curious that he could ask such a question. "No. I only play at school. Hiding is . . . *hiding*. You know. Being by yourself in the dark, where Mummy and Daddy and Nanny can't find you."

Nanny? Leo thought.

"Nanny's been given notice," Dominic explained to Leo, once mother and son had left. "She was a live-in housekeeper who cared for the boy during the day. He started school a few months ago at St Brigid's – pity to disrupt him just as he'd be settling in, but there's no other family."

"Is the husband's condition very bad?"

"It seems so. He's a prominent oncologist – very old family, thick with the Archbishop. *She's* a psychiatrist – fascinating, isn't it? Looks like a fashion model. Think the boy'll settle in?"

The abruptness of the question surprised Leo. "I think so. I wish there were other alternatives, though – other family to leave him with, I mean. What if he becomes ill? It's a big responsibility."

"Only other thing would be to leave him with Nanny, in the family house. And Doctor Parrish, while she didn't elaborate, somehow made me think that the woman may have been neglecting the boy. No, this is the only solution it seems. He'll just have to stay here during the holidays – the mother might be away for up to a year – or perhaps one of the other boys will invite him home."

"When's he arriving?"

"Day after tomorrow. Doctor Parrish leaves that afternoon for Los Angeles. Paid a year's tuition in advance – nice to have one parent we won't have to chase for the fees."

When Leo was next called to Brother Docherty's office, the mother and the child were waiting with Dominic in the corridor.

Even the smallest size of St Jude's uniform looked a little large on the boy, but he was neat as a pin, and very calm in the face of this long separation.

"Doctor Parrish is in a hurry to make several appointments before her plane leaves," Brother Docherty told Leo. "Would you like to take Mark up to the dorm and see him settled in?"

The question was, of course, rhetorical, this was Leo's job. Once more the boy's blue eyes surveyed him, calmly, and the small hand was placed trustingly in his. Over the boy's head, Leo looked at the woman. She seemed to regard the boy already as if from a great distance, and he was worried that her self-control would break, suddenly, and distress the child.

But she called his name, and when he turned to her, she bent, and kissed his cheek. Leo noticed the boy's arms come up towards her – and stop short of holding her.

Doctor Parrish straightened. "Be a good boy, and a brave boy, as Daddy and I know you are. We'll be back soon."

Leo glanced at Brother Docherty, who gave a faint jerk with his head towards the stairs. Picking up the large suitcase, and with the boy's hand once more in his, Leo led Mark up the stairs towards the dormitory. They were halfway up the first flight when the heavy front door shut behind them. The boy looked over his shoulder, pausing only for a second.

At the bend in the broad old mahogany stairs, the boy looked up at the large window. Being a warm day, the lower part was open.

"Can I look out and wave to my mother?" he asked.

Leo lifted him up, for the window was high and the stone sill a good twelve inches thick. Mark clung with one hand and waved valiantly with the other. A car engine started into life, and faded with the crunching of the gravel beneath its wheels. When he ceased his farewells, Leo set the child down on the stairs again. "Did she wave back?"

"No," philosophically. "She didn't see me. She didn't look back." He began to climb the stairs, matching his steps, in his small, new shoes, to Leo's. Only at the top of the stairs did he look back, once, through the huge window, at the now empty drive and the open gates.

Already, the boy had begun to tug at Leo's heart, the helplessness of him. Whether Leo knew then, instinctively, that Mark and his mother would become a part of his life, or, as Dominic later suggested, he was perhaps wishing himself into the place of the missing husband and father, Leo didn't know. He had murmured, later, to Dominic's suggestion, "I only want to do what's right. I'm not thinking of myself, I'm thinking of him."

For by that time, a year or so later, Mark smiled when he was with Leo. He prattled to Leo – all sorts of childish nonsense, and it was good to see the child be . . . *young*.

"You're favouring him. The other boys notice. The other brothers notice. You aren't the boy's father, Leo, nor an uncle, nor even a family friend. The mother could come home tomorrow and take the boy away – and he'd be distraught. You must discourage this dependence upon you. You're his teacher – *one* of his teachers – nothing more."

But, Leo wanted to say, if his mother came home tomorrow and took him away – at least he's had *someone* that he feels he can talk to – someone who cares about him. Isn't *some* affection and encouragement better for a child than none at all?

But Leo was only twenty-five, and Brother Docherty, already ill and growing understandably less patient these days, would not have listened to him, even if he *had* spoken up for what he believed.

But Leo did not try.

Brother Docherty smiled, and stood, and Leo stood also, with what he hoped was a smile, and left his office, smarting that he had had to be reprimanded for breaking so basic a tenet of the teaching profession: there must not be favourites.

And as Leo walked away from the door, a small shape in grey serge launched itself at him from where it had been hovering in the shadows of the hall. And, just as Mark later recalled, he went to take Leo's hand, his face alight – and Leo *did* – he pushed him away a little, for the boy's clamouring treble voice could not block out the criticisms of this, Leo's life's work. And, in that moment, Leo blamed the child. Why couldn't he be like other boys, more resilient, aggressive, gregarious? I did not know, Leo thought later, that I had another, a second life's work, and when it thrust itself into my arms, I pushed it away.

And Mark remembered that betrayal always, even though it only lasted a moment, for Leo took his hand then, and went with him, out into the playground, and left him, happily enough, to play with a group of other boys, while Leo went off to a cold cup of tea in the staff room. The bell to signal the end of recess rang, and the even tenor of the days at St Jude's flowed on.

Linda had lied to Dominic Docherty. Bill Parrish *was* in Los Angeles, but he had not suffered a stroke. He had flown there to begin a new life with his attractive young secretary, after months of careful, clandestine preparation. He had a lecturing position lined up at one of the large and prestigious medical schools, and managed – through Linda's pre-occupation with her own work and her reluctance, in those days, to socialise – to keep secret the fact that he had sold his share in his Macquarie Street practice.

He simply disappeared. Linda was frantic for hours, until she managed to locate Bill's former medical associate. The surprised and embarrassed man had had the sensitivity to come to see her, to explain in person all that he knew. She had pieced the story together, and the following day a letter had arrived from Bill, posted the same day she had driven him to the airport and kissed him goodbye.

I will never be what you expect of me, Linda. You call me shallow, and irresponsible – and I know you're undoubtedly right. But I am the same man you married. No, this isn't honest, either. I tried to be faithful to you – and don't feel that it was your fault that I wasn't. My shallowness and irresponsibility again. Whatever – as I'm sure you must have suspected – I was unfaithful to you many times before Sandra came along. I stayed only for Mark – and he is of an age now, he has begun school and will be making friends – I think he is old enough to understand at least the basic concept of divorce. He will not miss me so much.

"Perhaps Sandra posted it for him, he was busy packing all that morning."

It was some years later that Linda showed Leo this letter. He felt sickened, furious for her sake and for the boy's.

Linda had not known of Bill's other affairs, had not suspected. Bill had been her entire life, perhaps more than was good for her. When the initial shock was over, she made up her mind that she must, for Mark's sake, speak to Bill, reason with him. She tracked down his whereabouts through mutual friends, and flew to Los Angeles.

She did not return to Australia for more than two years. Cheques arrived regularly at St Jude's, and she and Brother Docherty exchanged letters concerning Mark's progress and welfare. When Dominic became ill, too ill to write, he charged Leo with continuing to liaise with Mark's mother. It was Leo who wrote to her to inform her of Dominic's death, and Leo who took the liberty, then, to ask her to reunite herself and her husband with her son, either here or in America.

Leo was finishing an MA in English literature – not because he was ambitious, but because he had always enjoyed study, and that year began teaching English and drama to the seniors. St Jude's was not a large school, so he was still able to watch over Mark from a distance, and was delighted when his mother came home to him. But she came home alone.

The first Leo knew of Linda's return was a telephone call requesting him to visit her at her home. She would explain matters then, she promised him. It would be best, for the moment, if Mark – then just turned eight – was not told she had returned. Leo received permission from Brother Orsini, Dominic's successor as headmaster, and drove, for the first time, to the house on Castle Crag Road.

For the first time, he had tea with Linda in the library, the stolid faces of Parrish forebears gazing down from their heavy frames, and Linda told him her story. She had stayed in Los Angeles, and found work there. Bill, despite all her efforts at a reconciliation, had wavered and vacillated between herself and the twenty-two year old Sandra for two and a half years. "Finally, I couldn't take any more. I had to think of Mark, so . . . I've come home." There was no contentment in her voice, only a wistful hollowness, but Leo responded positively: "I'm glad. Mark will be so happy to see you. Will he be able to stay on at St Jude's as a day pupil?"

For he presumed, as Linda had said there was to be a divorce, that the house would remain with Bill, or that it might be sold and she and Mark may move from Castle Crag. But no.

"You'll think me strange, cold-hearted, perhaps." She was twisting her rings around those fine, tapered little fingers. Beautiful hands, as delicate as everything else about this woman. "I'm looking forward to seeing Mark very much, and to spending time with him. But, these last two years . . ."

She would not cry. In all those years Leo was to know her, he never once saw Linda Parrish cry. He often thought that it might have been better if she had. Leo expected to see tears in her eyes, but she possessed such rigid self-control that it was up to him to guess at the extent of her pain. "You'd like

Mark to remain with us as a boarder for a while," he said.

"Yes," gratefully. "Would you think me unmotherly if I let him stay on at St Jude's? Until I adjust to being back home, until I can set up my practice again and find a routine . . ."

The new housekeeper, Maria, a plump young woman not long arrived in Australia from Portugal, came in at that moment. She had a round, pleasant face, and smiled at them both, asking if they would like more tea.

Linda turned to Leo. "Can you stay? Do you have to rush back to the school?"

Leo had the afternoon off for this visit, so he stayed, and they talked. She spoke to Leo as she had not been able to speak to anyone else in the past two years or more. There was so much hurt and betrayal in her life – she had struggled for so long to save her marriage, and there had been no one, in her limited circle in Los Angeles, whom she could really trust, in whom she could confide.

As Leo was leaving, Linda took his hand and smiled. "You'd have made an excellent psychiatrist, Brother Leo, or a good priest. I'm glad I found St Jude's. I'm glad I left my son in your hands."

She remained at the door as Leo walked down the steps. Looking back to smile at her, he walked into an azalea bush.

That same azalea bush bloomed, lay dormant, bloomed again, and was dusted with gold from the magnificent beech tree that grew close to a corner of the verandah, for ten more seasons before Mark left St Jude's and came home to live permanently in that house.

What was in the child's face as he ran to meet his mother in the corridor of St Jude's, seeing her for the first time in two years? Leo was behind him – he could not see Mark's features, but he could see Linda's. Her smile was warm, her eyes alight as she held her arms out to him – but the smile remained fixed, the eyes questioned, and by the time the boy had reached her she was gazing at him fondly, proudly, and with a kind of wariness.

It was very strange. Mark had slowed – Leo could recognise the set of the boy's shoulders, the drag of the feet of a child overcome by sudden shyness – but now Linda, too, was shy. It took seconds, long enough for him to draw level with them, before Mark could bring himself to hold out his hand. She looked at it, and at him, and took his hand in hers.

The words came before Leo could think. "For heaven's sake, Mark, give your mother a kiss."

Mark's blue eyes rolled up towards him like a frightened colt's, but, with a smile, he reached up on tiptoe and kissed Linda on the cheek.

Her hand was on his hair as he pulled away, and she gazed at him with affection and sadness.

Leo wondered all that night at her reaction, before he suddenly realised – *Mark must look the image of Bill*. This was confirmed when he finally saw the photographs. Gradually, over the years after the divorce, the photographs came out of their packing cases in the boxroom and were to be found on the mantels, the piano, the desks, the shelves. That tall, fair-haired, well-built man – perpetually young – smiled out at the world from the deck of his yacht; at his wedding to Linda; from the back verandah, holding a solemn two-year-old Mark in his arms; at an award night, his arm about a leading politician. In every photograph Bill was between the ages of twenty-five and thirty-three – his years with Linda.

And as Mark grew, he came to resemble more and more those photographs of his father. Visitors would often find it impossible to guess between images of father and son.

Was it hard, too, for Linda?

Bill Parrish died only five years after leaving for America. By then he was working in a cancer clinic in Washington, DC, and, ironically enough, he finally succumbed to a cerebral haemorrhage such as Linda, five years previously, had fabricated for him. The divorce settlement, however, had been most generous. The house had been deeded to Mark, with provision for Linda to remain there for the duration of her life, if she so wished.

The will was even more generous. Linda found that Bill had divorced Sandra not long after they had married. Everything Bill owned – assets amounting to nearly four million dollars – was divided equally between Linda and Mark.

This final, if belated, act of thoughtfulness for his family confirmed Bill's status in Linda's eyes. The betrayals, the lies, were forgotten. The fact that they had divorced was never mentioned. When Linda spoke of Bill, it was always "my husband", or, at most, "my late husband".

And still Mark did not come home.

Linda returned to her work, bought a terrace house in North Sydney and converted it into consulting rooms. She became, once more, a highly respected psychiatrist, and worked ceaselessly in the field of community mental health. She made speeches, wrote articles, and began appearing on television in her campaign to make the Australian public and its politicians aware of the needs of mentally disturbed people, and the fact that not enough was being done. There was also her charity work for the Church, and no one wondered, after a while, why such a committed and productive physician could not keep her son with her, but chose instead to board him at an excellent private school. Leo ceased wondering himself.

So did Mark. He was so very proud of his mother, sat entranced before the television screen whenever Linda was being interviewed, on one occasion, looking up to beam at one of his friends,

"She makes *sense*, doesn't she?" This last, at about thirteen, when the world itself did not make sense, let alone – to a thirteen year old – women.

Mark looked forward to the weekends he would go home to her, but they were relatively few, and when they did occur he would return to St Jude's quieter, more self-contained than ever. Gentle querying by Leo brought out the fact that his mother had been writing nearly the entire time, and had three times been called to the clinic for emergencies. Mark had spent the days with Maria in the kitchen, or wandering in the large grounds, alone. Those few holidays at Castle Crag were the same.

Yet many parents were busy with their work and did not have much time to spare for their children. Mark was never neglected, would never have said – never *did* say – that he felt unloved. Once Leo heard him tell Simon O'Neil (the beautiful Melissa's brother), "At least my mother doesn't *gush* like other mothers do. She's always let me think for myself."

Leo wondered if this had been bravado, but came to doubt it. Mark was growing up to be a strong-willed and independent young man. He was a quiet boy, but kind-hearted and fair-minded. Never one for close friends, his growing athletic prowess as a senior – when he suddenly shot up to stand head and shoulders above everyone, pupils and teachers alike – coupled with that aloofness that had discouraged friendly overtures, now made him something of a hero to the younger boys and gained him new respect

75

from his peers. David Papadimitriou and Simon O'Neil, closer to him than any of the other boys, described him to Leo as "a strange sort, but alright once you get to know him".

Mark topped New South Wales in his matriculation examination – the final crowning of those twelve years at St Jude's. At the graduation ceremony in the main hall, Leo saw him deep in disucssion with his mother. Later, Mark came up to him, smiled down at him – he was a good five inches taller than Leo, by then – and said, "I'm going into psychiatry or oncology, so I'll be at university for years and years. I told Mother I want to come home, instead of going to a residential college. That library's full of medical books – besides, it *is* home."

Leo was surprised, but pleased. He did not know that it had taken Mark two days to persuade Linda to agree to his plan. Now Mark was smiling at him. "I'll miss this place, too. You will come to visit, won't you, Brother? Often? Do you promise?"

How could anyone be blamed for feeling confident for his future? Though Leo admitted to Mark, and to Linda, that perhaps oncology might be a stressful field for him to choose – all through his medical studies Mark had found suffering to be distressing. For a long time, his naturally detached nature could not help him and he often made himself physically ill when a patient died. Perhaps, Leo suggested, family medicine, or, given his interest in sports, orthopaedics. Linda supported him in this, but Mark was firm. "I want to help people. I know I get involved with my patients, but I'll become inured to it as I get older. And shouldn't an oncologist care? If you had cancer, or a brain tumour, Leo, wouldn't you want a doctor who cared?"

And the boy was so sure, that he finally convinced them.

But if Linda had insisted that he go into a less traumatic field, he might have listened to her. He worshipped her – and why not? For she was beautiful, brilliant and captivating, and she had floated in and out of his life like an evanescent dream for so many years – a butterfly that was reborn each season, appeared suddenly in one's garden to take one's breath away, and was gone just as suddenly.

It would have been better for their relationship, Leo thought, if she had had more to do with the actual mothering, caretaking part of his boyhood – but Mark had no memories of Linda as a fussing, coddling, lovingly reproving figure who fed him, toilet trained him, laced his shoes, kissed away his minor hurts. Nanny had played that role, and she had long since vanished. And "Mummy" went away, and came back as "Mother" – and she was more a sophisticated and exotic aunt, or an older sister, than a parent. She was, by the time Mark

77

came to share a house with her, a stranger – a fascinating stranger – and so had more influence over him, in a way, than any of those mothers, whose love and opinions we so take for granted, could have done.

Leo went often to the house, his visits increasing further when he left teaching to return to the seminary, and after he was ordained. By then he was regarded as family, accepted, and – he knew – loved. Even the Archbishop did not query his visits to the Parrishes. And if he had, Leo would probably have found the courage to argue with him.

CHAPTER FIVE

Mark's beach house was at the end of a long drive through the rainforest property, where the trees met overhead and the trunks were hung with liana and bougainvillea, draping and shrouding the darker shadows between the trees, a darkness that seemed deep and ageless and impenetrable. There were no other houses about for miles, and it could seem, on that drive, as though one had taken a wrong turning and was driving deeper and deeper into the tropical wilderness.

And then the clearing, and the beach, and the house beside the wide expanse of sea, and the desire to take deep breaths, not realising until now how constrictive the driveway had begun to seem, how oppressive the encroaching wilderness, the waiting dark.

The house was large and sprawling and comfortable, set in a garden that seemed only a more colourful extension of its surrounding forest. "Hacked into submission," Mark said, as he had

had no time for horticultural endeavours, having been preoccupied enough with the interior of the house.

Inside, the house had been freshly painted, and something of the smell still clung about the rooms. In the spacious study, at one end of the house, Rosalind said, "It smells like a new home."

"It's the paint – I only meant to have the kitchen done but I got carried away with the colour cards."

"No, it's something else – fresh wood, carpentry smells . . ."

"The windows," Mark smiled. "I had some of the windows replaced. The salt plays havoc with the timbers."

"And what's in here?" For she had seen over the living areas, the kitchen, the bedrooms, all beautifully furnished – "like a shop window display" she had laughed, and Mark did not know whether to be pleased or not. Now her hand was on the knob of a heavy-looking door set into the far wall of the study.

"Don't look in there! I piled all my junk in there so the house would be tidy for visitors," he began. She was turning the knob, but it did not move. He said, "It's locked, anyway." And, as she looked up at him, "I lock as many doors as I can when I leave the house – a legacy from growing up in Sydney, I guess. That room was actually a recording studio, so it would have held a lot of valuable equipment. Would you like to help me make lunch?"

"Who'd want a recording studio out here in the jungle?"

Mark had turned towards the kitchen, looked back with a smile, "One of Australia's rock groups."

"Which one?"

"They disbanded years ago. Some weird name."

"You don't know?" She was laughing at him.

"Cole Porter's more my style."

She shook her head, "You're a strange boy."

Smiling, she moved off towards the sliding glass doors that led out into the timber deck. She was amused, Mark realised later, that he was twenty-seven years old and had no knowledge of popular music. But he was stung at the time, not by her laughter, but by her unfortunate choice of words, *you're a strange boy*.

"I'm not a boy, Rosalind. I'm a man."

She stopped, and turned back to look at him.

He stood there, six foot three of wounded sensibility, the blue eyes reproachful, and she regarded him fondly, apologetically.

"I'm sorry," she said, " 'matronising' you again. Leave the lunch for now – come and show me the beach."

He could never stay angry with her for long. By the time they had taken off their shoes and walked along the tidemark for a few metres, he had regained his confidence and his good humour.

But he could sense that Rosalind was a little guarded with him. The incident had jarred the accord between them and he had to concentrate very hard not to allow his frustration to communicate itself. He even made up a girlfriend in Cairns, a pharmacist at the hospital, and described her in glowing terms – only later realising that he was describing Melissa of the sugar bowl incident. And Rosalind was pleased for him, to his irritation. When they were about a mile away from the house, she looked back to study it. "If you marry," she said, "this would be a wonderful place to raise a family – a magic place for children."

It was a test that both failed and succeeded. She was more at her ease because he had mentioned the toothsome and fictitious pharmacist, but her very pleasure in the news, and these projections for his future, were bitter for him.

But he chatted on, about his plans for the house, for his new practice, and about the history of the area, for he had had time to study this in the days when the builders had been renovating one of the bedrooms, with its *en suite* bathroom, into the recording studio. The bricking up of the windows had been quiet enough work, but when they began on fixing the two soundproof doors, with a soundlock between them, at the far end of the study, he had taken his books down to the beach.

Mark had truthfully enjoyed the weeks while waiting for Rosalind to arrive. Professor Stewart had been right, he had needed a holiday.

Rosalind spoke of Geoff a good deal, about how she did not want him to expand the Harcourt Corporation at this time. Mark was surprised at her grasp of current economic trends – she seemed, in the three weeks since they had spoken, to be more aware of the dangers and pitfalls of what Geoff was planning.

"We don't know this Harry Manzone well enough. Geoff says it's the companies that matter, not individuals, but companies are *comprised* of individuals . . ."

He was smiling a little as he watched her, and she stopped, self-conscious. "Sorry, this must be boring."

"No, I'm as concerned for Geoff as you are."

I want Geoff to be happy, Mark wrote later in his diary. *I like the man. I only feel sorry for him, because he doesn't realise that he already possesses the most important thing in his life. If he wants more power, then I hope he achieves it – it'll be some compensation to him, when he realises the truth, and it's too late.*

Rosalind found a shell in the sand on the way back to the house, and was inordinately proud of herself. It was lovely, pink and palest apricot, with sculptured, flared wings that gave it the look of an elaborate oriental kite in full flight, banners streaming. Washed lovingly under the garden tap, it became the proud centrepiece on the table when they had their very late lunch on the verandah.

Mark had been studying cooking, he informed her, and this was true, of necessity. The quiche, he admitted, was store-bought, but the two different salads and the fried rice dish he had made himself. There were a lot of spices in the rice, perhaps too many, he pondered aloud – ginger, garlic, turmeric.

Rosalind set the table and they opened one, then another, bottle of champagne.

"Will your mother come to Queensland?"

"To live? No – all her work is in Sydney. Besides, I can't live all my life with my mother. It was convenient for a long while, but I have my own life to lead. She was becoming a little dependent on me."

"You're all she has." It was typical of Rosalind to see other people's point of view. "But you're right, of course. She'll miss you very much, though."

Mark did not answer because her words were uncomfortably close to the truth. And he had avoided thinking of his mother, except for the dutiful and prevaricating phone calls. He could not confront the thought of what she would say to his plans, to his relationship with Rosalind, to the fact that he may never return to Sydney. He had forced the thought of Linda out of his future, out of his life. He had been working independently of her for

84

the first time in ten years or more, and this was so new to him and he had succeeded so well that he did not want reminders of the hurt he may be wilfully inflicting.

Rosalind had risen from the table and taken her glass of champagne to stand with it at the railing, looking out over the sea. Like the sky above it, the intensity of blue was becoming muted, shadowed, as the light leached from the sky.

Mark looked at the table, the almost clear plates, the two empty bottles of champagne. Their first meal together in this house. He looked up at Rosalind, and stood, moving leisurely to stand at the railing beside her. One of her hands held the champagne glass, the other rested on her midriff. She was scowling a little.

"Are you alright?" he asked, concerned.

"I shouldn't have had that lunch on the plane – I'm such a pig."

"What's the matter?"

"Just indigestion. It wasn't your lovely lunch." She looked up at him in that bright way that never ceased to delight him, but this time he did not return her smile. He was watching her, carefully.

"It's getting late," and she glanced at her watch, "Geoff's phoning me from Los Angeles tonight. Hadn't we . . . ?"

He was standing rigid, he had not considered this. Why would Geoff ring *tonight*? Was she telling the truth? Wouldn't *she* be more likely to phone *him* in LA to tell him that she had arrived safely?

"Mark?"

"Sorry?"

"It's been a wonderful day," she glanced along the beach, her smile taking in the distant headland, the quiet sea, "but if we've got a couple of hundred kilom – "

She was already turning back towards him, but was drawn forward by the sudden pressure of his hand on her shoulder, and when her eyes came up to his, his lips were already upon hers.

She did not pull away. *She did not pull away.*

Could Rosalind have saved herself had she done so, Leo wondered. He knew so little of sexual matters, of the attraction between men and women. The Church wanted her priests to come to her pure in body and spirit – but to have known a few of the temptations that beset his parishioners would not have been a bad thing. He himself had never felt *driven* towards anything; God had beckoned him wherever He wished him to go and Leo had meandered cautiously along that path, less because of piety, he thought wryly, than because of his lack of imagination in thinking of alternatives.

Leo was in awe when he thought of those two people – caught in his imagination due to Mark's damnable tapes – standing on that balcony above a darkening sea. And he had tossed and turned at night, asking himself, *was* she in love with him? Was Mark more right than even she knew? Or was it a moment's passion? The champagne and the setting and this beautiful young man who adored her? Was she to be destroyed because of that one, understandable moment of weakness? Could she be blamed for giving herself up to what Robert Graves – who seemed to understand much more about love than Leo ever could – called that

> *Walk between dark and dark, a shining space*
> *With the grave's narrowness, but not its peace.*

The kiss did not last long. It was she who broke away, and she was afraid of what had happened. Even Mark, who wished he could believe otherwise, saw that she was appalled that she had responded. Embarrassed, she backed away a little. Her cheeks were pink, her eyes found it difficult to meet his, for Mark had not moved, was gazing at her intently, aware of her life and his in the balance.

Rosalind smiled, and said, lightly, "Well ... I suppose we always wondered what that would be like. And ... now we know."

He gave her no help at all. No smile, no shared embarrassment or feigned regret. He waited. He was close enough to be able to tell when the sharp spasm of pain seized her, the stifled short gasp of breath, the flicker of her lids, the unconscious movement as if to double over, stopped by the will after an imperceptible jerk of her shoulders.

He made to step towards her, but she was edging back, away from him. The same attempt at lightness in her voice, a deprecating little laugh, "Mark . . . my timing is terrible – but I feel awfully sick . . ."

He moved to her, taking her arm and guiding her towards the living room. "Where's the pain?"

"In my stomach – God!"

He had to support her through the sliding glass doors. "What did you eat on the plane?"

"I don't know. Who can tell . . . what they feed you in those little containers."

Think. He led her towards the couch.

"Some unidentifiable little roast with tiny baked spuds . . . Oh, God, Mark!" Laughing through her pain, gasping, "This is awful!"

"Was it beef? Chicken?"

She could only shake her head. He lowered her down onto the couch. "It was . . . too small for a chicken leg . . . and too big for a budgie . . ."

He was down on one knee beside her. "This is serious, I might have to ring the airline."

"Haunch of . . . guinea pig?" She gasped.

"Rosalind . . ." warningly.

"Rat roast?"

Her humour was her undoing. She gagged, and shot up from the couch and raced into the bathroom.

Mark was not quite fast enough and found the door locked against him. "Rosalind?!" for now he was truly worried. "Rosalind, open the door!"

Only the sound of her vomiting came to Mark. He knocked loudly. "Rosalind, stop being bloody coy! I'm a doctor! Open the door!"

Between retching, "You've got to be joking!"

CHAPTER SIX

ark had poisoned her. Leo's Mark, Linda's
Mark, had used – so he recorded – a
quantity of sodium warfarin, a common drug
prescribed as an anticoagulant to heart patients. It
also did service as rat poison. His tainting of the
seasoned rice dish on her plate was something he
was not proud of, and he avoided all but the barest
essentials of the matter in his reports.

He had been using the small, hand-held recorder
since coming to the house. Even when he spoke of
what he had done, his voice was more agitated, low,
hesitant with his discomfort.

*I am a healer – I've never wilfully inflicted
pain on any creature in my life – and now I
inflict it upon her, who means more to me
than my own life. When she began eating the
rice at lunch I nearly – so nearly – reached
across the table and grabbed her wrist to stop
her, nearly hurled the plate away, over the*

balcony. Instead, I ate my own safe meal and felt as if it were I, not she, who had swallowed the monstrous stuff. I felt the effects long before she did, and long after the pain was behind her.

It was late, nearly six o'clock, and Rosalind was worried. In just over an hour, Geoff would phone Silver Palms – she had been due there early that afternoon.

She fretted as she lay on the couch and suffered Mark to examine her – her chest, her throat, her heart, the glands in her neck. She was very embarrassed at having to unbutton her blouse, unzip her slacks, in order that he might palpate her abdomen. That his touch disturbed her, he could tell, even through her distress, when, by accident or design, his practised hands found a pulse point. But that happened with most women patients. He would have felt better had she clung to him in her pain, looked to him confidently to cure her, even exaggerated her discomfort.

Instead, she smiled, and said it did not hurt when it did, and held herself within herself, sharing nothing. And when she did speak, she spoke of her husband.

"Stop worrying," he told her. "Geoff will understand if you're ill. Phone him from here."

"No . . . it doesn't look right. Well, it doesn't," she repeated, when he looked a little amused.

"He's . . . any husband would be jealous in those circumstances. Ow!"

"That hurts?"

"Yes . . . a little. Can we stop, now?"

"That hurt?"

"Yes! Mark, I'll throw up on your head if you keep – "

"No, you won't. That hurt?"

For answer she gasped, and sat up abruptly.

Mark straightened, and made no effort to stop her as she quickly zipped up her slacks and almost ran towards the bathroom.

He pulled the stethoscope from his neck and began to replace his instruments in his bag. "You have salmonella poisoning," he said.

She stopped in the doorway just long enough to give him one black look.

This time he did not follow her. Instead, he walked out onto the broad verandah that ran the length of the living areas of the house. It stopped short of the dark corner of the house that was the recording studio. He did not look at that. Instead he watched the sea before him.

The sun must have all but set behind the house – here we face east – and the ocean was indigo, the wash of its waves muted, as if tonight even the ocean was holding itself still, waiting for some sign of portent. Yet I was confident. I was winning. I felt it, even if

Rosalind didn't. I gripped the wooden railing and felt that it was possible for the human mind to achieve anything, if one planned, if one ventured.

When Rosalind reappeared, paler, the recurring agony written on her face, she sat on the settee and asked Mark what she should do.

"I'm driving you to hospital," he said. Then, just as the consternation leapt into her eyes, "Unless you'd prefer to stay here and let me look after you for a day or so."

"I . . ." she hesitated.

"Here – while you're thinking, phone Geoff and tell him what's happened."

She took the phone on to her lap, and Mark handed her her handbag. She found her address book, began to dial – and stopped, replacing the receiver.

"But I have to tell him we're here . . . I mean . . ."

Mark merely looked at her, enquiringly.

"No," she half-muttered, "I suppose I don't." More quickly, "I suppose I could say that I was already at the resort – I will be, by tomorrow." She glanced at Mark, and noted his dubious expression. "I must, Mark." She swallowed against the pain, lifted the receiver once more. "This is terrible . . ."

He left her alone to make the call, but from his position at the deck railing, he could hear her voice quite clearly through the glass doors.

"No . . . no, darling, nothing's wrong. I've got a headache, that's all. It was very rushed this morning. I thought I'd ring you early and then go to bed."

She spent some time listening, then, to Geoff's news of his business meetings, until, "Why do you have to go on to London? Well, why couldn't they have come to us? I see. No, it's just . . . I'd have liked to come with you, that's all."

The moon hung in the darkest corner of the sky, above the place where the headland met the beach and the sea. Mark found he was gritting his teeth, and tried to relax, but it was hard.

"I have to go, now, darling – the waiter's just brought my supper . . ." It was such a smooth lie that he turned to look at her. She was standing, and obviously in distress, her body bent over a little.

"No! No, don't phone tomorrow. I met Lydia and Stephen Rosenshein at the airport. They were seeing a friend off . . ."

Even Mark could tell she was barely coping with the pain and the prevaricating. If Mark could tell, couldn't Geoff?

"They've asked me out on the boat tomorrow. I won't be back until late . . ." A long pause. "Yes," in some relief. "Yes, I'll phone you tomorrow or the day after."

Mark began to move towards the sliding glass doors, but Rosalind was saying, hurriedly, "And

Geoff, darling, since you're going on to London –
can't I meet you there? Even for a few days
together – we could drive through Wales again."

And Mark saw her smile, saw her smile at
something the man said, some mention of that
memory of Wales, and he hated Geoff, then, for the
first time.

"I love you," Rosalind was saying. "I love you,
my darling ... take care ... Goodbye ... I love
you ..."

Mark could not bear to look at her. He turned
and gripped the railing tightly, so tightly that his
hands hurt. He had heard Rosalind say these words
to Geoff before, bidding him goodbye ...

but everything is different, now. Geoff is in
LA. When he comes home, he will be in
Sydney – and Rosalind will be here, with me.
She has become my Rosalind.

And he had murmured into the tape recorder a
fragment of the Tennyson poem: *My Rosalind, my*
Rosalind, my frolic falcon with bright eyes ...

Leo knew the poem, one of Tennyson's works
written around a woman's name. He had never
realised how frightening a poem it was until he
heard it on the tape, in Mark's sonorous voice.
"Such a beautiful speaking voice," they had said,
from the time his voice broke in Year Eight at St

Jude's. He had won every recitation award in every eisteddfod in which he was entered.

"If only the boy could sing in tune," Brother Paul, the music teacher, lamented. "We'd really clean up!"

Mark phoned the resort and told them that Mrs Harcourt was staying with relatives for the next three days and to hold her reservation. When they asked for a contact number, he made one up. Rosalind, all this while, was once more being sick in the bathroom, though by now, after vomiting attacks each quarter of an hour or so, it was mostly a reflex action. Her stomach was empty, but her body was still attempting to reject the effects of the poison.

She was too ill to object when Mark led her to the main bedroom, where he had opened her suitcases on the bed. "Choose a nightdress."

"You wait outside."

"Don't be absurd. You'll fall over any minute."

He was as clinical in this as in everything else, and, once she was in the bed and the suitcases tidied away, he left a bowl and tissues beside the bed in case she should be sick once more, and returned to the living room to fetch his medical bag.

She did not seem to notice what he was doing in preparing the injection, but was more concerned that her presence was an intrusion upon him. "I shouldn't have your bedroom . . ."

"It's the only one with its own bathroom. Except for the studio – and you don't deserve that." And they smiled at each other. "Push up your sleeve," he ordered.

And she did so. "Mark, I will be alright to go to Silver Palms tomorrow, won't I? What's that?" she asked, deflected from her question by the coldness of the alcohol wipe on her upper arm, the sudden proximity of the deadly-looking little hypodermic.

"Stemetil," he said, truthfully enough. "It'll suppress the vomiting."

She watched as he held up the syringe and expressed the air from it. He noticed her puzzled gaze on his face as he bent over her, the needle poised.

"Don't worry, I'm very good at this. I practise on oranges for half an hour every day." And, when she smiled, "Turn away, don't be a masochist."

She turned her face away, obediently, and he watched the needle pierce the skin, and the lowering level of the Stemetil, and the line of her cheek and the pattern of the lace of her nightdress against her skin.

When she next looked at him he was scowling as he wiped the injection site with the cotton swab. "It'll make you sleepy, too. *And* . . ." shaking a tablet from a small brown plastic container, "take one of these. Antibiotics," as she looked at him enquiringly.

He sat with her for a while, and she told him – for she would not know that he had heard – that Geoff was extending his business trip to include London. "I'll only stay two weeks at Silver Palms and then I'll fly over to him." Her eyelids were closing.

It was the Amytal, of course. The tablets that Mark would be giving her for the next four days, ostensibly antibiotics, were, in fact, Amytal tablets. Amytal has a dual purpose: not only is it prescribed as a sedative, but many psychiatrists, including Mark's mother, used it to help lower a patient's resistance in analysis. Amytal could be described as a kind of truth drug.

Rosalind's breathing was slowing, she was not in so much pain now. Her eyes were closed, and he did not know whether or not she slept. He said, "I'm sorry you're ill, yet I can't be sorry that I found you and brought you here. I'd rather you were here than at Silver Palms, wouldn't you?"

She opened her eyes and surveyed him quietly for a second or two. "No ... I'd rather be sick by myself. I'd lock myself in my room for a few days – no one'd know."

"No one'd know if you died, either."

He realised her hair was still in its usual chignon and leaned forward to remove the combs and pins. Her hands fluttered at his, then she lay still, turning her head for him as he took down her hair. "I like doing things for you. Can you understand that?"

She smiled at him, fondly, and her eyes closed once more. He sat there, the hairpins and combs in his hands, his gaze upon her face.

"Rosalind?" softly.

When she looked up at him, "I'll be in the bedroom next to this. Call me if you need me."

"I'll be okay," she murmured.

"Call me," he said firmly. "Any change at all. I think it's salmonella, but I want to keep an eye on you."

"What else could it be?"

He smiled and stood, laying the pins and combs on the bedside table and taking up the syringe and the cotton swab. "Nothing life-threatening."

"Stop sounding like a doctor."

"It's hard."

"Seriously – I can go to Silver Palms tomorrow, can't I?"

"We'll see." He touched her hair, almost ruffled it, and it was wonderful to make such a casual, spontaneous gesture, to have her there, beneath his hand.

She said, "All this is very disturbing for me ..."

He had turned to the door, but stopped and looked back. "In what way?"

She was drifting into sleep, but he came back to the bed and seated himself upon the edge. "Rosalind? What is it about me that disturbs you?"

"No ..." her head moving on the pillow a little.

"Not you ... exactly. It's the situation ... I've always been in control of most situations ..."

Concerning him? He felt certain that this was what she would have said. Gently, "You feel helpless, and you don't like it, do you? You feel uncomfortable being dependent on me – is that it?"

"Yes." The heavy lids struggled, and she smiled. "Yes, you're a different you."

He brushed her hair back from her forehead, but she was asleep. She did not wake when he said, "I'm the same, Rosalind. I'll always be the same."

Mark awoke in the early hours to the rising wind, the first rumbles of thunder, and lay awake for some time. A glance at his watch – his bedside clock was with Rosalind – 3.00 am.

The storm rolled closer, the thunder and lightning becoming one force that shook the house on its foundations. He thought of Rosalind, and rose, pulled on his trousers and padded barefoot into the hall.

He was almost at Rosalind's door when he heard the noise – there, in the study, and quite close – a scraping and a sharp *bump*, and even through the floorboards he could tell that something heavy had fallen.

He turned on the light in the hall, and from the shaft that fell through the open door into the main bedroom, he could see the bed was empty. Moving too quickly, carelessly, into the study he almost fell over the small walnut table that lay on its side on the floor. His bare feet found the cold shock of wet carpet where the bowl of winter jasmine had fallen, harmlessly enough, on to the rug. At the same time he heard the glass doors in the living room sliding open.

He turned on the lights as he ran through the rooms and was just in time to see her, swaying slightly, her hand out, helplessly, to guide her, stepping from the lighted square that fell across the verandah into the darker shadows towards the railing. The wind blew the curtains back against the ceiling, the rain fell in such torrents that it blurred the floor of the decking with its force, and Rosalind seemed like a wraith rising from grey fog. He reached her before she could take another step, pulled her into his arms, gasping himself with the icy shock of the downpour. "Rosalind!"

She did not cling to him but pushed him away, her face wild in the flashes of lightning, her gaze fixed beyond Mark, out into the darkness.

"Geoff!" she cried out, and fought against him as he pulled her with him towards the open glass doors. Her bare arms were wet, both she and Mark had been soaked almost as soon as they had stepped outside, and she slipped a little from his grasp, would not be held – wanted to be away, crazily, into that maelstrom of a storm.

"*Rosalind*!" He had to shout over the roar of the wind, the sea, the palm trees by the balcony that whipped back and forth till their harsh leaves sounded like the clattering, gnashing teeth of devils above their heads. "Rosalind – it's alright! Come back to bed."

She looked at him wildly in the light that fell upon them from the living room – and in that moment, in another burst of sound about them, the lights flickered and the house was plunged into darkness.

"Geoff?!" The terror in her voice.

"He isn't here, Rosalind."

"Where am I? Where's Geoff? Where . . . ?"

It was difficult to hold her, but he managed, almost yanking her off her feet back into the dry dark house. He was struggling to restrain her and shut the doors while saying, calmly, "You're in Cairns, Rosalind. You're ill. It's Mark Parrish – you're safe, you're with me . . ."

"Mark?" She stopped struggling. He had managed to shut the door. They stood in the darkness, two shadows gazing at each other, shivering a little in the coolness of the air conditioning. "Mark? I have to go home. Please, I have to get home to Geoff."

He had to hold her up, the Stemetil, the Amytal, made her unsteady on her feet. In her sedated state he was surprised that she had woken, even with the thunderclaps overhead. "Geoff's in Los Angeles – don't you remember?" Patiently, "You ate something on the plane and you became ill. You're at my house. Now, come back to bed."

He steered her slowly but firmly, one arm about her, the other groping in the darkness towards the hall and the bedroom. In the *en suite* he found towels and took them back to the bedroom. It was useless, in the dark, to search the suitcases for another nightdress; he dried Rosalind as best he could and left her sitting naked on the edge of the bed, a towel around her shoulders, still muttering about Geoff through chattering teeth, and found one of his tracksuit tops in a drawer. It was enormous on her, he could not find her fingertips in the sleeves, and her sleepy and rather cross "What's *this*?" made him smile.

"This isn't very romantic, is it?" he said beneath his breath, safe enough to voice his thoughts aloud. "I'd envisaged it all rather differently."

"What's this *thing* I'm wearing?"

He pulled back the sheet and lifted her into the bed.

"I want to ring Geoff. Can I phone Geoff? I have to tell him . . ." Her voice faded.

"Tell him what?" Mark encouraged.

"Tell him . . . that I lied. I've never . . . lied to Geoff."

"But if you wait until tomorrow, darling, he need never know." The *darling* slipped out, but she did not seem to notice. Only the caring tone of his voice penetrated to her, and that was enough.

"Mark, I feel . . . so sick. I wish I'd stayed home. You've been so kind . . . but I want to go home."

He had to hold her gently on the bed. "Alright," he soothed her, "in the morning. What is it that worries you about Geoff? If you phone him now and tell him you're here with me, you'll only upset him. You don't want to upset Geoff, do you?"

"No . . ."

The questioning was so important. He did not know nearly enough about her. He had to know everything. He had not planned to begin so early, for she would be taking Amytal four times a day until the "salmonella" was cured, and there would be lots of time. But here they were and, drowsy as Rosalind was, she wanted to talk. He guided her carefully, for there could be no harm in planting some seeds of insecurity now. He was very tired, but he forced himself to concentrate.

"Rosalind," gently, "there's no need to be afraid of Geoff, is there?"

"No . . . but . . ."

"But what?"

"He trusts me. He wouldn't like it, knowing I was here . . . that you and I were alone."

"But he trusts you. He'd understand."

"He'd . . . be jealous. It's only natural . . ." Her voice was slurred as she drifted into unconsciousness, but they had begun their first session, and he could not let her rest.

"Geoff would be jealous," Mark repeated, carefully. "He'd be angry with you."

"Yes." A murmur.

Mark held her hands tenderly in his, and spoke in the same benign tone that he had heard his mother use on the tapes of her interviews with patients. "Perhaps," he said, almost paternally, "perhaps you were unwise to come here. I don't want to think that I've come between you and Geoff. Has he always been jealous?"

"Yes . . ."

"Possessive?"

"Nnno . . ."

He could tell she was unsure.

"What about the men who accompanied you to social functions, men like David Papadimitriou and Andrew Braithwaite?" Externalising their relation-ship, he did not include himself, "Was he jealous of them?"

"No . . . it's not . . . any single person. It's . . . a vague thing. He's afraid . . ."

Again she paused, and he had to prompt her, "Geoff's afraid of what, Rosalind?"

"Afraid . . . that he's out there . . . somewhere. The man I'll fall in love with. The man that will make him . . . lose me."

"*Is* he out there?" Quietly.

"No."

"There's no one? You've never met anyone else whom you could love as much as Geoff?"

It was a mistake to hold her hands. He was careful not to give any new telling pressure, but there were intangibles – invisible particles, impulses

105

that had nothing to do with sight and touch and smell, and no scientists had so far alienated them. Only the poets, Mark noted drily, afterwards, had them within their grasp.

There was a small pause, and what was held within it? Only the drugs, her tiredness, her subliminal suspicion of this young friend who held her? Or was it an effort to lie, despite the Stemetil, the Amytal, the hands that held her quietly captive?

"No. There's only Geoff. I've only ever loved Geoff."

She made a small strange sound in her throat, and he leaned forward and felt with one hand for her face. It was damp, though she pulled back and away from him. It could have been the rain – her hair, despite his efforts to dry it, was still wet. But he knew it was tears.

He moved closer to her and cradled her in his arms, rocking her a little. They were tears of weakness, and fright, he knew. She would have woken in terror at the storm, found her mind befuddled, her body not quite within her control. "Hush, it's alright . . . I'll make it alright . . ."

After a moment, "Mark?" into his bare shoulder.

"Yes?"

"What are you wearing?"

"A towel."

"Is that all?"

"Yes."

He could almost imagine the messages skittering through the neurones within the damp head that rested against him. As when one made a query of a computer, sometimes one had to wait . . .

"Mark?"

"Yes?"

"We won't tell anyone about this, will we?"

Mark continued to hold Rosalind until she was sleeping against him, then, in the quiet of the gentler rain, laid her down upon the pillow. The storm grumbled its way out to sea; still he sat there, listening to the rain and her soft breathing.

She loved her husband. She loved him more than he, Mark, had thought. In her fear, even sick and disoriented as she was, she had called for him. With the lowering of her inhibitions that would have come with the Amytal in her system, she had felt only shyness and embarrassment when he, Mark, had touched her, and her last waking concern was that these moments they spent together, this innocent intimacy, would become known – when Mark only lived for the time when they would stand together and announce their love to the world.

He was tired. There had been so much planning, and he had had so little sleep for days. He left her as the sun was beginning to wash the room with colour and went through the house, still draped in the offending towel, turning out the lights.

In the study he righted the little antique table and the fallen vase. Then he paused, and moved to his desk. He took a key from the bottom of a container of paper clips and unlocked the second top drawer. In it were the diaries, and the portable tape recorder. He sat in his chair, switched it on, and, as the horizon bled its scarlet light into the grey sea and sky and lifted the dark, he taped his record of the past twenty-four hours.

This is tape number eleven, side two. As with all the other tapes, the contents are not to be published or used in any scientific thesis or dissertation until after the deaths of myself . . . and my wife.

He took a deep breath. It shuddered a little, he was very tired.

Mark's motivation was his own. Of course Leo could not condone what he had done – no sane, right-thinking person could. But he was conscious of a terrible kind of logic in Mark's reports – his intelligence, even his caring nature, came through. Leo had an image of bright metal that had been twisted, blasted into hideous shapes.

Yes, Your Grace, Leo would have to admit, he poisoned her. And then, as Rosalind recovered, slowly, on Stemetil and Amytal – finally, after twenty-four hours, on Amytal alone – she was confused, debilitated, and could not even conceive of what he had done. It was too bizarre – Mark was too credible, too reasonable.

And she had trusted him. That was the terrible part. She had dismissed from her mind Mark's declaration to her, that night in Sydney. She had accepted his reason for it, the terrible stress he had been under. She believed their friendship could go on, as if nothing had changed. But, of course, everything had changed. Mark's words of love to her had been a cry for help, for understanding, a plea for affection from a man who had grown to manhood without receiving affection.

Until now, until confronted with the diaries, the tapes, Leo had not considered this: *I do not think Linda ever touched Mark with love. And he had come to live without it.*

It looked so obvious, in hindsight. The world would say that the man went mad – and that it was his mother's fault, that strict Catholic school and his repressed childhood. But other men – and women – have suffered worse as children.

There was a weakness in the boy, Leo agonised. Somewhere within that brilliant mind lay the unknown flaw that led him to do this terrible thing. Leo and His Grace might reason and reason, but the core of the problem remained in that dark space within Mark himself. It was this dark space that had separated him from all his fellow men who had received rejections from the women they loved –

and yet had carried on living. No one had understood Mark, Leo realised.

We who loved him can stand on the edge of the void, but we cannot see what lies within.

Mark woke later than he had meant to – the sun was bright through the bamboo curtains of the spare room. Ten o'clock. He checked Rosalind's room and found her sleeping, one hand beneath her head, the other invisible in the voluminous sleeve of his pullover.

He noticed something. Her rain-wet hair had dried into tight curls, almost ringlets. Her hair had always been straight, like his mother's, their hairstyles very similar, swept up into chignons or, if loose, brushed smoothly back from the face and held elegantly in place with a clip or combs. Linda's hair was shoulder-length, Rosalind's longer. He touched one dark brown corkscrew, pulled it out a little, and let it go. It sprang back amongst its fellows, and Rosalind stirred a little.

Mark smiled, and left the room quietly, without waking her. He showered, shaved and dressed, and for the next hour or so, sat at his desk writing out cheques for the carpentry, painting and other domestic matters that he had never before had to attend to. For nothing had ever changed at the house on Castle Crag Road, and when, by chance, some repairs were necessary, his mother had arranged them.

Rosalind ate very little breakfast. He would not let her dress and come to the dining table; instead he brought her a tray on which rested a sprig of jasmine, a glass of watered-down fruit juice and a slice of dry toast.

"It's all you should be having at the moment. Eat up."

"I suppose you'll tell me it's good for me."

"Would I do anything that wasn't good for you?"

They exchanged a look of tolerant amusement, but, even with encouragement, she could not manage more than half a slice of the toast, though she drank the orange juice. Before she had quite finished it, he handed her another Amytal and watched as she swallowed it.

"How long will I have to take these?"

"Five days."

"You'll have to give me some to take with me."

He looked down at her. She was not joking. It was impossible for him to understand. How could she say such things when she must know that she did not want to leave him?

Even yesterday her behaviour had puzzled him, grieved him. They had spent hours together since the fateful lunch, and he had received no clue from her that she was overjoyed to see him again, nor were there any of the subtle feminine signals that could lead a man to assay the warmth between them. He had hoped that she would flirt a little,

111

say, "I've missed you," then he would have had no need to take matters further. And last night, holding her naked in his arms, the pliancy of her ... She *must* see that they belonged together.

He tried to be patient, wished that last night had not happened, for it made it more difficult than he could have imagined. He sat on the edge of the bed and chatted with her, or so she thought. His questions were carefully, skilfully chosen, and just as thoughtfully placed to elicit the best response.

He learnt of her early career in dancing, how she had taken it up in the face of her mother's reluctance, her father's downright disapproval.

"He was a teacher, wasn't he?" Mark prompted.

"Yes, a very gifted one. I was coached and coached as a child. I didn't mind, there wasn't much to do in Bega besides study. I didn't spend too much time at the beach – I freckled all over in summer – ugh!"

"Did you do well at school?"

"I topped the State in maths and science," she said with a small and rather touching pride in herself. "I really did," she added.

"I believe you," he smiled.

"Most people don't. Most people don't think I'm much good for anything other than giving fabulous dinner parties."

Mark stored this away. And he said, "I topped the State in maths and science, too."

112

"Not just in maths and science – you're being modest. Your mother told me," she teased. "*And* that you won a scholarship to America that you decided not to take up. You ..." she sobered a little, "you *did* something with those results – just look what you've done with your life, how many children you must have made well ..."

"Did your father have high hopes for you, academically?" Mark interrupted smoothly.

"You can imagine – science, medicine, law ... I hated disappointing him. I was a coward. I went off to stay with an aunt who was living in Sydney, and I phoned him and told him I was going to concentrate on my dancing."

"You were that good?"

"I was offered a place at the Australian Ballet School when I was fourteen, but my father ..." she stopped.

"Prohibited you?"

"Discouraged me."

"Did you resent him?"

"Not then. Later I did. Dancing ... was what I wanted to do. I spent less than a year at the Ballet School, and then went into the Company."

"How successful were you?"

She was drowsy. He had the feeling she would like to sleep, but, "Corps de ballet ... soloist ... I never became a principal dancer."

"You didn't give yourself much chance, did you? Marrying Geoff at twenty-two?"

She opened her eyes and looked at him, surprised perhaps, at his bluntness. "Twenty-two is middle-aged for a dancer. I knew my limitations. Besides, I tried to keep on with my dancing, but ... it was ..." Her voice faded.

"It was what?"

"Too much trouble. I was performing nights, Geoff was working days – that was before he began working both."

Mark did not share her smile. "And your father?"

"I'm so sleepy ... why am I so ...?"

"Did your father ever come to approve of your dancing?"

Rosalind frowned, remembering. "He died when I was twenty. Only a few months before, he and my mother came to see me dance. In the greenroom afterwards my mother was effusive – she'd been captivated by the whole experience – and she was glad for me, then, I think. My father ... kissed me on the cheek, and said nothing about the ballet at all."

"*Nothing*?"

She did not answer. The look in her eyes told of her hurt – twenty years ago, and still causing her pain.

Rosalind drifted in and out of consciousness, and Mark spent most of the day with her, speaking with her in her brief intervals of wakefulness and, often, remaining to watch her sleep.

She did not press him about leaving for the resort, nor to telephone Geoff. Each Amytal came

114

before the effects of the previous one had fully worn off. Rosalind dozed, or wakened in a twilight state to Mark's gentle smile, his gentle voice, and never doubted that he was anything but – as she would breathe, in that half-waking state – "So kind . . . what a good friend you are . . ."

In the mornings she was a little brighter, muzzy-headed, but more alert than usual, until the first tablet, taken with breakfast, began to take effect. On that third morning, after an uneventful night, she was arch enough to say, "Porridge? I *hate* porridge."

"It's good for you."

"Please, Mark, I'm not hungry, really."

"Will you eat it yourself, or . . .?"

"Alright, but don't stand over me."

He left the tray on her lap and wandered to the window. This room looked over the garden and the driveway. One could not see the ocean, but could hear it whispering, all the same, wherever in the house one might be.

Mark found himself praying, and he did not pray often, these days. *Let this be the day. Let her say something. Just one sentence, one phrase. "Mark, I don't want to leave you." "Mark, being here with you like this . . ."*

"I'm not hungry." He glanced over his shoulder. She was gazing regretfully at her plate.

He felt a rush of anger, and turned to face her. By now she must see – she was being wilfully

115

obtuse. They had been together for nearly forty-eight hours. He had held her, naked, against him, controlled himself because he wanted her only when she reached for him. He had cared for her, nursed her as a parent would a child, and she could give him no word, not a word.

"You're very stubborn, you know that?"

The words were out before he could stop them, and he cursed himself.

She looked up at him, her eyes puzzled; she did not understand what he meant.

He looked at her, there in his bed, in her innocence, and he loved her, wanted to run to her, kneel by the bed, hold her. The thought came to him, *either she's lying to me – or her reasoning is not my reasoning.*

He came to the bed, sat down on the edge of it and took up a spoonful of porridge, purposefully.

Rosalind began to laugh.

"Stop it. Eat up."

"This is crazy, Mark . . ." The spoon hit lightly against her teeth and she had to take the proffered mouthful. Mark wrestled silently with his new and distressing thoughts while she studied him. She had lovely eyes, disturbing, and never more so than when they were directed at him and filled with humour. "I've come to the conclusion that you're a sadist."

His hand, stirring the spoon in the porridge, slowed.

"You waylay travellers and keep them prisoner, feed them diets of dry toast – "

"And I jab them with needles," he added, coolly, "and force-feed them porridge. I get a lot of jollies out of force-feeding porridge." He held another spoonful towards her.

"Let me do it." She went to take the spoon, but he held firm. Her hand closed over his.

"No."

"If I do it, I can stop when I want."

"I know."

Her fingers tried ineffectually to prise his from the spoon. He made her take another mouthful of porridge, but it was dangerous – she was laughing so much, and so was he. She had touched him, touched his hand of her own accord . . .

She swallowed, still laughing. "Do you remember all those games when you were small and your mother couldn't get you to eat? 'I'll give it to the cat', or, 'Think of the black babies in Africa', or pretending the spoon was an aeroplane . . ."

Mark's eyes were lowered once more to the plate. "I didn't have that kind of mother."

When he looked up it was to find the green eyes probing him quietly.

She had looked at him in that way before, he realised, but it was hard to find a pattern of when, or why. And still he did not know what lay behind that look, sympathy, empathy – pity? The thought soured his enjoyment of the moment.

And he almost said, "Don't think you understand me. I don't want you to understand me. You have too much power over me already. It's I who must understand you. When I know what makes you afraid, I can offer safety. When I know what you need, I can provide it."

But of course he did not say this.

He waited, all that day, for some sign from her, another touch, a look that was more than fondness, or gratitude.

He left her sleeping in the afternoon, and went for a run on the beach. He ran until he was exhausted and fell upon his back and lay there, pulling the salty air into his lungs and gazing at the sky.

What was wrong? Was it Geoff? What was it that they had, that he could not break through, share even a little of that secret world she and Geoff seemed to possess so jealously? She seemed more completely Geoff's here, four thousand miles from him, than she had seemed in Sydney.

For the first time, in all those months, Mark suddenly wished himself free of her. Let her go. Stop the Amytal, give her several cups of coffee and drive her to Silver Palms Resort. Release her back amongst her own kind, the glossy-winged, the sharp-taloned – let them all tear each other apart . . .

When we have lured you from above,
And that delight of frolic flight, by day or
*   night,*

118

From North to South,
We'll bind you fast in silken cords
And kiss away the bitter words
From off your rosy mouth.

He smiled at the sky, closed his eyes against the warmth of the sun. He had planned for everything, every eventuality. In the planning, the long weeks of preparations, he had never expected an immediate victory. Only now, having her here, so close to him and yet so distant, did he feel impatient, and too easily became discouraged. He thought of the falconer in the documentary, the bearded Tasmanian, dragging his feet about his home while the bird clung to his wrist and tried to outguess him, withstand him.

"When we have lured you from above . . ." She was here, now, as dependent upon him as if jesses and a leash bound her to him, and him to her. That was it. He rolled over on to his stomach in the sand. He was as dependent upon her as she was upon him. I can no more escape than she can, he thought. And how could he expect otherwise?

He felt calmer now. There was no way to go but forward, and it was not as if it were into the unknown – he knew exactly what he had to do. But there was still time. He had promised himself four days, four days in which time she might come to him of her own free will. He grinned at his own foolishness. A wild creature does not come on command. The falconer would have laughed at him.

He walked slowly back towards the house and, once before it, turned down towards the sea and plunged into the surf, briefly, before making his way up the sand, drying himself with his shirt as he went.

Rosalind was not in the bedroom. He stopped in the doorway, frowning, then saw the door to the *en suite* bathroom was shut. Approaching it, he heard the shower running.

The door was locked.

"Rosalind?" He knocked sharply on the door, furious with her. "Rosalind, I told you not to lock the door! If you faint..." How long had the shower been running? "Rosalind?!" There was no answer. "*Rosalind*!"

Now he was hammering at the door. How long had she been in there, the room filling up with steam faster than the exhaust fan could expel it ... Three days with little to eat and the bloody Amytal... "Rosalind, can you hear me?" No answer but the steady sound of the water running. "*Rosalind*!?"

He could put his shoulder to it, it would yield easily enough, and he must just hope that she had not collapsed close to it.

The shower was turned off. "Just a minute ..." came, barely audible, from within. He was still staring at the door when it opened a moment later.

A bath towel around her body, another wrapped about her head turban-like, Rosalind leaned forward in the doorway and he caught her, almost shook her.

"Sorry," she muttered, "did I worry you? I just had to have a shower – it's been three days . . ."

"Don't you know you could have fainted? You could have drowned in there!"

"I did faint – I slid down the shower recess wall in a graceful heap . . . must have been the steam . . ." She leaned against him. "The only shampoo and soap I could find was your Pierre Cardin – I prob'ly smell like you."

Mark held her to him, and it did not matter, at that moment, whether she was in his arms for safety, or for love, or for any other reason. For a few seconds, he had believed he had lost her. It was enough; he would not lose her, not to Geoff, nor to anything else that threatened to take her from him.

They had dinner together, and she picked at her fish and salad half-heartedly while he asked her about Geoff.

He had avoided facing this for too long, and it was as difficult as he had imagined it would be.

"People say he must have changed since I married him. He was only twenty-eight, then, and buying and renovating houses in Balmain. When we first married we moved seven times in as many years – but I didn't mind. And when the projects became bigger – the building of office blocks, shopping centres – well, it was easier, then. We began to have a permanent home.

"I'm his best friend – that's rather marvellous, to be able to say that, after eighteen years of marriage, isn't it? He still rushes through the door to find me, to tell me what's been happening with his day. We talk everything over together. Good things, bad things ... That's why it's been such a strong marriage – we aren't afraid to confront each other, and we're willing to compromise, if it will make the other happy."

Mark noted mentally that she had not said that Geoff was *her* best friend. He asked, "Don't you get lonely when he's away so often?"

She frowned a little. "He wasn't away much – and I always went with him – until the stock market crashed. Something changed inside Geoff, then. It was as if we were facing utter ruin, and of course we weren't. We were just very rich, instead of being mega-rich." She smiled drily. "I saw that he was afraid for the first time. He couldn't face the thought of losing anything, you see. He never thought he'd suffer a setback – it's all been growth, movement upwards, for him. Every share in the Harcourt Corporation was accounted for, equated with some victory, some sacrifice. He has to sell something soon – probably Amalgamated Media – but he's been fighting for years to avoid it. *That's* taken him from me, more than all the years of our struggling to build the empire – it's holding onto it that's destroying Geoff. He's fought for so long to make his life a success that he can't see life without that success. He can't see *life*. There's only work."

She looked over at Mark, on a chair by the bed. "This is very boring talk. Why are we always talking about me, lately? I'm the invalid – you should be entertaining me. Why don't we talk about you anymore?"

"We talked enough about me back in Sydney."

She was very tired. He was distressed to see that her eyes were beginning to hold dark shadows beneath them. "Try to eat something more," he encouraged, "you're worrying me."

"I was thinking in the shower, before I keeled over, how unfair this is. I should have gone to a hospital, Mark. I'm not being sick anymore, I don't have those dreadful stomach pains, but I feel so weak – sometimes it's hard to keep my head up straight, let alone have the energy to walk across the room. What's wrong with me?"

"It's just natural debilitation after the poisoning. Try to be patient. Another day or two and you'll be back to normal. Will you trust me?"

He smiled at her. And she returned the smile, fondly. "Yes, of course."

The following morning was the fourth day.

He woke her at nine, the tray with her breakfast of the hated porridge already beside her on the bed, but she was having none of it today. Did she sense that today was different, or was her mind, so active despite the effect of the drug, simply rebelling at last? She insisted on getting up, refused to take the tablet until she had had her shower, "I always feel better first thing in the mornings. I'll have the tablet with my breakfast, at the table."

For a moment she must have thought she would not get her way, for Mark had plans for that day, and had already been busy. But then he smiled, and agreed.

He made the bed while she showered, the bathroom door just to, and dressed herself in slacks and blouse and put up her hair. She insisted on making up her face and, knowing that she barely had strength to stand, he admired her for her courage. She sat at the dining table, by the glass doors in the living room, and ate the fresh porridge with her chin propped up on her fist, barely awake. She had taken the Amytal with her orange juice, and Mark, drinking his coffee, watched her and hated himself for what he was doing to her.

His eyes on the sea, he took a deep breath, exhaling it slowly. "You should be almost well, you know."

She looked up at him. His face was cool, regarding her with his professional look. "Do you mean, I'm not getting better as fast as I should? Should I go to a hospital – for a blood test, perhaps?"

"I'm not sure that would tell us anything," he said, carefully. "Rosalind, I care for you very much – do you really want to go to Silver Palms?" There were different ways to accept this statement, this question. Mark waited.

She smiled a little, puzzled, or pretending to be. "I don't understand. They're expecting me. Why would I make the reservation if I don't want to go?"

And Rosalind waited.

Mark gazed at her, and thought of the hawk on the falconer's wrist, awake, distrusting, watchful, but tiring. He chose not to speak. This was unfair, and he knew it. The Amytal would be clouding her thought processes, slowing down impulses that would normally take one thousandth of a second. Yet he must make *her* be the one who considered, who doubted.

"Are you saying," slowly, "that I'm well over this . . . salmonella, or whatever . . . and that what I'm feeling now, this tiredness, and depression, it's all in my *head*?"

Depression?

Mark leaned forward – and the phone rang.

He almost looked at his watch, only just stopped himself. They were early, they had to be. He cursed them, and looked at Rosalind to find her gazing at him, puzzled, wondering, no doubt, why he did not immediately go to the phone.

"That'll be Geoff ringing back," he said, and watched her eyes fly wide. "I called him earlier, but

he was out. I left a message for him to call here."
He stood, unhurriedly.

And Rosalind, too, had pulled herself to her feet.
"You didn't! Mark, how could you! You know I
wanted to be the one to explain . . ."

"It shouldn't matter. I was worried about you.
He's your husband, and I think he has a right to
know that you're ill."

He walked very quickly across the room, into the
study, with Rosalind's voice following him. "But I
told him that you were going to Thredbo – and
now . . . Mark, let me talk to him!"

The telephone operator was young, bright-
voiced, cheerful, "Good morning, Mr Parrish, this
is your eleven o'clock call."

"Thank you," Mark murmured, and with relief,
he heard the girl disconnect.

Rosalind had entered the room, but Mark
remained turned from her. She heard his words
clearly.

"Geoff? Yes, Mark Parrish. It's to do with
Rosalind . . . Yes, she is in Cairns, she has been
taken ill . . ." And a long pause, during which Mark
made several attempts to interrupt. Finally, "It's not
what you're thinking! . . . Yes, I am in Cairns,
but . . . It was a coincidence, that's all. It was damn
lucky I *was* here! Don't you even want to know . . ."

Rosalind had made her way to him, leaning on
the furniture for support, her face distressed. "Let
me talk to him!"

Mark moved away a little. "Just . . . ! She's just here, if you'd . . . She didn't lie to you, she just didn't want you to worry . . . Listen, you stupid bastard . . . Harcourt?"

Rosalind tried to take the receiver from him and he allowed her to have it, stood and watched as she spoke into it, her face alight. "Geoff? Geoff, darling . . . ?"

She was close to the edge of Mark's desk, and leaned against it as the light went out of her eyes, slowly. Even more slowly, her hand lowered, and the receiver was replaced. She stood for a long time, her hand still resting on the phone as if in disbelief. "He hung up," she said, and turned to gaze at Mark. "He didn't want to talk to me. He hung up."

Mark moved to her, placed his arms about her, and she clung to him as if he were her only safety in her shifting, nightmarish world.

"It'll be alright," Mark promised her. "I'll make everything alright. You're safe here. Stay with me here and nothing will harm you."

Something in his words gradually began to penetrate Rosalind's confused mind. She looked up into Mark's handsome, concerned face and, lifting her hand, she touched his cheek tenderly. "You're very sweet," she said faintly, "but I have to go home to Sydney. I'll catch the first flight to LA tomorrow. Will you phone the airport for me?"

CHAPTER SEVEN

Nothing Mark said could deflect Rosalind from her purpose. She fetched her handbag, found her return ticket within it, phoned Cairns airport and booked her flight home. Mark watched her. It was not the booking of the ticket that worried him; he could cancel it, in her name, any time in the next few hours.

But he had failed to make her love him. No, he thought, as he made his way to the kitchen and poured two glasses of orange juice, he had failed to make her *admit* she loved him. What Rosalind thought, what Rosalind felt, was locked away inside that pretty head, and he had no access at all to the information he wanted.

There was not quite enough orange juice, so he turned on the juicer, sliced two oranges in half and squeezed the juice into the glasses.

Now, trees – you could cut down a tree and take a horizontal slice of its trunk and read there all that that tree had known, all its history, ring by ring. It was fortunate, perhaps, that one couldn't under-stand the human mind so easily, or half the world's population would be murdered by the axe-wielding other half.

He could hear Rosalind's voice, still speaking to the reservation desk. Without hurry he took the small salt shaker from the back of the cupboard and tipped part of its contents – Amytal tablets crushed that morning – into one of the glasses.

Rosalind was waiting to have her booking confirmed. Mark handed her a glass of orange juice and took his own over to the glass doors, where he stood, looking out. He felt very calm. The worst had happened, but he was not about to give up yet. There was still the studio – but surely, surely that would not be necessary . . .

He was too hesitant, too bloody well-mannered for his own good – or hers. He had been very stupid in wanting the ego-gratification of Rosalind coming to *him*, reaching for *him*. Would Geoff have waited for her while she played her silly games and watched him dance attendance on her? Of course not. Geoff was a man of action, of ambition, and even a kind of cunning recklessness. Well, he, Mark had learnt.

The room was silent, and he turned. Rosalind was seated on the couch, holding the now half-empty glass of juice, gazing at him thoughtfully. When his eyes met hers she looked away, but still she seemed worried, or perplexed.

"You're really afraid, aren't you?" he said, more as a statement than a question.

"Afraid?" She looked back at him, then.

"Of Geoff. Of his disapprobation, or of losing him – or both."

She swirled the orange juice about, frowning. "We'll sort it out. We've weathered worse than this."

"Why was he so angry? Did you tell him that I was in love with you?"

"No, of course not." She looked almost startled.

"Why 'of course not'? You would have told him when Andrew Braithwaite fell in love with you. Didn't you usually tell him when some man began to get serious?"

She was beginning to appear uncomfortable, looked away from him. As on that night in his car, she gave the impression of wishing to be somewhere else.

"Did you tell Geoff about me?" he asked.

"No."

"Why not? What was the difference between me and, say, Andrew?"

"If you don't know . . ."

"I'm asking you."

"Mark, I'm very tired. Must we talk about this now? It's futile."

"Why didn't you tell Geoff about me? He'd have been amused, wouldn't he?"

"No. I mean . . . I don't know. If I told him . . .

130

then you and I couldn't have remained friends. I thought ... that you spoke the way you did that night because you were depressed, over-worked – you mistook kindness for affection, many people do. I knew that after you came back from your holiday you'd see things in perspective."

"I didn't need to go to Thredbo for that."

Their gazes locked, and there were no games between them, no politeness, no fondness, in those seconds. Mark turned, began to walk out the open glass doors, but her voice stopped him.

"My staying here – it was a very bad thing. It's made you think that ... " Any moment, now, she would put her head down against the back of the settee, and her eyes would close. She scowled, suddenly, trying to gather her thoughts. Mark did not want to watch her, did not want this discussion keeping her awake, making her fight the drug.

"You shouldn't be here, Mark. This is a lovely house, but you shouldn't have buried yourself away from people. When one's alone too much ... "

The orange juice in her hand almost spilled. She became aware of it and placed it on the table beside her. In the pause, Mark moved back into the room, behind the settee. He sat on the back of it, touched her hair gently. "Stop worrying about me, Rosalind. I'll miss you, but if you feel your place is with Geoff, then what can I do? It's just that having you here, being so close to you for four days ..."

"I know. It was a mistake." She made as if to move, but she could not. "Mark, I feel very faint ..."

His hand did not stop its soothing motion on her hair. "I never knew you had curly hair," he spoke quietly, his tone even. "You've been straightening it for years, haven't you? Why?"

"Geoff ..." she murmured.

"Of course. You'd wear your hair to please Geoff. Straighten it and torture it to keep the same style as when you first met him. He has you in a timewarp."

"Mark ..."

"Women can be such fools. Like my mother. You'd never believe what my mother went through in order to keep my father.

"While you're here – and I really would like you to stay a little longer – you mustn't straighten your hair, you must be yourself." Her head rolled sideways a little, and was still. "I love you when you're yourself, you see. I don't want you to be anything but what you are, what you want to be."

He waited until the evening, because he wanted her to *know*. There is a nasty and simple method medical folk use to test the consciousness of a patient. The base of the thumbnail is very sensitive, and one has only to press hard with one's own

132

thumbnail and, if possible, the pain will pull a patient back to wakefulness.

Rosalind woke to the pain in her hand, and the last light of the day coming through the half-closed blinds, and to the knowledge that she and Mark lay naked together beneath the sheets of his large bed. In that terrible consciousness that is awareness without voice, or movement of any kind, his words came to her – but they were Tennyson's words. In a ghastly parody of those moments of safety and warmth she had known as a child, tucked between her parents, Mark was reading to her:

> My Rosalind, my Rosalind,
> My frolic falcon with bright eyes,
> Whole free delight, from any height of rapid
>   flight,
> Stoops at all game that wing the skies,
> My Rosalind, My Rosalind,
> My bright-eyed, wild-eyed falcon, whither,
> Careless both of wind and weather,
> Whither fly ye, what game spy ye,
> Up or down the streaming wind?

She lay upon his chest, her head against him, his left arm about her. When she moved, his grip upon her tightened. Unconsciousness was almost a relief, the nightmare seemed to end, and yet that voice, as deep and mellow and ominous as a bell, kept calling her back.

> *. . . the very wind . . .*
> *is not so clear and bold and free*
> *As you, my falcon Rosalind.*
> *You care not for another's pains*
> *Because you are the soul of joy . . .*

She must have slept, for when she next awoke his voice had changed, somehow. His heart was thudding in her ear, and she tried to say his name, but no sound came. Only the words, and his arm about her, more tightly.

> *Come down, come home, my Rosalind,*
> *My gay young hawk, my Rosalind . . .*

Her father's words! He used her father's words . . .

> *Too long you keep the upper skies;*
> *Too long you roam and wheel at will;*
> *But we must hood your random eyes,*
> *That care not whom they kill . . .*

She could not open her eyes, she could not call out. The darkness lapped over her and threatened to drag her down – and that would have been better, perhaps, but even she knew that he did not want this. He must know the poem by heart, for his lips were upon her hair, and the terrifying words, the terrifying voice went on:

. . . We must bind
and keep you fast, my Rosalind,
Fast, fast, my wild-eyed Rosalind,
And clip your wings, and make you love.

And Mark rolled over to cover her, and dropped the little book beside the bed, and told himself that the cry she gave was not one of fear.

For it was too late, now. I had waited too long. I murmured her name, over and over, and hoped I took her with me – for it was all I hoped it would be.

Afterwards she lay beneath me so quietly. I spoke to her, but she didn't answer. I asked for her forgiveness, and whether I had hurt her – though I had tried to be as gentle and patient as possible – but she seemed to be sleeping, and I didn't want to turn on the light and spoil the quiet and the joy of what we had shared. "We're part of each other, now," I reminded her, "we're lovers, you and I." This was what was needed, what I should have made certain of, from the beginning. Women need a sense of belonging, of commitment – why else would so much of their popular literature feature the heroines being raped by the men they loved? It must be a very deep, primeval desire, some sort of courting ritual, or proof of the man's strength and virility. It

135

always amused me, but I see the need for it, now.

That night Mark slept with Rosalind in his arms, and felt secure in the future. What had happened could never be erased. It was a bond forever.

But when he woke in the morning, she was gone.

CHAPTER EIGHT

M ark's heart was beating wildly. He pulled on
his clothes, ran through the house, all the
time thinking ahead – had she left the grounds,
taken the car? Had she called the police? Were they
even now on their way?

Empty hall, empty study, living room and
kitchen – front door locked and bolted – back into
the living room ... Then, at the glass doors he
slowed, for through that wall of glass he saw her.
He leaned against the frame, then, and closed his
eyes for a second in the sudden ebb of panic, the
safety of relief.

Rosalind was sitting huddled on a patch of grass
at the edge of the sand, some distance from the
house. She had found her nightdress beneath the
pillow, and now sat, knees drawn up, looking out
to sea.

Her hair was a tangle of curls and approaching
her closely, Mark smiled. No photographer would
recognise her now. In this tousle-haired, windswept

little creature there was nothing to be seen of the sleekly fashionable and glamorous Mrs Harcourt.

He stood above and a little behind her, thinking – *my woman; she's my woman.* And he touched the slender neck beneath the coiling mane – it was the colour of dark cedar in the bright sunlight.

She slapped his hand away with a force that jarred his knuckles, and turned to look at him with vicious reproach.

Mark was furious. Didn't she know that he could sweep her back upon the sand – with one arm he could do it – have her pinned there beneath him and take her again, as he had last night, and with none of his patience?

"Why?" she said. And he heard, in the one word, the tremor in her voice, the anger, the fear.

Calmer himself, somehow, he went down on one knee on the spiky grass beside her. He looked at her troubled face and said, patiently, kindly, as if to someone struggling with a problem of great complexity, "You knew it was bound to happen. Try to put aside all those preconceived notions you have about virtue and propriety, and realise that the human condition doesn't often take laws into account. What happened between us last night was a very natural thing. I'm not sorry. Are you?"

Of course she would say yes.

"Yes! How can you even . . . " She turned from him and lifted her hands to her face, pressed the heels of her hands to her eyes, ran the long fingers up into her hair until he thought she would pull at it.

"Mark ... " A real effort in her voice to keep it calm. It had begun, he realised, without him meaning it to – she was moving towards the edge. He made a mental note to remember the point exactly for his report. And should the remainder of his plans – his exigency plans – have to be put into play, then it was best to remember her state of mind at this moment and to take that into consideration.

She was not, he thought, looking at her critically, as strong as he had assumed. That pleased him. She was sensitive, of course – it was the artist, the performer in her. She was affected by her surroundings, was almost a victim of them.

He was surprised to find that he was, momentarily, without pity for her – probably because she was saying such negative, hurtful things. Still, he felt the barbs. She's like a patient, he thought, and wondered that it had not occurred to him before. His mother had been right: one must always keep a sense of objectivity. How else could he have hoped to continue as an oncologist? How else could Linda care for her mad women, her lunatic men, with the same tranquil concern that she showed towards her own son?

"It wasn't *natural*. You didn't ... you weren't thinking of me at all. I never gave you any encouragement to think that I wanted to make love to you. And it wasn't lovemaking, Mark – don't look at me and try to tell me that it was! I couldn't move – I couldn't speak ... " Her breath was coming in dry sobs, she glared at him through her wind-whipped hair, and he had never seen her so malevolent.

In the pause, he said, calmly, "You do see what you're doing, don't you? You're looking for reasons to avoid taking responsibility for what happened."

She stared at him and, for a second, even the anger left her face. "How can you suggest that, knowing ... You're a doctor, you must have known! I couldn't even say no, though my mind was screaming it!"

She rose to her feet. He went to take her arm, but she pulled back, stumbling a little on the rough grass. Then, finding her balance, and her tongue, "Don't you touch me. Don't you ever touch me again." And her voice broke with the sudden tears in her throat, "What am I going to tell Geoff?" Her voice as soft and keening as the wind about them, "What can I say to Geoff?"

She turned away from him, would have left him there on the beach, and he could not bear it. One stride and he took her arm, "Don't go yet."

"Let *go*!" her voice rose in hysteria.

"Rosalind, listen, it's just ... "

She pulled away, turned her back to him, and began walking away towards the house.

"I've never made love to a woman before."

For a dreadful moment he thought she would

stop, and turn and laugh. But she stopped, and turned, and before her spite could find voice, he said, "I've . . . I've never known if I could. There was never a woman that I wanted. And then you . . . and I wanted you so badly. Last night – it was wrong, and I know it, but . . . four days with you, holding you, caring for you . . . That first night, when you ran out into the storm, and you were wet and cold, and I dried you and warmed you . . . Can't you understand how difficult it's been for me?"

She was looking away, colouring a little, the small bare feet moved backwards, away from him, through the sandy soil.

"Last night, when I put you to bed, you reached for me, you said my name," he lied, "and I thought . . . I'd lie beside you, hold you . . . but it was the first time I've known the closeness of another human being – the first time I've lain beside a woman, held one in my arms . . . "

"Oh, Mark," she said softly, "what a terrible beginning."

"I can make it up to you." He came to her, stood close to her, but that was a mistake. Gone was the friendship, the trust, their easy way with each other's closeness. He towered over her, and there were other memories now – his closeness was an intimidation, a threat.

"I meant . . . " she said awkwardly, "a terrible beginning to your sex life, not – "

"Other couples have bad beginnings and go on to . . . "

"*We are not a couple*!" Her shrill voice, almost a scream, cut across his words. "Mark! I am already part of a couple! I'm *Geoff's wife*!"

She would have turned away, but he said, coldly, "Geoff thinks we've been sleeping together for months." Her gaze swung back to his, in surprise, and in the fear that he could be right. "Why do you think he was so furious? Why was he making those threats?"

"What threats?" she began, but Mark continued over her, despite, and because of, the fear in her eyes. "I didn't want to worry you when you were ill, but it's as if he knew there was something between us, as if he were waiting to have it confirmed."

She was so easy to read. He had been wrong, so wrong, to think that there was no understanding, no way into the tidy feminine labyrinth of her mind. Her fear led him into its depths like a skein of twine, glowing there in the darkness. Sometimes he lost the thread, but he was clever – and he knew her, and loved her – and he had no difficulty in taking it up again.

He said now, softly, kindly, "Geoff's always been afraid of losing you. And, like many a brave man, he confronts his fears. Did you believe he allowed you your string of glossy young men because he was naturally unselfish, or thoughtful? Of course you did. I've heard you speak of him to friends at gatherings – your darling Geoff, whose generosity wouldn't allow you to miss out on your round of amusements – "

"Stop it!"

"And all the time he was playing just another game of chance, with his pride as the stakes. Gambling on your loyalty, Rosalind, your sense of duty and commitment."

"My love for him!" she burst out.

"Did he gamble on that, too?"

"No! It's just . . ."

"He's lost, Rosalind."

She stopped her protesting, stared at him. Then, "No."

"Yes."

"*No!*"

She walked back to the house, stumbling often, for her motor nerves and balance were still affected, but her pride gave her impetus. Mark watched her go, thoughtfully, but easily caught up with her as she was about to cross the balcony to the living room. He took the stairs from the beach to the deck three at a time, and when she whirled to face him, startled, he pinned her against the narrow space where the deck railing met the side of the house.

He felt possessed of an almost professional calm. The same practised calm that he used for that first encounter with a patient after the results had come back, or for the dreadful, gut-wrenching speeches he had to give in those small rooms at the end of corridors, where parents raised terrified eyes to him over the tea that Sister had provided – terrified eyes that asked for a miracle, another day, another hour – and all he could tell them was that their child was dead.

"I've done everything that I could." *No more explanations*, he told himself. Now it was merely a battle of wills, and the less she knew the more at a disadvantage she would be, but, "Even last night . . . " he began, wanting to say the words that he later spoke into his little hand-held tape recorder:

I thought the joining of our bodies would have meant something to you. Even if I didn't bring to you the ecstasy that being with you, possessing you, brought to me. Somehow I thought that you'd know how hard I tried, and my gentleness might have moved you. I thought your fondness for me would, when the last barriers were gone and we were part of one another, deepen and broaden until even you could no longer ignore that change and call it by another name.

He thought of speaking those words then, on the balcony, with Rosalind leaning back, away from him, but realised that it was too late for words. He finished, sadly, "It doesn't matter now."

Holding her by one wrist, he twisted her other arm behind her back, hard, and deafened himself to her cries. He pushed her, thus, across the study, pausing only at his desk to fetch the keys, and opening both soundproofed doors, he thrust her into the darkened studio and left her there, sobbing and screaming his name.

CHAPTER NINE

Mark did not phone his mother as often as he had promised. She told Leo on one of his visits, that she had a suspicion that Mark had found himself a girlfriend amongst the crowds of skiers at Thredbo.

"Wouldn't he tell you about it?"

"Not he – you know he keeps things to himself lately. It was twenty-four hours before I heard that young Michael Halvorson had died. Mark told me about Michael and about leaving for Thredbo all in the same breath."

"You're pleased, though, I presume, that he has some kind of romantic attachment at the moment?" Leo wanted to say nothing that would remind Linda of Rosalind Harcourt.

"Yes . . . " Linda said, but the word came out leisurely paced and sounded, not uncertain – for Linda was never uncertain – but somewhat considered.

Leo glanced at her, but waited for her to speak voluntarily. They were walking in the garden, something they often did, unless Sydney turned on one of its brutal rain storms. In milder showers, they often took two of the large striped umbrellas kept by the conservatory doors and went out anyway, to squelch their way across the lawns and splash along the mossy and uneven paths between the trees.

But this particular day was clear – the pond reflected an oval of blue sky and the frame of nodding irises that bloomed about it. Above the deep purple flowers, two *Azalea Indica*, some eight feet tall, were a mass of pale pink pearl blossoms. Leo gazed at this, one of his favourite corners of the garden, but a full appreciation of the scene was only allowed him in retrospect.

For Linda asked him, "Have you read the latest gossip columns?"

Leo had been thinking of Mark, alone in a remote cabin in the snow country, avoiding his mother's natural curiosity and concern over the telephone. It had not always been that way. Now Leo's surprise at her question knocked the frown of consternation from his face. Linda laughed.

"No, of course you haven't. I can't see you reading Adrian Darlington's column over morning tea. But I do. There's a touch of devilry in me, you know, that you haven't guessed at." She threw him a sideways glance from her tip-tilted hazel eyes. "I dearly love hearing gossip about my friends. None of them actually confide in me, in case I draw unfavourable conclusions about their mental health, so," she lamented, "everything must come to me second-hand."

Leo was about to remind her to tell him what Adrian Darlington had written, when she volunteered the information: "Adrian writes that Rosalind Harcourt has left her husband."

Leo looked at her, sharply, but Linda had stepped forward to the pool to peer down at the transparent lives of her half-dozen golden carp. "She left for a holiday in Queensland earlier this week, but that was just a cover. None of her friends have heard from her, and neither – rumour has it – has her husband. It's just like her to wait until he went overseas. She's probably up on the Gold Coast, closeted with her lawyers, scheming how best to get half the Harcourt empire."

"That's a bit uncharitable, isn't it?" Leo said, gently. It was unlike Linda. Jealousy, he thought, suddenly. Still jealous over a woman years younger than herself, whose only crime was that she had, perhaps unwittingly, captured what had been Linda's own prerogative – the exclusive friendship and affection of her son.

He was moved for her. Linda was, he realised with a kind of anguish, too much alone. She should have applied for an annulment and remarried years ago. Why had he not seen it before? Why had he not noticed her growing dependence on Mark? But who would have thought that Linda, with her great heart and strength of character, could become dependent on anyone?

"I'm not being uncharitable, I'm just noting matters as they stand. Just look at the life she lives." And, as Leo began to interrupt, "I am not saying she was *sleeping* with all those men, but she showed an absolute disregard for whether or not the world thought she was. And no consideration at all for her husband's pride."

The goldfish all seemed to be present and healthy. They loafed in shadows or gathered in common insouciance beneath the water lilies. Linda looked up at Leo, thoughtfully, "I can't help but feel rather sorry for Geoffrey Harcourt. It's been very hard to find anyone who speaks ill of him, do you know that? Don't you think that's very odd?"

"Certainly," Leo muttered, thinking it was almost as odd as Linda diligently searching for someone to malign Geoffrey Harcourt, which was what her phrasing seemed to suggest.

"Come and look at the camellias," she said, and took his arm. "The *Polar Bear* is just superb this year – every petal as white and pristine as porcelain." She smiled at him, delighted with her metaphor, but then sobered, and patted his hand, abstractedly. "I wonder if the rumours are true?"

"What rumours?"

She sighed with heavy patience. "About Rosalind Harcourt running off to Queensland. Mark said that it would be quite in character."

"Mark said that? When?"

"When he phoned last night."

"Was he upset? I mean, they were friends, and when he comes back from Thredbo . . . "

"Oh, no. He was genuinely amused. He's well over that infatuation.

"There! Isn't it marvellous? They look delightful in a blue bowl – help me break off some blooms for you to take home."

Mark in Thredbo, no letter, not a phone call, and when in Sydney he called Leo at least once a week. Then, just three weeks after Mark's departure, Rosalind Harcourt disappears.

That evening Leo gave pre-marriage counselling to two young couples planning to marry the following month, and made final arrangements for a funeral later that week. Then he was able to sit down with a sherry and consider.

Was it possible that Rosalind Harcourt had not gone to Cairns? Or had gone, but then left immediately for Thredbo?

He shook his head. "And I called Linda uncharitable!" he muttered.

Mark had seemed so unhappy, so tense, on the eve of his departure. That was not the mood of a young man about to be reunited with his mistress.

Yet . . . what were his words, his last words on the matter, just before they turned the topic to the merits of Balmain and Parramatta and their chances for Sunday's game . . . ?

Don't worry. I'll come back from Thredbo a changed man.

No, Leo concluded. There was nothing in his rather sordid hypothesis. Mark's words had been said in a flat, dead voice – he could still see the look on the boy's face. The words were hollow bravado, his spirits so low, at that moment, that he did not even bother to lie convincingly. Whatever had been between Mark and Rosalind Harcourt, Leo was certain it had ended that night – and, for Mark, it had ended badly.

Geoff Harcourt had lost precious time due to the casual wording of the resort telephonist.

"No, Mr Harcourt," she had said, "I just checked, your wife isn't expected in until tomorrow."

"Leave a message for her, will you? Just say to call Geoff in LA. She has the number."

That had been on the twenty-third. He had been busy in meetings since, and whenever he had managed the time to phone he'd found, with irritation, that it would be too early, or too late, in Cairns.

That Rosalind was not expected back that night did not disturb him. All their friends in Cairns had sizeable yachts, all were made for sailing about the Reef. Other trips with Stephen and Lydia had lasted days.

Another thirty-six hours passed, and Geoff called again. This time he spoke to the assistant night manager, who had taken Mark's call on the twenty-first. No, Mrs Harcourt had not yet arrived at the resort – no, not *at all*. He was *certain*. As a matter of fact, they were planning on calling the Harcourts' Sydney home the following day. Mrs Harcourt's brother-in-law had said she was spending a few days with family, but . . .

"You didn't query? You didn't *check*?" Geoffrey Harcourt did not often raise his voice; he no longer needed to. But it was raised now, and the unfortunate young man in Cairns paled beneath his tan.

"We had no reason to doubt him, sir. He was well-educated, confident, he knew exactly the time she was booked in, even the number of her bungalow – "

The icy voice cut across him, "Did he leave a number?"

A terrified silence, then, in a strained voice across the miles of Pacific, "Yes, sir, but . . . we tried today . . . and no one at that number had heard of Mrs Harcourt."

Geoffrey Harcourt was forty-three. Nearly six foot tall, thick-necked, powerfully built, he had the face of a man who had spent his boyhood engaged in the various wars of the narrow streets of Newtown. He grew a beard that covered two razor-slashes on his left cheek, but his broken nose – of which Rosalind had claimed to be very fond – he left defiantly as it was. It made a nice contrast to his beautifully tailored dark suits. He liked it when new acquaintances stared at his face, wondering how it came to be as battered as it was, and if he had been put upon, how was he here, and what had happened to the other guy? The broken nose gave him the look of a man who did not mind descending to the physical, should the need arise. It never did, but such a reputation never hurt in the corporate world, where all claws were manicured.

Three years before he had begun to put on a lot of weight, and Rosalind had, in his words, "made his life hell" until he had slimmed down to an acceptable weight. Now, like most other things in his life, his weight was under control, due to a self-discipline and exercise regime that was as strict and demanding as his business practices.

His blood pressure was harder to control. Not yet requiring medication, it sometimes took him by surprise, as it did now, in his hotel room, sixteen floors above Wilshire Boulevard.

He sat on the edge of the bed, feeling the blood charging through his brain, and – for a few seconds – thought that he might die. And that it may be a good time to go, if this was the truth. If the little bastard was telling the truth, then there was not much point in debating Manzone's terms. There was not much point in anything.

Rosalind did not have a brother-in-law. And she had told him, four days earlier, that she *had arrived* at Silver Palms.

There was some mistake.

He turned the pages of his address book and began to phone all Rosalind's friends in Cairns starting with Lydia and Stephen. Three quarters of an hour later he rang Angelina at the Sydney house. As he had feared, she knew nothing, and he rang off knowing that he had now worried her. Then he phoned former Deputy Police Commissioner Jack Risley.

"Jack? Geoff Harcourt. I need your help."

Mark had bought exercise equipment and he worked a good deal with weights. He also ran. Jogging, now, was not enough. He ran until he knew he was pushing his body to the limit, up the white beach to the headland, back down the white beach to the promontory, until his eyes were dazzled by the blur of the pale sand rushing past him, and it came up to meet him, half-offered, half-accepted.

Still he could not stop his thoughts. They ticked away like the second hand on his watch face. This watch, an expensive Omega given to him by his mother for his twenty-fifth birthday, now seemed to possess him as much as his appointment diary had ruled his life back in Sydney. And he felt the same resentment; he always seemed to be looking at the damned thing.

I have no precious time at all to spend,
Nor services to do, till you require.
Nor dare I chide the world-without-end hour
Whilst I, my soverign, watch the clock for
  you . . .

Shakespeare's words came into his head late on that first night of her captivity, while he was leaning on the balcony railing, waiting for the appropriate hour to turn on the tape. He repeated the words out loud to the black sea and grey sand, and laughed to himself. With part of his brain, he thought, *I'm going mad.*

For it was harder, much harder than he had thought possible. He realised that he had become as much a prisoner as Rosalind.

You should never let yourself care about someone. It's the greatest weakness, the ultimate self-betrayal.

His professionalism had left him. Once the struggling little form was out of his arms, and he had only the scratches on his hands and his memories of her – earlier, warmer, more pliant memories – he had felt bereft.

The contact between them, so close for four days, had been reduced to this tape deck, pulled from its packing case beneath the bed in the spare room, his alarm clock, and the wires that ran from the rear of his desk, up the wall and along the ceiling, to disappear into the wall of the studio.

Every two hours for the first twenty-four hours. Thence every four hours, for twenty-four hours. He could not play the tape more frequently, nor leave her alone for any longer than forty-eight hours. The first might send her mad, and the second might kill her. No food for two days ... His fear gnawed at him as her hunger must be gnawing at her. He found that he, who could eat at will, had no appetite.

She had already been in a weakened state when she entered the studio. He should have made her eat more, but how was he to know that she would prove so stubborn?

Until she came to the house, she had been very healthy, very fit. And there was water – by now, even in the dark, she would have found the bathroom and the taps. It was a complete bathroom – toilet, shower, washbasin – there were towels, soap, a drawer full of everything she would need. Except food. And light. And human companionship.

Very soon after she had realised that he was not coming back, that the lights would not be switched on, surely she would have begun to explore her surroundings. Cement walls, the small table and the straight-backed chair, the narrow single bed – a valuable one, brass, with a porcelain trim. It was psychologically unsound for his purposes, the room should be bare, functional and souless, but he had been unable to resist the bed. Some rules were made to be broken. Like her hair. It would have been best to cut it close to her scalp, a valuable demoralising measure; but he loved her hair now, the tangled mass of it. Change from her old life was important, but this wild-haired Rosalind was change enough.

The studio was fifteen feet square. By now she would have its size paced out. And the bathroom. Both air conditioned like the rest of the beach house, these two rooms were her domain. And every few hours, the tape. On hearing it for the first time she would, perhaps, have addressed the voice, thinking it was he, that he could hear her. Yes, he thought, she would undoubtedly have tried to argue, to plead . . . but the voice would have rolled steadily on.

He had been very careful, on the tape, to make his tone just so – paternal, caring, understanding, but with a note of quiet firmness.

What would she say to the relentless voice? Perhaps he should, after all, have installed a microphone in the ceiling, but it was too late now. A pity. He might have learnt a great deal. But again, he had not thought, he truly had not believed, that any of this would be necessary.

Remember your feelings, the tape began, *when we stood on the balcony, and I kissed you. You enjoyed it, because you love me. You came here with me willingly and happily.*

You had all your belongings in the back of my car. We were happy – we sang as we drove from the airport to the house.

We're together now, as we were meant to be. Geoff belongs in your past. He's furious with us – with both of us – we could be in real danger. Our only hope is to face it together.

You came with me because you wanted to. You'll stay because you want to. You know you're safe with me.

You love me.

On that third day, as the time approached to enter the studio Mark grew more and more tense. A few hours earlier would not matter . . . but no. He had to stick to the programme. There would be reasons enough to be deflected from it later, when her behaviour and needs demanded it.

To calm his nerves, to make the final hours pass, he left the house and drove into Tilga for supplies. He took the keys to the studio with him and, as he fetched them from the second drawer of his desk, he caught sight of the black leather case that held his father's revolver. It was an instinctual thing – perhaps born of his emotional state, his suspicions caused by lack of sleep and his dread of discovery and persecution – but he took the revolver, loaded it and placed it in the pocket of his windcheater. Thereafter, whenever he left the house, the gun went everywhere with him.

When the lights finally came on, they were blinding for Rosalind. There seemed to be lights in every corner of the ceiling as well as above her, and they exploded onto her vision. The glare woke her from her sleep, and she sat up on the bed with a cry, her arms about her face.

Mark's footsteps made no sound on the carpet, but there had been, she was sure, a faint noise close to where she knew the door to be. She sobbed with relief and terror.

"Where ... where have you *been* ... Oh, God ... my eyes ... " For she could not open them, they streamed with tears, part trauma, part desperation.

"Keep your eyes closed." The voice was so calm. She could not know what emotions lay behind the clinical tone. When he touched her, she started, felt his hand take her chin and raise her face upwards, but still she could not see him, as blind in the light as she had been in the dark. His hand left her face, took up her wrist and held it, the fingers moving to find her pulse.

"I can tell you what my heart's doing. It'd be obvious, don't you think? You were taking a chance, weren't you – "

"Be quiet," mildly.

"What if I'd died? What if I'd hung myself from the shower curtain railing?"

"You've too much sense for that."

Mark was very pleased. Even when he had

entered the studio, it was a relief to see her sit up with such alacrity, to see colour in her face. And she was defying him, making demands upon him – it was a great relief. He almost touched her hair, fondly, delighted with her, but stopped himself in time. Instead, he said, "I've brought you some soup", and he took her arm to help her rise, would have guided her to the table.

She let him help her to her feet, but then one talon swiped hard at his arm, catching, painfully, for her, in his sleeve. She walked in the opposite direction, still almost sightlessly, feeling her way around the high and ornamental foot of the bed.

He watched her go, and decided not to insist. Passivity was the best weapon, let her flutter herself into tiredness. She did not yet realise that there was tomorrow, and the day after, and the day after . . .

Rosalind was lost in the centre of the room, but Mark made no move to help her. She walked to a wall, and made her way around it, edging, he could tell, towards the door. "How long have I been here?"

"Come and have your soup."

"How long have I been here?" And when he still refused to answer, "It's been days, hasn't it? It must have been days . . . " Slowly her vision was clearing, she managed to focus upon him, still shading her eyes.

There was a short silence, and then she half laughed, but there was no humour in the sound. "You look . . . just the same. So . . . healthily good-looking, so . . . earnest. It's all I can do to believe . . . "

His calmness, his stillness, seemed to enrage her – all the more, perhaps, because she knew him so well, and sensed some private strategy to which she was not privy. And this was true. It was fortunate for her that she did not know, could not guess at, the extent of his study, his preparation, the strength of his will.

Her shoulders drooped a little. He saw this, knew that his obduracy was tiring her. Woken for the first twenty-four hours, every two hours by a piercing whistle and the sound of the taped message, then sent almost mad for the next twenty-four hours on less than four hours sleep at a time – he knew her defiance could not last long.

"When you first dragged me in here," her voice was lower, softer, "I thought you were going to kill me. And then . . . the hours went by . . . and the days – I know it's been days – and I thought, he's locked me in here, and he won't ever let me out. He's walled me up alive."

Still I stood there and gazed at her without expression, Mark recorded later, *and this waiting game was by far the best tactic to use. For she'd been too long in the silence, and the sound of my voice, saying anything, was already becoming important to her.*

"Are you going to kill me?" Her voice was only a whisper, and for a moment Mark was appalled at the fact that she could so fear him.

"Of course not," he moved towards her, speaking as patiently as to a child. "Just stop worrying and come and eat your soup."

"No." She shrank away from him.

"Alright," he made his voice velvet, "but I'll be turning the lights out when I go. If you don't want to eat now, you'd better use the time familiarising yourself with the layout." He would have led the way to the bathroom, to explain the contents of the drawers, but she interrupted him. "I've worked everything out myself. I even had a shower in the dark. When are you going to let me out?"

He turned back to her, and once more his face was closed.

"*Are* you going to let me out?" She took a few paces towards him.

He thought she would reach for him, and came forward to meet her. With more intensity than he felt he should have betrayed, he said, "It depends on you. I'd never do anything to hurt you, I care more about you than my own life, but I *won't be played with*." He said these last words because she had not sought closeness to him at all – his own steps towards her had made her shrink back. "All this," he finished, jerking his head at the rest of the room, "it shouldn't be necessary. It's for your own good, your own protection."

She repeated, in a dead voice. "My own protection . . . "

"Your own happiness, eventually. Sit down on the chair, Rosalind, I want to talk to you."

When she did not move he stepped forward and took her arm, but she pulled out of his grasp with a cry of "*No!*" and fled to the door.

He watched her, pulling futilely at the handle. Then she calmed and turned to him, her mouth closed tightly against her rising panic. There was something of the old Rosalind there, the Rosalind of their Sydney days, who would send him off to buy an opera programme, or to fetch a glass of champagne from the bar. Her face was ravaged by tears, but there was dignity in the lift of her chin and in her voice. "Give me the keys, Mark."

It stirred him, oddly, to see her. He almost wished he could hand her the keys, as the old Mark had once handed her the programme or the champagne, to see her smile with that quick grace of hers, the way the green eyes lifted to him, her murmured "Thank you". With a shock, he realised that those days were gone forever. In what he was destroying within her, in what he would build within her, there would be no place, however he regretted it, for that old charming arrogance.

"Give me the keys!" she shrieked, and woke him from his reverie as abruptly as if she had dashed cold water across his face.

He would have liked to have stayed longer with her, but she had to learn that such behaviour would drive him away. He said, coldly, "You disappoint me. I'd have thought you had more sense." And he stepped forward to the door, and Rosalind, purposefully.

She did not shrink, as he thought she would. Instead, she attacked him, and so coolly was it done that he felt certain she had had some lessons somewhere. On the balcony he had had the element of surprise, but this time it was he who moved back abruptly, suffering a sharp kick to the shin and just – only just – dodging a well-aimed knee to his groin, which he caught on the hip. She was off balance in that moment – he grabbed one arm, and her other hand came round and delivered a stinging blow across his ear. He imprisoned that hand too, and twisted her left arm hard behind her back.

"You're breaking my arm!"

"I think I'm in a better position to judge that. What *will* happen is a dislocation of the shoulder – and I'll set it for you. But you can avoid that by doing what I tell you. When I let you go, I want you to walk to the middle of the room and stay there. You're not to try this again. Do you agree?"

"*Let go.*" Through clenched teeth.

He could not bring himself to tighten his grip, but forced himself to keep it steady, and waited.

"Alright! Let me go!"

He walked her three paces forward, then backed quickly against the door. Even then, she made a move toward him. "Don't try it!" For his patience was quickly coming to an end. "We can go through it again if you want – as many times as you like – but I'm ten inches taller than you and I'm twice your weight. I'll win every time. All you'll do is make me angry with you. It'll be easier on your arm and my temper if you just let me come and go without … " he paused to find the right word, " … molesting me," he finished, with what was almost a smile.

She stood there, unmoving, in the white nightdress she had pulled on that morning two days before, and it was if she, too, had learnt stillness.

He glanced over towards the bowl of soup on the table. "Your dinner will be cold," he said, and taking the keys from his pocket, he opened the door.

"Mark."

He looked back at her.

Icily, "Change the tape. It's getting boring."

He gazed at her. How long will it take to break you, he thought, when you can weaken me so easily? He made no reply and had almost pushed the door shut behind him, when:

"How about Olivia Newton-John? She's pretty pacifying." The door, which opened out from the studio, hid his smile. "Barry Manilow? John Denver?"

He paused.

"Kamahl?"

He opened the door again and looked at her. She had not moved, and from the defiant tilt of her head it did not seem possible that she had spoken. But he looked into her eyes and could not hide his smile, seeing in their depths her humour and her courage, and loving her.

He shut the door upon her, thinking, yes, it will be worthwhile. I know it will.

He locked the door to the studio, and the outer door beyond, with the little sound lock, and went to his study, where he flicked off the light switch to the studio. As he went to his desk and turned on the tape, he tried not to consider how she would be feeling now. But the process had begun. In four hours he would see her again – but then he stopped to consider.

No. She had to worry that he would not come back. The struggle at the door had been a bad thing, and it mustn't happen again. He would avoid her until late that evening, say ten o'clock.

Mark was shaken, but elated also. Finding he had an appetite, he finished the remainder of the soup he had heated for Rosalind, then went to bed and slept for six hours.

CHAPTER TEN

Geoff heard it first in his old friend, Jack Risley's voice. The polite silence, the unvoicing of thoughts that might hurt, then the decision to speak out.

"Geoff, mate – Roz called you to prevent you calling her ... and later, some bloke calls the resort and postpones her arrival. It doesn't sound like a kidnapping. It sounds like she and the bloke were stalling for time."

She and the bloke ...?

"Time for what?" testily.

Again the hesitation, "Do I have to spell it out? How does it look? She's obviously – "

"I don't care how it bloody *looks*. Rosalind isn't having an affair – and she hasn't run off with this bloke!"

"Geoff ..."

"Jack, are you going to help me or not? Have you got contacts in Queensland? Can they make sure they find her, without getting her name all over the papers? I know how it'll look if this gets out, and she'll hate it."

"If she's gone off with a boyfriend she deserves what she gets." Jack's tone was acerbic. "Stop fooling yourself, mate. If she was being held somewhere against her will they'd have contacted you within the first twenty-four hours. Instead she phones you with some cock-and-bull story about being with Lydia and Stephen Rosenshein – and if you've told Lydia that Rosalind's missing then you can bet that everyone in Queensland knows by now."

Geoff's head was pounding. He heard the words, knew that they made sense, but still he could not believe it. Am I that arrogant? he thought. Was I that sure of her, did I take her so much for granted?

"You still there?"

"Yeah."

"Look, I'll tell you what I'll do. I'll make a few phone calls to some Queensland mates – but in the meantime, there's a bloke you should call. He started on the force with me, made it to inspector before he retired, but couldn't keep out of the field. Still can't. He's a private detective – fussy about what he does, but he's the best. Face like the old bloke who plays Santa Claus and a mind like a steel trap. And charm – he can talk a nun out of her knickers. Give him the job. He won't want it, but offer him a lot of money. Do him good to get off his butt and go trailing round Northern Queensland."

168

"Jobs for the boys?" Geoff grinned.

"When the boy can get the job done. Ron'll stay on this 'til Roz is found, I can promise you that. But . . . you might be better off waiting for her to contact you. You might not like what Ron Christianson will report."

Jack was wrong. He didn't understand. Rosalind hated lies, hated any kind of deception. This . . . this thing that had happened – there had to be some other explanation.

Eighteen years they had been married; and they'd known each other nearly nineteen. Is is possible to live so close to someone for so long and not know how she thinks?

The next day Geoff phoned Silver Palms once more. Still there had been no word from Rosalind. Next he phoned Ron Christianson in Sydney and explained matters to him. After some persuasion, Ron agreed to leave for Cairns, as soon as Geoff had arranged for his office to deliver a cheque for the retainer. Finally, Geoff rang Julia, his secretary, then took the next flight home to Australia.

Mark brought her fresh clothes that night, and sat upon the bed, leaning back against the foot, while she showered.

As he heard the shower being turned off, he called out: "Bring the towels out, too, and I'll put them through the wash". There was no reply, but when Rosalind came into the studio, dressed in fresh jeans and blouse, she was holding the towels and her nightdress rolled up in her arms. She brought them to him – for a moment it seemed as if she might throw them in his face. He made no move, and held her gaze. She threw them down on the bed beside him.

Mark unfolded himself from the bed. It was a small but valuable psychological advantage, never to sit while Rosalind stood – always, she must look up at him.

She did so now, studying his face, trying to read within his eyes some key to his mind, and her freedom.

"Have you heard from Geoff?" she asked.

"No."

"You're lying."

"I don't have any reason to lie. Geoff made his feelings quite clear – "

"When he finds you he'll kill you. Do you know that?"

"So he said," drily.

She looked unsure at this, and moved back a little, the better to study him. He could see the questioning fear in her eyes, the words unspoken, the demands for truth that she wanted and yet was afraid to make.

Mark said, "Sit down, Rosalind. There are some questions I want to ask you." For the time had come to begin.

She glanced at the chair and table where she had sat, some half an hour before, and eaten a meal of rice, bean shoots and diced chicken while he stood over her. If she had not been so hungry she would have choked. And yet this was harder; not knowing what he wanted of her, she was afraid to agree to anything. She scowled at him. "Only if you'll promise – "

"No deals." Bending to the bed he picked up the towels and would have left . . .

"Alright!"

That was the look she would come to hate – his eyes were always cool, but when she bent her will to his will there was a faint, such a faint, stirring of interest, one could not call it warmth, in their blue depths, like a silent shadow in the sea.

Then it was gone, and his expression was cold and unreadable. She seated herself upon the little straight-backed chair, crossing her feet at the ankles, placing her hands loosely together in her lap, and gazed up at him with mock respect.

He didn't seem to notice. He moved to the table beside her, and pushing back her plate, seated himself on its surface.

Once there, he did not speak immediately.

And she refused to look at him.

Mark let the silence settle, and let her mind begin to question, before he said, with a sweet sadness in his voice, "You no longer think of me as your friend."

A slight movement of her head, a tensing of her shoulders, her fingertips moved. Nothing more.

"Do you?" his voice prodded gently.

Then the green eyes came up to him, venomous. "How can you even think it? You're a madman. Only a little more mad than I – because I couldn't see through you. I trusted you. I cared about you . . ."

She stopped. He did not understand why, could not know that his unreadable gaze, those eyes long practised in seeing all yet giving nothing, had betrayed him. He did not know the dark shadow that was his desire, his wanting. He only knew that she was attempting to shut him out.

"You cared about me," he repeated.

"As a friend," she said, watching his eyes.

"The kiss on the balcony wasn't the kiss of a friend," he reminded her.

"Stop it, you sound like that bloody tape!" And she would have stood, but for his hand suddenly on her shoulder. She had no other way to shrink from his touch but back into the chair. She sat still.

"So you trusted me, and you cared for me. That's more than many a man can hope for from the woman he loves. But there was more than that. You know it, too."

"No!"

"Why did you come with me, Rosalind? After I'd . made my feelings for you very clear when I last saw you in Sydney, why did you watch me place all your

172

luggage in the back of my car and drive into the unknown with me?"

"I . . ." She ran her hand through her hair.

"But it wasn't the unknown, was it? You drove off with a man who loved you very much – you knew where we were going."

"I can't follow your reasoning! I can't! You twist things, innocent things, until I feel guilty and I haven't – "

Again she stopped. And he knew, then.

She's reading me as I do her. She has her own skein of twine leading down to the Minotaur. When she knows what I want her to say, she refuses me.

He smiled a little, and was disturbed to see that this seemed to make her more afraid.

"Look," reasonably, "I'm going to be honest with you. What I want from you is for you to be in touch with your own feelings. I believe you love me, Rosalind. I wouldn't have done what I have unless I was very sure that I know you better than you do yourself. You just have to trust me . . ."

"No! You destroyed that! You destroyed any . . . good feelings . . . that . . ."

"*Good feelings?*" he was amused. "You're an articulate woman and you can't do better than 'good feelings'?" And, quietly, "Say 'love', Rosalind."

173

She stared at him. "No."

He laughed aloud. "One little word . . . !"

"No."

"Why?"

"Because . . . because you want me to. And whatever you want is part of your plan. And I'm not going to be part of your plan."

He had promised himself not to use physical persuasion of any kind, even though all the case histories he had read made it clear that destruction of the self was facilitated by the fear of death, of beatings, of rape and any number of physical indignities. Such tortures were all very well for political conversion – no military psychiatrist had ever demanded that his prisoner form an emotional and permanent attachment to him. Her very imprisonment made Rosalind afraid of him – more than he needed for his purpose. To terrify her would be to gain, in the end, only a slave, and he wanted more than that. But, at times like this, he burned to take hold of her upper arms and shake her, just enough to rock her equilibrium, to remove that look of bitter defiance from her face. But words would do as well.

"Do you want to get out of here or not?"

Now he had all her attention. But she said nothing.

"No one would blame you," he said, in that calm and reasonable tone, using the knowledge that his voice was part of his weaponry, "no one at all, if you lied to me, deceived me, seduced me, only to be free of this place."

"I thought of that. But you're too intelligent," she said bitterly, "you'd see through it."

He took her chin in his hand and turned her face, her guarded eyes, towards him. "Try it," he said.

Another silence of guessing paths in the dark, each of them there in each other's eyes, driven separately by love and hate, groping their way forward.

"No," she said coldly.

"Then you'll be in this room forever," he said, his neutral tone accentuating the horror of his words.

She did not push his hand away, as once, even that morning, she may have done. He noted it and was pleased.

"I'll kill myself." Her words were as well-chosen, as carefully spoken as his own. His hand dropped from her face before he could control it, and from the spark of triumph that glowed for an instant in her eyes, he saw he had betrayed himself to her.

"Foolish, don't you think, when escaping is so easy?"

"By admitting that I'm in love with you? *That* easy?"

"No," honestly. "But it's a beginning. It's the truth."

"It's not!"

"It's the truth," he continued calmly, "and if you say it, you'll come to realise it's the truth."

She turned away, away from his eyes and their demand of her, to better understand this tactic. Her hands came up to her face and she rubbed her eyes, tiredly. "You've studied this, I can tell, as well as all your mother's psychiatric text books – probably when you were eight. But you've studied *this* in detail." She gestured at the room before them. "All I know is what I read years ago about Patricia Hearst . . . and other things . . . they always seem to happen in America. Australians are too . . . prosaic . . ." Her voice faded, and she frowned and looked up to find him listening, quietly.

She said, "That's part of it. Wanting me to talk, looking for something . . ."

"Looking for what?"

Her voice suddenly low, vehement. "No. That's it. I give myself away with everything I say."

"Give what away?"

"I don't know! I don't know!" Once more the hands were covering her eyes. Mark stood and reached for her, drawing her to her feet. When she would have pulled back from him he held her firmly, but not close to him.

"Listen to me. You trusted me once – you must try to trust me still. I do want you to speak to me. There are things I want to know about you – it's only natural. It's up to you. If you don't want to speak to me I can come with your meals and leave again immediately. But that won't get you out of here."

She still leaned away from him, so he set her down once more upon the chair and stood in front of her. "I'm not going to explain my actions to you, nor my plans – partly because they're complicated, and partly because I want you to learn to trust me again, and this is as good a time to begin as any.

"But I will tell you this: we're going to have long hours together, you and I, where I'll be asking you a lot of questions. Some will seem so trite, so insignificant, that you'll wonder why I bother. Others may brush close to things you'd rather forget – but I want you to be honest with me in everything. There'll be a lot of repetition, so you'll have to be patient. If you are, and you co-operate and avoid playing senseless mind games with me, then you'll be out of here very soon."

"How . . . ?" she began, but he ignored the question, speaking over her.

"If you're stubborn, or lie to me, or lose your temper, then I'll simply stay away – and you'll be postponing the time of your release from this place. Do you understand, Rosalind?"

He was all business, and it was a dark and frightening business that she could only guess at. And what good would that do? In the dark of that place, in the silences between the tape of that deep and beautiful voice with its gentle poison, she had tried in vain to understand his strategy, his aim. She was tired. Living with her terror in the darkness had made her tired.

His voice was like honey, his hand on the nape of her neck, "Do you understand, Rosalind?"

"Yes."

He studied her, as if checking for any deception or trace of sarcasm – but there was nothing. He let her go and straightened up.

In a matter-of-fact voice, "I want you to start at the beginning. Every detail, from as early as you can remember."

He could see that Rosalind did not understand. "The beginning?" she repeated, and then, as she thought she understood, "*My* beginning?"

Mark waited.

Her voice was small, "You want my life?" She looked up, and was caught by his gaze and the irony of her own words. "Yes," she whispered, "of course you do."

He seated himself once more on the edge of the table, close to her, aware of the growing fear that came with her understanding. Kindly, he said, "Rosalind, it'll be much easier if you don't try to outguess me. Nothing's as frightening as you believe it to be. Just trust me. Don't think, just answer. Where were you born?"

She had told him before that she had been born and raised in Bega. He knew this, knew a good deal already about her background, but that was not the issue. She looked up into the emotionless blue eyes and knew a little – knew enough. To speak was her only means of escape – yet to speak gave Mark the very weapon he wanted.

CHAPTER ELEVEN

M eal times were staggered, so Rosalind had no idea of time, and Mark did not tell her. All meals were the same now that she seemed to be regaining her strength. Brown rice, vegetables and a little chicken or fish. He brought fresh orange juice or sometimes milk. He brought vitamin tablets, too, C and B Complex and calcium. At first, being suspicious, she would only take the vitamin C, easily recognisable with their orange flavour. The following meal time he brought two of each tablet and let her choose her own, watching him as he swallowed the others. They continued this practice. She was always suspicious of him.

She did not want to talk about her past, tried to steer the conversation to her release and what it was he wanted, but Mark was adept at ignoring her questions, and he had time on his side. He simply did not answer, directed at her the calm intelligence of his gaze until, in desperation, she took up the narrative again. To Rosalind, it seemed futile, almost as mad an obsession as keeping her there at all.

Mark would interrupt her with questions. "How big was the oak tree in your garden?"

"I don't know – *big*! It was eighty years old."

"And did you have a tree house?"

"No, but we climbed it, and it was Tarzan's house, a castle, a sailing ship – whatever we wanted it to be."

"You and the Carson children."

"Yes."

"Tell me their names again."

It was difficult, she found sometimes, when it was a pleasant memory, a fond one, not to smile, for it seemed he came with her into the past, so close was his interest, so great his desire to be there. Mark smiled also, and the old games, the oak tree, the ponies, the rope swing over the river, seemed to become as real to him as they were to her. He knew the Carson children and the ponies by name, and sometimes began questions about them. "Did Danny Carson ever kiss you when you blossomed into pubescence?" "When Taffy died, did you cry?"

She grew more and more highly strung, he noticed, she cried easily. But with her emotions so close to the surface, her defences were very low. His power over her, she had begun to realise, was absolute, and Mark could feel a subtle dependency building up inside her. There was a small smile for him when he came with her food, and she always thanked him. He never commented on this, for he sensed that she did not know it had come about.

She had been right, of course, to be reticent in speaking to him, in telling him all the small details of her past. He took no notes, for he had an excellent memory and was able to retrieve information and confront her with it, subtly. "When Danny Carson kissed you in the cinema, why were you so shocked? You'd flirted with him, hadn't you?" And when she denied it, "Come now, all the preparations you made – this was your first date – the way you dressed, the way you looked at him . . ." He was knowledgeable enough to pinpoint the right moments and had her thinking back and seeing her own culpability in a thousand small incidents. "When your grandmother died, why did you refuse to kiss her? It would have meant a lot to your parents, to see that last farewell kiss on her cheek. Couldn't you have overcome your horror by thinking of them?" "How do you *know* your mother wasn't brokenhearted by your choosing ballet over an academic career? If she never spoke of it, perhaps her disappointment lay too deep to express."

"Yes . . . perhaps." She would always admit to these small crimes and, though she often offered defences, excuses for her behaviour, he was content. The seeds of doubt had been planted.

And if he scattered the spores upon the long-fallow fields of her childhood, he drove them deep into the soil of her marriage, always interrupting her in the middle of some innocent anecdote, when she was at ease, when she least expected it.

"What do you know about Geoff's business contacts in America?" he asked during a long session on the sixth day in the studio.

"I . . . I only know one – Harry Manzone. He's heavily involved in mining, but he . . ."

"He and Geoff met in Brisbane, over plans for the Lotus Island development."

"Yes . . ." her eyes were wary, for this had been one of Geoff's mistakes, not costly, but embarrassing – though even Harcourt shares had suffered a morning of hesitation before lurching forward again, like Geoff himself.

"What do you know about Harry Manzone?"

"Nothing. I only met him socially, two or three – "

"Has anyone else spoken to you about him? Did anyone mention *anything* to you about Geoff going to the States for these meetings?"

Her gaze slid away from him. He watched her closely, and now, after six days of intensive 'discussion', she was wary of lying to him. "Some of his business friends didn't approve."

"Why?"

"They didn't say. A friend of Geoff's, Neville Bruce – he's a banker – he said at a dinner I gave . . ."

"Yes?"

"That Geoff was overextending himself."

"You had the impression that Bruce didn't like Manzone?"

"Yes, but ... Neville didn't like Geoff's global expansion – he always said that there were avenues here in Australia – "

"A cautious man, and a patriotic one – and he thought Manzone was dangerous ..." Mark looked thoughtful. Rosalind would have questioned his choice of words – she had not used the word 'dangerous' – but he changed the subject again, abruptly.

"Do you think your father's death had anything to do with his disappointment over your career?"

She stared at him, then jumped up from her chair before turning on him. "That's a *horrible* thing to say! A ... a malicious and senseless thing to say! My father had a heart condition ... he died nearly three years after I started dancing!"

The moment Rosalind leapt to her feet, Mark casually stood from his seat at the table. Now he moved to lean against one of the walls. He said nothing, let her pour out her invective on his tastelessness, his cruelty – and all the time it was there in her eyes, the proof that she had been afraid of this very thing, ever since her father had died.

"How can you claim to love me? God, you can't have any feelings for me *whatsoever* and say things like that!" She was weeping now. Mark waited until the sobbing became uncontrollable, then stepped

184

forward and placed his arms about her tenderly, holding her unprotesting body – so thin now! – against him.

"Hush, now. I'm sorry. I was wrong." He kissed her hair, her face, gently, and she was too distraught to pull away. He had no compunction about apologising, using a little humility – if she remained in his arms it was worth it, and the necessary damage had been done, after all. In the long hours of darkness between his visits, she would think about his words. If she did not consciously dwell on them, she would face the fears in her dreams.

He stood rocking her in his arms, allowing himself, for this moment, to feel the terrible tenderness against which he constantly had to guard himself.

"It's ... it's my own fault, isn't it?"

Her words took him completely by surprise. He pushed her gently back from him in order to see her face.

"I shouldn't have come here, and ... and when I became ill I should have done as you suggested and gone to a hospital. Having me here ... where you've been so alone, lonely ... I should have *thought*. And ... after you ... made love to me ..." – she had always called it "rape", so this, too, was new – "... you felt committed to me in some way. But ..." And here she ruined it, for his heart had begun to pound hard in his chest and his spirits rose with hope – "... but sex doesn't have to mean *anything*. Can't you think of all the other women you'll have in your life? You're so good-looking, Mark – just because I was the first ..."

And she stopped, looking up and seeing what he knew must have been written upon his face.

"The *first*? You honestly believe there'll be others? Do you think you've left me with anything to give to another woman?"

"Yes!"

"What?"

She wanted him to let her go, glanced down at the hands that were avoiding squeezing her arms, but she did not break out of their grasp. "You ... yourself," she said. And when he looked sceptical, "Your love."

"My soul, perhaps," Mark suggested.

"Your ... yes, I suppose ..." But she was unsure, sensing, once more, that he was leading her, but not knowing where.

"You can't love if you have no soul. You've already taken mine. I can't give to someone else what I no longer possess."

She started to move back, to pull out of his grasp. His voice was as reasonable as ever, "You know I'm speaking the truth."

"No – "

"You have my soul – and I have yours."

"No!" She turned away in his grasp, and he allowed the slight movement.

186

Then, "It's the truth, isn't it?"

"No!"

"Rosalind . . ."

Only her name, and she was afraid, summoned the strength to pull back, out of his grasp, and found herself up against the wall of the studio. "You can't make me say it. I won't say it. You're mad, and this place is driving *me* mad, but I won't join you. I won't give up the last of myself. Do you understand?"

"But I know that you loved me. I know that you still do, at this very moment. How many times must I explain to you?" he spoke carefully, patiently. "Say the words . . ."

"No!" she screamed, seeing him move towards her. "I won't say I loved you! I didn't love you! I was attracted to you, that was all! You can't destroy us both because of that!"

She turned into the wall, her face half-buried in her arm, the hands, like a small bird's talons, looking for purchase on the smooth grey surface. She started when he placed his hand on her shoulder, turned her about to face him.

I could have cried myself, he declared later, on the tape. *It was all I could do not to hug her, kiss her, laugh into the coils of her hair. To stand so still, so close to her, was the hardest thing I'd done since locking her in this room six days ago – a lifetime ago.*

187

"Say that again."

Her face showed puzzlement only, the fear and her puzzlement.

"You weren't in love with me, you said. But you were attracted to me."

"Yes . . ." Unsure, now.

"Say it."

"I . . . was attracted to you."

"From the beginning? When we first met?"

She felt the trap now, "I . . ." His hands tightened on her shoulders. "Yes."

"Define attraction."

She looked at him helplessly, "I don't know . . ." But seeing something hard in his eyes, realising that he would not let her go until this was confronted, and he had gained whatever emotional victory he needed, she became cunning. Mark saw the green eyes narrow. "If I do, can I go to sleep? We've been talking for hours – and no tape. I just want to sleep for a few hours, *really* sleep, without the tape."

"Just tell me the truth – that's all I'm asking of you. And then – yes, you can rest – eight hours, and no tape."

It took a few minutes, he saw her trying to gather her thoughts, calculating how to give him as little as possible, how to satisfy him yet still retain the essence of herself, her right to lie.

"I . . . I liked being with you," she began.

"Go on."

"I . . . we were friends . . ."

"Not good enough, Rosalind."

"You . . . I thought, when I first saw you that you were very handsome. I didn't know who you were. Everyone watched you, that evening. And you seemed so unconcerned, you didn't notice. You don't, you know. You don't think of yourself as attractive at all, you don't think of yourself as being in any way worthwhile . . ."

"We're drifting away from the subject," he reminded her. "I want *your* feelings."

"But . . . that was it – or almost. Your mother introduced us, and you were charming, and courteous. And when David Papadimitriou couldn't accompany me to the ballet, and mentioned you, I was pleased."

"Why?"

"Mark, sometimes we don't consider these things much. You agonise so – most people avoid looking too closely at their feelings. Can't you understand that? I liked your company, I'd even thought, in my ignorance and vanity, that it helped you to talk to me. I admired your *caring*, your strength – *such* strength – working against your own sensitivity to save those children . . ."

"You loved me, Rosalind."

"No," almost a sigh of weakness. "Oh, Mark, what victory is there for you in doing this, in having me say it? If I did say I was in love with you – they're only words. Don't you understand? They can't bring the *feelings*."

"Say them. Say them anyway."

In anger, exhaustion, defiance – to show him how meaningless they would sound against his ears, within his heart – she looked up at him coldly. "I was in love with you." The silken cords drew tight.

Mark studied her face for a moment, his slow smile beginning in his eyes.

"There. Was that so very hard?" He let her go then, and exhausted, she leaned against the wall and began to turn away. "Say it again," Mark persisted.

She looked back at him; he could read the refusal in her eyes. He said, "Say it again and we'll go out to the kitchen and have coffee." It was almost touching, the hopefulness, the pleasure that flooded her gaze. "Would you like that?"

"Yes . . ."

"Say it. Just trust me, and say it."

"I was . . . It doesn't make it true, Mark!"

"Say it."

"I was in love with you."

"Again."

"I was in love with you."

She was weeping now, those silent tears of exhaustion. Mark placed his arm around her and walked with her to the door, speaking soothingly to her as he found the keys in his pocket and unlocked the first door. "There. That wasn't difficult, was it? Now, when I ask you to repeat it, you must. And we'll have you out of here very soon."

"How soon?"

"A week or two," he lied smoothly. "It depends on you. You have to be honest with your feelings. That's all I've ever asked of you. You can't learn from your mistakes unless you face them. Do you understand?"

She did not answer. How could anyone answer without – as Rosalind had refused to do, earlier – joining Mark in his madness.

The morning sun slanted through the broad glass doors on to the pale carpet of the study. Outside, a pair of early courting gulls screamed to each other and were swept like children's kites along the beach, dipping and rising without the beat of a wing. Rosalind stared and moved forward. Mark, suspicious, left the two doors to the studio open, in case there was a necessity for a rapid and perhaps violent return, and followed her, standing at the window close by her shoulder.

"Morning," she murmured. "You never tell me whether it's day or night. Time has no meaning in there."

Standing, looking down upon her, he almost placed his arms about her. Would her head come back against his shoulder? In the sunlight of the familiar room she was suddenly less his troublesome captive and more his Rosalind – perhaps more than she had been before. There was no way of knowing if she would turn in his arms and hold him, if she would relax in his embrace and go with him to the bed they had shared, unless he first held her. And what if she grew afraid, fluttered and bated in his arms, and all these long hours work would have been for nothing.

His impatience was his greatest enemy, not Rosalind, who was being true to her nature, after all. He took a deep breath and allowed the thought of her rejection to cool his blood. When he did reach for her it was the lightest of touches on her shoulder, and she turned, calmly enough beneath it, towards the kitchen.

He had planned for this, and the room was devoid of any weapon, any missile that she could easily reach. Rosalind's own small dinner plate he placed in the sink. All surfaces were bare, except for the coffee percolator on the bench, and he himself filled that and took down mugs from the cupboard above his head, watching Rosalind all the time. He said, lightly, "Don't think of running. If you do we'll have to start all over again."

Her eyes became unreadable with her reaction to these words. But she said, calmly, "How bothersome for you, 'starting all over again'. One would think you didn't enjoy it. How long have I been in that room?"

He was not angered by her words. Her voice shook – it was bravado, and the sunlight, and the memory of the woman she had been in the outside world. He considered her question, decided to tell her the truth. "Six days."

She leaned back against a kitchen cupboard as she digested this. At the same time, her eyes moved casually about the room. In his heart he knew she was restless, that she was going to turn upon him.

"You were so kind when I first came here," she said, "when I was ill. I can't believe that you're the same man. How empty is your life, Mark, that you have to take your joy from making me repeat empty words?"

"Because they're the truth. And the more you repeat the truth, the more in touch with your feelings you become. You don't understand," seeing her scowl. "Just trust me." He opened the refrigerator door for the milk.

Only a second – and the dinner plate that had been placed in the sink was shattering just above his head on the cupboard doors. No, more than a second, even for her, light and quick as she was. A shard of broken china struck his cheek. He turned, knowing she would be gone.

The closest escape route was out onto the balcony and down the steep flight of stairs to the sand, but he vaulted the settee and reached the glass doors before her. She almost collided with him, and he could see, by the fear in her eyes, that days of work had been ruined. It was his own fault; she had not been ready. Her frightened gaze moved from him towards the front hall and the door to the driveway, measuring her chances. "All the doors are locked," he said, "the keys are in my pocket."

He moved towards her, edging her gently back towards the kitchen. "You know what you've done, don't you?" His voice held his disappointment.

Surprisingly, she stopped. "What? What are you talking about?"

And he thought, I don't have to threaten her. I don't have to try for the necessary physical fear – she does it herself, her imagination does it. I only have to *be* and she thinks me capable of anything.

"I was going to leave the lights on," he lied smoothly. "All day, until ten o'clock tonight. I might even have given you a book."

"You're lying!" Her hysteria was born of her disappointment. "You're just saying that!"

"I'm not lying. I was very pleased with you." He regarded her for a moment, then added, almost puzzled, "Just where did you think you were running to, Rosalind? Geoff won't help you – the police won't believe you. All you've done is make me annoyed with you."

He wished she would not look at him with such hunted eyes. Was his power over her so great, so soon? He continued to move towards her; there was nowhere for her to go but back into the kitchen. Her short reprieve was over, and she knew it, but he had not expected the loss of it to have such an effect upon her.

"Mark . . . please . . ." She was actually pleading with him.

And then it happened as he had feared it would.

She ran for the drawers, opened them, one by one – and one by one left them gaping – one, two, three, four ... No silverware, no sharp cooking instruments, *no knives*. What would she have done if she had found what she was searching for? His furious sense of betrayal must have been written on his face; certainly he had not felt so angry before, so close to striking her.

"It's your own fault!" she cried out, as if she could read his mind – and why not, after all they had been sharing? Her body was half-curled into itself, as if she expected a physical blow from him. "It's your own fault! You make me afraid of you! You can't blame me!"

He broke angrily through her words, "Have I hurt you? *Have I?*"

"I ... You ... Yes, you do!"

"How? When?" His words were like a whip.

"Everything! Everything!"

He lost patience with her, reached for her, but she pulled away, quickly, backed along the cupboards. "*No!* No, I'm sorry! I didn't ... You haven't ... hurt me! I shouldn't have run, I know I shouldn't have run ... *No, Mark!*"

He only wanted to get her back inside the studio, without harming herself, or him. But his effort to calm himself, even though successful, seemed to frighten her more, as if his intent was enough to send her into paroxysms of fear.

"I'll be good," she said, and there was a child-like

pleading to her voice, tears held in check, a child trying to be grown-up and unafraid. "I will. You haven't hurt me. I shouldn't have run ... I won't anymore – and I'll say whatever you want me to say! Only let me stay out here, don't make me go back in there."

"You must, just for a while ..."

"No!" And it was then, when he had her pinned into a corner and could have reached for her at his leisure, that she stood her ground and turned on him with all the nerve that she had left.

"Why are you doing this to me? Can't you get a woman to come to you willingly? What's the matter with you? Are you afraid she'd see the truth – that you're a pretty face with nothing behind it except something twisted – and dirty!"

He leapt for her then, cutting short her scream as he took her by the hair, pulling her face around towards him. He had had no idea how much she could hurt him. To think that she had said such things, cutting at the very heart of his existence, for – and he could admit it, later – she was right. These were his fears, and nothing hurt so much as that which might be true.

This was why he lost control, amazed that she was, in her desperation, using upon him the tactics – cruel, but necessary – that he was using upon her, confronting her with her fears, destroying her sense of herself. Later he regretted it bitterly, but in that moment he could not prevent himself.

Holding a fistful of her thick warm hair and speaking into her ear with a controlled voice that demanded all his restraint, he said "That was good, very clever. I don't mind you knowing the rules of the game. But you're not allowed to play."

CHAPTER TWELVE

J ulia Wainwright was waiting for Geoff when he
    stepped off the Qantas flight from Los Angeles.
She smiled at his look of almost comic surprise
when his concentration broke and he found himself
suddenly confronted by his secretary.

"Julia . . ." His smile seemed to her subdued,
strained. Fond of him as she was, she watched him
worriedly as they fell into step, walking through
the crowds, Geoff looking about warily for the
press.

"Any news?" he asked as they headed for the
baggage retrieval.

"Nothing from the police, but Jack Risley
phoned late yesterday and said to give you his
best."

"Nothing from Ron Christianson?"

"He's been in Cairns for two days, but he hasn't
phoned yet. Maybe he's waiting for you to arrive,
or perhaps there's nothing to report. If Rosalind
doesn't want to be found . . . "

He threw her a black look. There was no one about to overhear, but Julia lowered her voice nevertheless. "I'm sorry, Geoff. But if it hadn't been for that phone call she made to you . . . Why would she lie, say she was at the resort when she wasn't? Unless she was stalling for time."

These had been Jack Risley's exact words, a few days before. Geoff felt a hot rush of irritation, knowing that these words, from both a friend and a trusted employee, who had proved her loyalty over more than ten years of working closely with him, were nothing less than what he could expect from the world.

"We'll find out," he said, grimly. "It's not what you think. Not what anyone thinks. I feel it in my bones, in my blood. She wouldn't do this to me. She just wouldn't."

He felt Julia's pity for him. Was he going to appear a figure of pity to the entire nation? What was the old term for it that they used in Shakespeare's plays? A cuckold, that was it. A figure of fun.

But Geoff realised that it did not matter. He only wanted one thing – to have Rosalind back. Even if that meant eventually confronting the fact that she had left him, that she had been sleeping with this other man, the one who rang the resort – it didn't matter. What tightened within him was not jealously, as he had always imagined it would be in such an instance, but determination. *I don't care if*

you've had fifty lovers. I don't care if you've lied to
me, cheated on me in my own bed, with my best
friends. Come back, Roz. Just come back.

Going home to their house terrified him. Going to
the office was almost as disturbing. More of his
marriage had been spent there than at home with
his wife. The house *was* Rosalind; the office was all
those hours that could have been Rosalind. The
evenings with her reading or watching television
curled beneath his arm; the mornings making love
with all the day ahead of them.

We have more than enough, she had pleaded,
only about a month ago, when he had broken the
news to her that he was going to the States to
explore the idea of mining in Colorado. He hadn't
listened to her, had refused to speak of
consolidating, of selling Amalgamated Media and
ploughing the money back into the other
enterprises. He had not wanted to sell anything, to
let go of anything. And now, that which meant the
most had been torn from him and, for the first time
in his life, he was helpless.

Or *had* it been torn from him? Had she perhaps
merely drifted away from him, tired of being
ignored, of having no place in his schedule of
important events?

He had said to her that day, almost crossly,
"What do you want me to do? Give up? Let it all
go, everything we've worked for?"

"We were working for each other. For ... for the children we might have had."

"Roz ... " he began.

"But even if Jamey had lived, I wouldn't *want* him to inherit an empire like this, Geoff. I wouldn't want his life to be ruled as yours has been."

He had come home from the office at lunch time – unusual for him – to explain to her about Manzone, about this need of his to try for the US deal. But she seemed to be taking the opportunity to heap on his head all the hurts that she had stored up for months, for years.

"You haven't been the same since the crash. Before that, you were possessed – now you're driven. Other people have had to sell off – "

"Not Amalgamated Media. That was the *first* – I *am* Amalgamated Media. I *am* the Harcourt Corporation. And before anyone else sits in my chair at the head of *any* of those board tables, I'll blow the buildings up with my own hands." There had been a silence. "Do you understand?"

Rosalind had lowered her gaze to her plate, pushed the food about a little. "Yes. Yes, I suppose I do."

"It's not that I love the businesses any more than you ... "

"I know that."

"But we're part of it. I know more than anyone how you've helped me get where I am. You gave up your dancing for me to play hostess to people that you despised – some of them, at least. And I haven't

201

been able to give you anything in return except money, and you're not too impressed with that."

She had looked up, smiled a little.

"And my love," he'd said seriously, "though you've practically had to make an appointment for that."

They had smiled at each other. Rosalind had left the table, and he followed her, to the large glassed area that overlooked the pool. He recalled that he'd said to her, "I wish there could have been more babies."

"Why?" She had sat down on one of the couches, her gaze on the view of the garden. "To keep me occupied? That's not a good enough reason to take on the responsibility of another life."

"Maybe I should have let you adopt when you wanted to."

"You don't 'allow' your wife to adopt a child, it's something two people do together."

"Don't go for me like that, love – you know what I meant. I don't use the right words, sometimes . . . "

She'd put a hand out to him, and he'd taken it, had sat on the broad arm of the couch, feeling helpless, wanting what he wanted, but not knowing how to give her what she wanted, not knowing that it was going to end, so soon, and that he would not have the chance again to say, "You were right. I want to give you my time. Take all of it, and, with it, give yourself back to me."

Her cheek against his hand, she had tried to comfort him. "I'm happy with my life the way it is," she'd said, and he knew it wasn't a lie, just her attempt to make the words true. And he'd chosen the easy way out, and believed her.

"So am I," he had said. "But I've put everything I have, everything I am, into that corporation. To lose any of it is to lose part of myself. What I've built is all that's left when I'm gone. My ... immortality. Try to understand, Roz."

He knew she tried. She always tried. But, "I don't understand immortality – outside of heaven perhaps. But earthly immortality ... if we'd had children, perhaps. But I no longer think about that, about the future. I want to be happy with you, here and now. That's all I want, Geoff. All I've ever wanted."

He had bent down and kissed her lips. It had been a gentle kiss, but when they drew back they came together once more and again, and each kiss became more passionate, until she had been lying back upon that couch, her face raised to receive his kisses.

Geoff had stopped suddenly. "Where's Angelina?"

Rosalind had smiled. "I gave her the afternoon off when you said you were coming home for lunch."

"Geoff?" He looked up as Julia came into the office. He was still standing there, in the middle of that sea of pale carpet, holding his briefcase. The view of the harbour, the expensive Italian furniture, designed to look as uncomfortable as possible while being very comfortable indeed – it all meant nothing to him now. It was a place in which to waste one's life – he had thought that on the plane. Now, standing here, he felt that it was a *waiting* place. Empty, as if expecting some new tenant. For the first time he felt that life was going on elsewhere.

He never did find out what Julia wanted. Probably she was simply voicing her concern. He turned to her abruptly. "Where's Allen Myer? Melbourne? Get him for me." Allen Myer had wanted Amalgamated Media very badly.

Julia was staring at him. "Geoff? Can you use him any longer for delaying tactics? He's lost patience – he won't fall for . . . "

"He'll talk now." Looking through her, "It's okay – I'll do it." And going to his desk, dropping the briefcase, he looked up Myer's office number and phoned.

Ron Christianson advised Geoff not to come to Cairns. "You'll have all the media in the country thinking you're going to be buying up the Marlin Coast. Besides, if your wife calls – and I think she will, any time now – you should be there." Christianson had no news beyond the fact that Rosalind had been on the flight. He was questioning crew members and ground staff, and was attempting to bribe a contact in the airline to give him a passenger list.

"I'll need some more good pictures of her, too, and some of her recent boyfriends."

"She didn't have *boyfriends*." Icily.

"Those blokes that used to squire her around town, then. You know the ones I mean." Christianson was getting impatient. Geoff, who had so far only spoken to the man on the phone, did not like him, but had to admit he seemed to be working hard. Christianson did not think Rosalind would be long in contacting him, did not even think that the separation was necessarily permanent. Geoff could forgive the man a lot for that.

The passenger list was, after a lot of haggling, forthcoming – and then, silence.

Geoff found himself going ahead with the sale of Amalgamated Media. It was not that he did not care any longer, but that his mind was elsewhere. His bankers were delighted; so were his nervous stockholders. The Harcourt Corporation, after rocking on a stormy sea for some years, now cleared the bilges and sailed sturdily on. The pressures eased immediately, and Geoff wanted Rosalind more than ever, to say, "Look, you were right!" But she was not there.

The day the sale was finalised, he tried to make his escape as soon as possible. He had never liked Allen Myer, and the little turd would want to sit over a few drinks and gloat. Geoff made his excuses, shook the hand of the man himself, all the lawyers and accountants on both sides, and was at the door when Myer caught up with him. They were out of earshot of the others.

"Thank you," Myer said. "Away from all this," he jerked his narrow head towards the rest of the room, "I know what it took for you to do this."

"Really? You'd be surprised how little it took."

"Of course. Yes, well, it was half-expected, once we heard the news. Rosalind will be out for everything she can get, of course. Good idea to keep liquid and go for a cash settlement."

Geoff's tone was deadly. "What are you talking about?"

"Oh, come *on*, man! I heard it through a source in the Police Department. You don't even know where she is yet." He gave a small smile. "Shouldn't be too difficult to find her – she'll be off with one of those young studs you used to set her up with, won't she?"

The press were waiting on the other side of the door. There was a fierce pleasure in imagining Myer greeting them, burbling his triumph through bloodied lips and broken teeth, but then there'd be the lawsuit . . .

Geoff stood very close to Myer, pushing the man up against the door, delighting in the sudden fear that sprang into the pale eyes. "You just bought

Amalgamated Media – it was my toy, now it's yours. Enjoy it. But keep your snotty little nose out of my personal life. If I hear that you've breathed one word of malice about my wife, I'll personally tie your balls in a knot on top of your head."

Why should it bother him, surrounded as he was now by the world giving him its opinion? Why couldn't he accept it, shrug it off? It wasn't even that he found he still loved her in the face of the evidence of her betrayal, for he could not, no matter how he considered it, even believe in that betrayal. Even that last phone call – she had wanted to come to him in London, and it had been no lie, no 'stalling for time'. She had mentioned driving through Wales again. That first trip, five years ago, had been one of their best holidays ever. Rosalind across a tea table set with high tea in a farmhouse living room; Rosalind striding out beside him, up twisted mountain tracks to gaze at purple mountains sheering away into mild green valleys, slopes so sharp they seemed sliced with a knife. On the point of leaving him, she would not think of the best of times.

And she would not lie. She did not do it well, and she hated those who did. *She would not lie.*

But, to those around him, it merely seemed that he was not facing up to the facts. He found himself thinking up new arguments – Julia was one of the few people he spoke to about them. Why would

Rosalind leave with only her light clothes, five suitcases full? She had a room of clothes, some she was very fond of. Why didn't she take more things, back a truck up to the house and take *everything*?

Julia fiddled with her dictation pencil, said almost unwillingly, "But she had enough clothes for Queensland, or for Sydney, weather. And she probably had all her favourite pieces of jewellery with her." *And she had.* "I know women who've left their husbands and taken only an overnight bag. To this day the poor bastards don't know why their wives left them. We women don't like confrontation; we skirt around it, avoid it. But when we can't take any more of a situation, we leave. As cleanly as a surgeon snips out a diseased organ, we can cut a guy out of our life. And no regrets."

It was his banker friend, Neville Bruce, who said, "Open her bank statements – you'll see where she's been withdrawing money." And added, "Then move her things out of the house and divorce her. Don't *brood* about it. I liked Rosalind, but let's face it, you two have been going your separate ways for years now. You don't have a thing in common."

Ron Christianson returned to Sydney for the birth of his daughter's first child, and reported back to Geoff. He also made enquiries in Sydney, and the very fact that there was a private detective about, asking questions, fuelled the rumours. Christianson came to see Geoff at his home on a Saturday.

"In my opinion, she probably flew to Cairns then flew out again – maybe even on the same day – under an assumed name."

"Someone should have remembered her ... " Geoff began.

"I got up to Cairns five days after she flew in, wearing a sun hat and dark glasses, your housekeeper says. I'm still contacting staff and passengers, but so far no one's remembered her. A thousand women in sun hats and dark glasses walk around Cairns airport every day."

Geoff swivelled his chair away a little, unhappily. Christianson sensed his sudden depression. He said, blithely, "Look, I wouldn't give up hope yet if I were you. She'll be back, even if it's only to get the rest of her things. Maybe she'll come back to you – I see this sort of thing happen all the time. Three weeks in Alice Springs with her tennis coach or the bloke who cleans the pool, and then she's on the doorstep, all tears and pleas for forgiveness. I tell you, I see it happen all the time to women when they reach your wife's age. They need to know they're still attractive to young men."

Geoff turned in his chair, slowly, and gave the man the sort of look he would give a creature he'd found under a rock. *It was not like that. It was not.*

He opened her bank statements. The last transaction was a cheque made out to one of her favourite boutiques in Double Bay. The date was the twentieth, the day before she had flown to Cairns. After that, nothing.

Rosalind had vanished without trace.

He went back over every man Rosalind knew; *who was the man on the phone?* And he kept coming back to Mark Parrish, because he had been the last man to befriend Rosalind before her disappearance. And because – Geoff confronted the memory only unwillingly – because of the expression he had sometimes seen on the handsome young man's face when he looked at Rosalind. But Geoff shrugged the thought away; Rosalind would not do this to him. She would not. Not with any man.

"Who is it?"

"Doctor Linda Parrish. She sounded rather agitated, says it's important."

"Put her through." It was only while waiting for Julia to connect them that he remembered who Linda Parrish was – Mark Parrish's mother. Geoff's heart rose.

"Hello!" he almost barked down the phone.

"Mr Harcourt?" He had never actually met the woman, but had seen her, looking very cool, very beautiful, giving advice on various television programmes, being interviewed by journalists whenever they needed her professional comments on some newsworthy matter. Her speaking voice was extraordinary, very low for a woman, and musical.

"Yes . . . " Geoff began, but could get no further. The lovely voice was speaking coolly, rigidly. "I have received a visit, unannounced, at my consulting rooms from a man I believe to be in your employ. A Mr Ron Christianson. Is his claim correct?"

Oh, shit. "Yes, that's . . . "

"I want to tell you that I object very strongly to the man's assumption – which I presume stems from you – that there was anything . . . untoward . . . in my son's relationship with your wife."

"I know that," he hastened to interrupt, "of course I know that."

"I've read the rumours in the newspapers that your marriage has ended, and I'm very sorry. But I will not have slurs made against Mark – he has a brilliant career ahead of him. He's a fine young man and a devout Catholic, and . . . "

"I can't apologise enough for Christianson's clumsiness. I spoke to him on Saturday, and he asked for a list of Rosalind's friends. She has friends," and he placed a subtle emphasis on the word *friends*, "of both sexes, and I'm sure I didn't in any way give him reason to believe that I thought . . . "

"Mark has been in Thredbo for the past seven

weeks. He left a good three weeks before your wife disappeared."

"I see, of course. Doctor Parrish, I promise to speak to Christianson today. . ."

What had happened to the famed Christianson charm that Jack spoke of? Or was Christianson's suggestion of even the most tenuous link between Mark Parrish and Rosalind enough to ruffle the feathers of his protective mother? He seemed to remember Rosalind telling him that Mark was overly influenced by Linda Parrish. "I'd like to come and see you myself, if I may, to apologise in person."

"There's no need for that." Only slightly mollified, he could tell.

But he persisted. "There are things that I feel I should explain. Please – can you spare me half an hour or so?"

"It was the most astonishing thing," Linda recounted to Leo afterwards. "I ushered my last patient out, and saw this stocky, well-dressed man sitting on one of the chairs in the waiting room. And on his lap three dozen – *three dozen* – of the most perfect red roses. He sprang up like a boy, just like a little boy, and all my preconceived notions of him went out the window. We talked for two hours. There's an ingenuousness that still clings about him, and it's not a pretence. He faces everything squarely, like a child does before he learns to play games, to hide himself from the world . . . " Her voice faded a little. "Yes," she said reflectively, "I liked Geoffrey Harcourt."

But she had been quite firm with him, as she had been with Ron Christianson.

"Your wife is an attractive, charming woman, and she and my son had interests in common, but his feelings for her were those of admiration – and a kind of pity. She was a lonely woman. This is no criticism of you – my own late husband's work was extraordinarily demanding in energy and time – but it's harder for those wives without the benefit of a career. I've been fortunate in always having my work, and my son. Rosalind didn't have those kinds of responsibilities. Sometimes they can be a refuge – a lifeline, even."

He had nodded, agreeing with her. She had the feeling that in these weeks of being alone he had been seriously thinking about the life his wife had led. He had confronted many truths that he had hitherto been too busy, too preoccupied, to face.

"Even so," he had said, "the fact that Rosalind and Mark were friends – and she did spend a lot of time with him over the past six months or so – made me wonder if she may have said something to him. If she was unhappy in any way, she may have confided in Mark rather than in some female friend of her own circle."

Linda had given a small smile, "If she chose Mark for a confidant, then she chose well. He rarely confides in anyone, even me."

"Then may I have his telephone number in Thredbo? I'm sure he won't mind if I talk to him about this. Mark and I always got along very well, and he may be worried about Rosalind's safety, too."

"There is no telephone in the cabin." She had explained to Geoffrey Harcourt what she had already told Ron Christianson – that Mark was writing an article for the medical journal, that he did not want to be disturbed.

"But surely, given the circumstances ... " Geoff had interrupted. So Linda had told him then, sensing that his doggedness would not easily let the matter rest, "My son has been under a lot of strain. There's even some doubt as to whether he wishes to continue in oncology. He had three young patients who died – two of leukaemia, one of heart disease – while undergoing treatment. The prognosis for cancer in children is quite good, but these three deaths – unavoidable as they were – came in as many months. Mark and the team at the Children's Hospital did everything possible, but he took their deaths to heart. He's a caring boy, a sensitive boy.

"So, you can understand in the circumstances, why it would be best if he were not distressed any more than he is."

"But if Rosalind had ... "

"Mark phones me every four days or so. We've spoken about Rosalind's disappearance – if he had

214

any clue to her whereabouts I'm sure he would have said something to me. As you say, you and he had a mutual respect, and I'm sure he'd alleviate your worry if he felt it was in his power."

"When he next phones . . . "

"I'll mention that you called and pass on your message. I know he'll phone you if he has any news that may help you."

"Thank you." He ran his hand through his dark hair. "I know you've read the papers, heard the gossip, but I wanted to tell you that I don't believe what they're hinting at. I know my wife. I know she loves me. But even more than this – I know her *character*. She doesn't hide her emotions, and . . . and she's *forthright*. This . . . going off like this . . . it just isn't like Rosalind. It *isn't* Rosalind."

Linda looked at him with pity, thinking of her own marriage. "The sudden disappearance," she said, "the cutting of ties in so cruel a manner . . . it's like a death to the spirit. It's a murder of the spirit."

Geoff looked up at her, surprised by her words, her empathy.

"I don't know why I opened up and spoke to him," Linda told Leo, "perhaps his predicament touched my own memories. Perhaps it had been a long day and I was tired, my usual resistance may have been down. Or it may have been the roses, that extravagant and ridiculous peace offering.

"No man has brought me roses in thirty years," she murmured.

CHAPTER THIRTEEN

For Mark, it was as if the incident in the kitchen had never occurred, as if he could put it from him, that act of violent rebellion on Rosalind's part. Of course, he *had* to put it from him. It would not do to remind her of it; she already suffered from the knowledge that she had failed.

The programme continued without change. The tape played every four hours that Mark was absent – and he was absent for anything from five to twenty-four hours at a stretch. Their 'discussions' usually lasted about seven hours – but sometimes nine, sometimes only five. He would break off, coolly, and leave if she became hostile – and she was hostile after the kitchen incident, often flaring at him suddenly, without warning.

"How many lovers did you have before you married Geoff?" It was a question she did not want to answer. For two hours they were locked in impasse, Mark repeating the question, Rosalind staring in front of her, her arms folded, obdurate.

Finally, "There are prettier women than me . . ." she began, turning to look at him for the first time in all those hours, "there are more intelligent, younger women than me. You're good-looking enough to – "

Over her, "How many lovers before you married Geoff?"

"I just want to know why me, for God's sake? Can't you answer a simple fucking question?! I'm forty years old, you're twenty-seven."

She looked at him, hard. "Is it because I look like Linda? When you made love to me were you imagining – "

He leaned forward and roared at her, "How many before Geoff?!"

"No one!" she screamed. "Only Geoff! He was the first! Alright? *Alright*?!"

And she broke down and cried, her head on her arms, leaning on the table. He was seated sideways on the table, and her arm touched his leg. Even then, she moved away, a little jerk, telling in its abruptness. He took a handful of her hair and pulled her face up to look at him.

"Good," he said quietly. "Now if you'd said that two hours ago, you wouldn't feel so upset and exhausted, and it would have meant two hours less that you were in this place. Two hours of stubbornness, indulged in too often, adds up to days of imprisonment – all totally unnecessary. Think about that, won't you?"

Mark drove into Cairns to study old newspapers at the local library. He ordered back copies of the *Bulletin* and read as much as possible about Geoffrey Harcourt's past.

This section of her programming was easier than he had expected. Geoff had been so foolish in shutting her out of his business plans. And Mark knew her now, knew when she was unsure of her self. He found he enjoyed embroidering, embellishing, distorting; creating his own truth for Rosalind.

"Geoff only met Manzone a few times – this trip to the US will be the first time they've talked in detail . . ."

Mark probed, ". . . but what about the Lotus Island scam?"

"It wasn't a scam!" she was stung to reply. "It wasn't Geoff's fault – a lot of people were interested at first. Geoff heard about it through friends and – "

"Joe Castellan was instrumental in setting that up."

"Yes," unwillingly, when Mark paused. She had become wary now when he paused in the middle of a sentence. It was the laying of a snare, and she could not tell what kind or where, just that he was there, knowing, waiting.

"Geoff knew Joe Castellan very well – they were friends."

"No, not *friends*. Geoff used to say Joe was an operator, whatever that means. They didn't . . . do business in the same way."

"But they were going to, with Lotus Island."

"It was to be a syndicate . . ."

"Until things became too hot, and the publicity broke – Geoff knew that Joe Castellan had drug links with the US," he lied, smoothly.

"No!"

"And Castellan introduced Geoff to Harry Manzone."

"No! Yes! But . . ."

She stood from her chair, and Mark stood also. When she moved around the room he followed, a little behind her, but there when she turned, a little close, always too close for her to feel at ease.

These discussions about Geoff's work were very productive. She was unsure of her own character, her own strength in being able to defend herself against Mark. She was even more eager and determined to defend Geoff against Mark's accusations, but she did not have the knowledge of Geoff that she did of herself. It was hard to fight Mark, and he knew it, so they spent whole days talking about Geoff Harcourt.

"Rumours!" she hissed at him once, having talked herself clear across the studio and into one of the corners. Mark leaned against the wall beside her, and thought, for a tense moment, that she was about to rear back and tear at his face, but he remained calm. Nothing new was learnt if he did not sometimes goad her too hard.

"All you're doing is repeating rumours! Or worse – making things up out of your head!"

"Like the rumour of Geoff getting his first big break with the Carlington contract?"

She was two, three, moves ahead of him. She even moved a little closer to him, such was her rage. "How dare you!" Her voice low, her face white.

"Two union leaders murdered . . ."

He would have paused there, but she did not allow it, spoke over him, her voice hard with her anger. "There was in-fighting in the union – and you know it. You *know* it! That was how the strike was broken! Geoff had nothing to do – "

"Two union leaders murdered." The deep, heavy voice was expressionless.

"By someone within the union!" There was a kind of desperation in her voice. "There'd been some embezzlement of funds and . . ." She stopped, and her face closed. She gazed up at him, then said, "You know all this. I'm not going to talk about it anymore."

"Trying to block it out won't – "

"I don't have to block out lies!" She pushed past him, headed for her chair once more.

"You're blinding yourself to a lot, Rosalind – "

"Leave me alone!"

"Why are you so afraid to confront what Geoff – "

"Stop it!" She threw herself into the chair, turned sideways away from him, hands over her ears.

He pulled her hands down. "Everyone in the country knows what sort of man he is!"

"I'm not listening!"

"What do you know about him?"

"What do *you* know?!" She slapped his face, hard.

The blow shook him, made his head ring. For a moment he could not believe that it had happened. But there was Rosalind, pulled back in her chair, like a young peregrine eyas, newly perched and unmanned, and ready to bate and strike out at him again at his first move.

Mark straightened, using all his self-control to say nothing, to keep his hands from her. He walked out of the room, locking the door behind him on the voice that screamed at his back, "I won't beg you to come back! Lock the door! Turn off the lights! Go *fuck* yourself!"

Mark leaned against the second door, stood there in the quiet of the study and tried to come to grips with the fact that he had nearly, so nearly, hurt her. He walked around the room a little, went out onto the balcony, but the heat was too intense, the glare of the sun on the white sand burned into his eyes and made his head ache. *Rosalind* made his head ache.

He felt alone. He telephoned his mother and smiled to hear her delighted and familiar voice, "Mark, darling! It's wonderful to hear you."

He closed his eyes in his sense of relief, the sense that he was not alone, that someone *did* care.

"Mark?" questioningly from Linda, for he had paused for too long. "Is anything wrong?"

How he wished he could tell her, just blurt it all out, share his pain ... "No," he smiled sadly, "no, I'm fine, just very tired. I haven't been getting much sleep lately."

"Mark, dear, is this project worth it? It seems to be causing you a lot of strain, and you had enough of that in Sydney. You went away to try to relax."

He recorded the conversation in his diary that night – it had been almost hysterically funny; hysteria was so close.

"No, Mother, don't worry. It'll be worth it in the end ... No, there was no real reason to phone – I just needed to hear your voice. I get ... lonely, sometimes."

"Is this isolation good for you? Don't you think you should come home, dear?"

"Not for a while ... Yes, I promise I'll get out more. Uh-huh, I'm making friends – slowly."

"And how's the weather down there?"

Shit. Usually he had the newspaper ready. "Sorry?" he covered the mouthpiece and looked around for the newspaper on his desk. It was a Brisbane newspaper, but it carried reports of the snow levels at the alpine resorts ... Mark traced the description of Thredbo with his finger, "The

222

sky's clear, but we had another four inches of snow last night".

"And the cabin is warm? You're not suffering in that cold, are you?"

Mark smiled, drily, "Oh, I'm much too busy to feel the cold."

CHAPTER FOURTEEN

He left her, locked away in total blackness, for a day and a night, twenty-four hours without food or light, he did not even play the accursed tape. It was this, more than anything, that broke her of her defiance – the absolute silence, the lack of any human presence. When, finally, Mark returned, she could not hide her relief and joy. Even blinded as she was, her hand came out towards the door, and he took it briefly, pressed it reassuringly. Then, coolly, he told her to eat the meal he had brought – and afterwards the questioning began again.

For Rosalind now, there was only the reality of the studio. For Mark, there were two realities – his life outside the room, and his life, with his recalcitrant guest, within it. "Time has no meaning in there," Rosalind had said, and time began to have no meaning for Mark either, inside or outside their prison. He had to keep glancing at his watch, not merely to remind himself of the hours, but of the days also. Rosalind offered fewer challenges to him, since her attack upon him. She argued with him tearfully, but she stopped short of actual mutiny. But she was still stubborn – their conversation went round and about, and it was hard on both of them – but harder for him, Mark felt, for he could not afford to indulge in his emotions, could not act upon his impulses. He had to be impersonal, clinical and constantly alert; he could not afford to be otherwise.

"Say you love me."

"I love you."

"Do you mean it?"

"No."

"Why not?"

"Because I don't. I love my husband."

"Why did you come here?"

"I came as a friend. Only as a friend."

"You were attracted to me."

"Yes, but . . . I came here as a friend."

"You're lying."

"I'm not lying."

Five to eight hours of this usually reduced her to tears of exhaustion, and finally, before he left her, he could ask her once more, "Do you love me?"

"Yes."

"Say it."

"I love you, Mark."

"Do you mean it?"

"Yes."

"Say it again."

"I love you, Mark."

And he would hold her, uncomplaining, against him and kiss her gently, and she would allow this. He never presumed any further upon her, knew it was an acquiescence born of fatigue and helplessness, but he would embrace her and kiss her anyway, for she had to become accustomed to his touch, had to come to accept it as normal, even pleasurable. As the weeks passed she began to lean in to him when he embraced her, for she knew the session was over then and she could rest. Besides, all humans, all living creatures, need the touch of another. Mark's touch was necessary, although Rosalind did not know it in her conscious mind. His hands, his lips upon hers, were vital to her vision of herself as alive and functioning, and she accepted it, even coming as it did from him.

The hardest time, for both of them had she but known it, was when he made her speak of her son.

"I think . . . he would have grown up to look like Geoff. He had Geoff's blunt nose, Geoff's wide-set eyes, direct gaze. That sounds silly . . . " she murmured. She was sitting cross-legged on the bed, did not look up at him, was speaking almost to herself. "But they were Geoff's eyes. He was a special baby . . . a special little boy . . . " Two tears made a gentle splashing sound as they fell upon her hands, clasped before her.

Mark leaned against the wall and folded his arms across his chest, against the desire to hold her.

"Why didn't you have another child?" he asked, quietly, "Why didn't you go back to the IVF programme? If it worked once . . ."

She was shaking her head and there were more tears, but still she did not look up. "To lose Jamey – after four years of trying, unsuccessfully . . . We . . . we lost heart somehow. I never went back. Geoff never asked me to. We never discussed it again."

"Did you feel resentful towards Geoff?"

"Why should I resent Geoff? He'd be more likely to resent me." She sniffled. Mark walked to the bathroom and came back with a handful of tissues. Handing them to her, he asked calmly, "Why should Geoff resent you?"

She blew her nose. "It was my fault."

"Why?"

"It was my body, wasn't it? That . . . didn't work."

Mark watched her quietly for a moment, then, "*Did* he resent you?"

She looked up at him, but he felt she was not seeing him. "He . . . he never made it obvious."

It was enough. More than enough. Mark touched her hair, gently, and turned towards the door.

"Are you going?" She had risen from the bed.

"Yes."

"Leave the lights on. Please?"

Mark came back to her, kissed her lightly, noticed that her face came up to his, anticipating the kiss and receiving it.

"Do you love me?"

She did not answer immediately, but he read the struggle in her face.

"Are you still afraid of me?"

"No," she lied. But that did not matter, rather it was a positive sign.

"Do you trust me?" he asked, holding her lightly in his arms.

"Yes." And even for him it was hard to tell if she told the truth. Perhaps it was hard, also, for Rosalind.

"Say it," he suggested.

"I trust you."

"And . . . ?" It made it easier, to begin with a small request.

"I was . . ." An inner struggle, she lowered her head to avoid his gaze.

"Rosalind," patiently, "we agreed. I only want the words."

She lifted her head. "I was in love with you. I came here because I wanted to be with you. I liked it when you kissed me."

Three separate lessons – and no tension in her, no obvious resentment. "Good girl," he smiled.

"How long?" eagerly.

He walked towards the door, and she followed him. "Twenty minutes," he conceded.

"Can I have a book? A magazine? Please?"

He came to an abrupt halt. Her hand was on his arm, her face looking up into his with the smile of a child, and his heart almost stopped. "Yes, alright," he said, before he had realised that he had spoken.

It is the first positive physical contact she's initiated in the four weeks and three days she's been in the studio. The arguments are fewer, the tears less frequent. Every day I see some of my logic breaking through her wilfulness.

Slowly, it was happening, the disintegration of the woman. He was without pity. Slowly, she came to realise that he was her only lifeline – not simply to the outside world, but to her sense of herself, her sanity. Not knowing what to do, what to think or believe any longer, she turned more and more to Mark, who seemed so sure. It became difficult, almost impossible, to lie to him. Difficult, even, to tell him the truth when it was a truth he did not want to hear. Sometimes even he could not tell, but it did not anger him. She had no guile, by now. She had no defences at all.

What was unusual, what surprised even Mark, was her reluctance at the thought of returning to Sydney. It was not merely her growing wariness of Geoff; it seemed that there was truly very little of her old life that she missed.

"The theatre," he would suggest, "and the ballet season?"

"Yes," slowly, "but the crowds, the parties, the same people, all pretending friendship . . ." Her nose wrinkled. Mark gazed at her in amazement.

They had several discussions on the matter, and he was convinced it was not a pretence. Of course, she had come from the country, from an area close to the sea – was their beach, and the stripping away of the accumulated experience of years, bringing her back to what she really wanted, the kind of place where she was truly happy? Had he succeeded even beyond his expectations?

Her placidity, these days, was almost worrying. She seemed calm enough, as if she had begun to accept these grey walls, her few pieces of furniture. He wondered if she was becoming afraid of the outside world. When he gently offered to take her into the main part of the house, her expression froze.

"Why?"

It was difficult to hide his surprise at moments like this, difficult to know exactly how to handle these new fears of hers, unnatural, unexpected. Finally he realised that she had to be encouraged, like a frightened child.

For I've done it – and it was awesomely easy. This is a new Rosalind, a Rosalind in transition. Who she is, what kind of woman,

is dependent entirely on me. It fills me with
fear – if she only knew that she's being led by
a man as blind as she is herself.

It was much more difficult, this building of a new Rosalind, than destroying the old had been. Then, in the dreadful glare of the studio, any mistake, any ill-chosen cruelty, had only pushed her closer to the edge of her sanity, to that point where she gave up her autonomy, was no longer able or willing to form her own conclusions, to act upon them.

Now, she had almost to be coerced into leaving the studio, and sat as uncomfortably rigid on the living room couch as if she were a creature of the wild air, suddenly unhooded, finding herself in a strange place.

He watched her closely, but there seemed to be no reason to worry. She stayed close to him, even startled him on her third brief respite from the studio, by staying close behind him when he made his way to the kitchen to pour them drinks. Not threateningly, simply there, waiting for him. "Can I help?" she'd asked, and he had replaced the bottle of fruit juice and taken her in his arms.

In this, the physical contact between them, he was consistently disappointed. She never held him. He could touch her as he wished, but there was never any response, merely a gentle acquiescence. To know that she would go with him to his own bed any time he chose to lead her there was no victory when he realised that his own passion and tenderness would be met with ... gentleness, acquiescence.

That she had loved Geoff he was no longer in any doubt, but there is love and there is love. Her sexual relationship with her husband was one subject he had not covered in those "discussions" in the studio. He had told himself it was not important, that her love for Geoff had long since ceased to be a passionately physical union. At twenty-seven, inexperienced himself – except through textbooks – until Rosalind, he had never been close to a couple who had a vibrant, close marriage that had lasted through long years.

But now he began to consider. He had despised the young women – and the not so young women – who had looked at him with questing calculation, the small smiles, the lids half-lowered over eyes that slid from his hair to his groin, and back again to linger on his face, hopefully, until he turned away. Now, he felt pity for them, and a kind of gratitude that temptation had spared him for so long. The Church was right to declare fornication and adultery heinous sins, to lock sex safely away within marriage. Lust – that richly evocative word, these days heard only when flung across the pulpit – was truly the most dangerous emotion in the world. He would do without it. He wished to God that he *could* do without it.

He began to wonder if Geoff had some hold upon Rosalind's emotions that was at such a deep and basic, primitive, sexual level, that he, Mark, could not know about it. He did not want to ask her. He did not doubt that he could wring any information at all from her, these days, but did he want to hear? She had become so much his belonging, an extension of himself, that the thought of her lying with any other man, breast to breast, thigh to thigh, filled him with a sickening rage. Could she hold memories, something of Geoff's manner of loving, that he, Mark, lacked, that all his textbook technique could not compete with? Had she lain in his arms, even on that one occasion he had possessed her, and made comparisons?

His doubts about Rosalind, and about himself, began to control his thoughts. It was all he spoke about on the tapes for days. Yet still he avoided confronting her – as much afraid of what she would tell him, as that she would deny anything, everything, frightened of displeasing him.

He walked with her on the beach one afternoon. Her light summer dress blew about her knees – barefoot, her face free of cosmetics, she looked young and vulnerable beneath the brim of her straw sun hat.

She kept blinking, rubbing her eyes a little.

"You okay?" he asked.

"My vision's a bit blurry."

Of course, so many weeks now with no distances upon which to focus her gaze. He explained this to her, "Your eyes will adjust themselves in a while – we'll have to come for walks more often."

She looked about at the white sand, the encroaching forest, the steep hills that rose around them, towering over the house.

"A whole day outside . . . There are red tips on some of the gum trees. Has it been that long?" She looked up at him. "Tell me. How long has it been?"

It was the first sign of interest in matters outside herself for two weeks or more. It was, perhaps, a good sign. "Six weeks," he admitted.

Her voice was so soft that he barely heard it above the surge of the waves upon which her gaze was fixed. "Six weeks . . ."

It was the first time she had seen the world outside the beach house for a month and a half – he could almost hear her mind acknowledging the fact. Her face looked closed, her eyes grave.

As for Mark, he wondered at the wisdom of allowing this walk – perhaps it was too soon. They were at such a distance from the house and, though he was ready for any emergency, it was a long way to drag her should something go wrong.

He brought it on himself. Later he would be amazed at his stupidity, his lack of self-awareness, of forethought.

"What are you thinking?" he asked.

She looked at him suddenly, and he was aware

234

that she had forgotten him for a moment, but now was afraid of him again. "Nothing."

He took her shoulders, lightly, paternally, "Come along. Out with it."

He waited, and she knew him now, knew he could wait and wait.

"Hasn't ... someone missed me? You've never told me. Is Geoff so angry that he hasn't ... ?" She started a little when his grip tightened imperceptibly on her shoulders.

"Not just Geoff. I have aunts in Bega, and friends in Sydney ..."

"I thought you didn't care about your so-called 'friends' in Sydney?"

"I don't. It's just ... I've vanished, and no one seems to care."

"I care. Isn't that all that matters?"

"Yes. Yes, of course."

She was lying. *Lying.* He stood close to her, very close, and she looked into his face and *lied*.

His courage flared with the force of his jealousy. "It's Geoff you're thinking about, isn't it? Don't lie."

"I won't! I was only thinking ... when a marriage breaks up, it doesn't happen so ... suddenly. It's not like Geoff. That's all."

"He shouldn't matter."

"He doesn't. He doesn't, Mark."

"What do you think about when you think of Geoff?"

"I don't think about him – I was just wondering!"

Her neck was so small, so close to his enveloping hands – a few inches to the left, to the right, and all he had to do was close his grip . . .

She went to step away, up the beach a little, but he turned them both so her back was to the surf. A wave, cool, startling, rolled over their feet, hissing about them and tugging them insistently back into the sea.

He made his voice calm. "Geoff belongs in the past. You know that."

"Yes."

It was useless. It was as he had feared – she locked him out with her terrified lies. And he had only himself to blame. There was no trust between them. Geoff held that trust, but not Mark. Would Geoff go to such trouble to possess her, care for her, the way he, Mark, had done? In that instant he hated Geoff. Hated whatever it was that still held her to him.

"All that time you've been with me, you've been thinking of him. Haven't you?"

"No! No, I . . ."

"What is it? What is it that he's got that I haven't? Money? I've got two and a half million of my own, you know, thanks to my bastard of a father!"

"No, Mark! Please don't be angry . . . He was my husband, it's only natural that . . ."

She stopped, seeing her mistake written in the expression of his eyes. The waves were surging around her knees, and she realised that he was edging her towards the sea.

"Even when we made love . . . you were thinking of him – weren't you?"

"We didn't make love!" In her terror she forgot herself and told the truth, the words forming before she could stop herself, "I never wanted to . . ."

A wave broke. It surged about her waist in a rush of foam, and beneath it the sand slithered away from their feet. They were pulled by the tide, and Mark seemed to go with it, obeying the ebb as if he were part of it, and the water grew deeper around them.

"I thought . . . I wanted to give you more time . . ."

"Yes," she breathed, and such was her dread of him and the encroaching waves that she actually clung to him. The unaccustomed feeling of her fingers on his arm, his shoulder, the slight grip that grew stronger with the tug of the current, his own steps downwards into the sea –

"I was a fool, to believe that you were becoming fond of me . . ."

"I am, Mark, I am! Please, don't! Can't we go – " A wave struck her forcefully in the back, the explosion pushing her against him.

"But not fond enough. Not as fond as you are of Geoff. You liked making love to Geoff, didn't you?

You wanted to make love to Geoff. *Didn't you?*"

"Stop it! I want to go back!" Her eyes were on the shore as it retreated from them. He saw the white sloping stretch of beach reflected in her eyes – her eyes that were the same green as the water that rose and rolled about them.

"How often did you make love to Geoff? Once, twice a week? Every night?"

"Stop it!" The water covered her shoulders. Unable to see the incoming swells, she had to guess when the waves, high enough to close over her head, were about to heave towards her. "Please . . . !" She was crying.

He could not understand his own cruelty, indeed did not even consider it. But that morning he had been so pleased, walking with her. Everything had been going so well, and now it was spoilt, spoilt . . . Later, the strength of his own jealousy would surprise even himself.

"Do you belong to Geoff or to me, Rosalind?"

"To you. I belong to you, Mark."

He kissed her hard, in anger, frustration and, perhaps, the excitement of possessing total power over another human being, hitherto unknown in his life. Harsh and uncivilised, his actions were primal, intoxicating enough for him to forget his strategy, his discipline, his self-control.

Later, on the tape, he recalled dragging her back towards the shore, her hat long gone on the tide, her hair dark and clinging to her head and back.

She tripped on the saturated dress that hung, salt-water heavy, about her. That she was struggling to escape from him *still* infuriated him. He wanted to reach the beach, the point above the darker, hard-packed sand where the tide had turned – that blazing white sand, fine-grained and giving.

She escaped from him, but he recaptured her, pulled her down with him in the shallows. He remembered the struggle, her voice pleading with him. And that was all, until he awakened, with the sun-drying sand under his cheek. And it was strange, he could not understand it – he could not move.

Something tugged at him, and he stirred. Rosalind crouched beside him – only a few minutes must have passed. She was dripping sea water like a siren and would have pulled back from him, had he not reached out to take the arm on which she rested part of her weight.

He half sat up, took in the drag marks from the water to where his body lay, the small footprints that led away, down the strand, then doubled back, betraying her, to where she stood. He tried to look up at her, but his head swam and he wanted to vomit. His head *hurt*. He reached up, felt the raised lump just above his ear . . .

He brought up water, lots of it, and understood then. He pulled her down on the sand beside him. "Why?" he croaked. "Why did you come back?"

He knew that she had struck him, probably with one of the rocks that lay below the water's surface. But she had come back ... "Why? Why didn't you run?"

"I don't know." Their faces were close together; he could see the faint glints of salt and sand on her skin.

"Yes you do."

"No." And she had twisted, suddenly, out of his grasp, had risen to her feet, "No!"

He did not hear the noise until he saw her fling up her head, the damp hair flying back from her face as she looked back towards the house.

A car. A car was coming up the drive.

"Rosalind!" Not a command, rather a warning. He tried to rise, but the movement was ill-timed, too abrupt. He passed out again, for two seconds, perhaps three. When he came to, she was not so far from him, but she was flying on the white sand, back towards the house and the drive and the sound of that intruding engine.

The gun was gone.

Whenever Mark left the house he took the gun with him. Not knowing how far they would walk, or who or what trouble they might encounter, his suspicious mind now felt safe only when the small revolver lay close to hand. Now he stood, felt in his pocket, looked around him.

Rosalind had taken it.

But no, he could still see her, just about to disappear into the tangled overgrown grounds of the house. Her hands were empty. Mark lurched slightly, finding it difficult to keep his balance. He hadn't had concussion since his final year rugby match when St Jude's played Christian Brothers, and it was horrible. He looked around again – there was the gun, lying half-buried in the sand like some deadly sea creature, the waves swirling over it, tugging at it.

More salt water could not make any more difference to it. Rinsing the weapon in the next clear wash that swept in, he shook it free of as much water as he could, and wiped it on his already drying shirt. The tropical sun beat down on his head like a knife driving into his brain. He turned and stumbled up the beach, hearing from the direction of the drive a car engine pausing, changing gears. For a second it whirred, helplessly, as if the vehicle were bogged. They've run off the roadway, Mark thought, for the driveway itself had been built up, two or three feet in places, and the tropical rains never bogged it, such was the run-off.

The engine sounded far away, as though it hadn't quite reached the house. Or perhaps it had, but then the driver had discovered he had the wrong place, had reversed and turned, taking the car off the soft shoulder of the road. Get out of there, Mark willed the invisible spinning wheels, get out before Rosalind reaches you. Get off my land, get out of my world.

The engine was switched off.

His heart thudding, he broke into a trot, then slowed as he reached the darkness of the drive where the branches of the melaleucas almost met overhead and the lantana webbed them together, shutting out all but a green and sombre twilight.

The first voice he heard was Rosalind's, raised in panic, the words unintelligible – then she screamed, the sound, cut short, seemed to throb in the dank, steamy air.

The driveway made a shallow turn, as he rounded it he could see them through the trees, above the ferns, or rather he could see their forms, struggling, caught a glimpse of the pale blur of Rosalind's dress amid the greenery, turning with the men in some grotesque dance that was taking them deeper into the rainforest.

The battered utility was parked almost across the roadway, as if they had just pulled free of the soft earth and were about to turn. There were two of them, there below in the shadows.

"Let her go." He was surprised by the calmness of his voice, the steadiness with which he held the weapon, pointing it at the head of the taller of the two – the one who held one hand over Rosalind's mouth, the other at the torn shoulder of her dress. The second boy – for they were both no more than twenty years old – held Rosalind's arms, and was kicking at the back of her ankles, trying to dislodge her, to force her down to the ground.

There was a fifty–fifty chance that the revolver would not fire. Mark felt the explosion, the comforting thrust backwards into his palms, and saw the taller boy's head jerk back, the black hole at his temple, the dark gush that sprayed backwards, soiling the forest before the rest of him fell . . .

But it did not happen like that. Rosalind spoke his name, and was suddenly free of the trespassing hands, was moving towards him.

Slipping a little on the rising ground, she stumbled up the slope, through the young ferns and tripwire vines, to stand on the roadway. Behind her, vaguely, he was aware of the two pale faces turning towards each other, shifting nervously from one foot to the other.

All I could focus upon was Rosalind, coming towards me, sobbing drily, but coming towards me of her own volition, reaching me, leaning her body up against mine, her head turned, the better to fit against my shoulder.

He let them escape, as he might have done a spider from his kitchen, carefully, warily, without fondness, but with an innate respect for the creature's meagre contribution to Nature.

For me, I had enough. She was in my arms. While not holding me, I was, to her, the source of her safety, her freedom, perhaps her very life at that moment. I watched the dust of the utility rise into a green cloud between the trees. It could not have worked out better if I had paid the animals to appear. It is an enormous victory.

CHAPTER FIFTEEN

R osalind was puzzled by his silence. The truth was, he did not know how to handle this new development; he needed time to think. Rosalind had presumed that she was to be thrust back into the dark of the studio, had even started meekly towards the study and the double doors of her own volition. The fact that she did so made him call her back.

She was shaking. "We make a fine pair," he murmured into her salty hair as he held her. "You're in shock and I've a brain knocked half-loose from its moorings." She stiffened a little in his arms, the shaking became more pronounced. He looked into her face, but not her eyes – she wouldn't meet his eyes. You did hit me, you little bitch, he thought mildly. He was too tired to be angry though, too relieved to be safely home.

He considered sharing a shower with her, but did not trust himself. Instead he took her satin kimono from where her clothes now hung in the wardrobe next to his, and sent her into the *en suite* while he showered in the main bathroom. There was a risk that she would be gone when he returned, but somehow he doubted it. Like a wounded animal, she was seeking a safe, quiet haven. He was not surprised when he came out of the bathroom, having pulled on a pair of shorts, to find her curled in a corner of the living room couch, the kimono about her and her damp hair already curling on her shoulders.

He left her there while he made them both tea, handed her mug to her silently. Just as silently, he spread some newspaper on the dining room table and began to clean the little revolver.

Rosalind watched him from her seat on the couch. The few times he looked up at her she was studying his face, trying to read his feelings, his mood. He gave her nothing, for it was all she deserved, the little spitfire. With part of his aching brain he admired her for her courage, but he could have died from the blow, or drowned.

The tracks along the sand appeared in his mind's eye, as clearly as they had indented themselves in the white sand. *She had come back for him.*

But why strike out at him in the first place? Wasn't it natural that he would want her? Hadn't he been patient enough?

"If you're still angry," Rosalind said, "why haven't you locked me away in the studio?"

He looked at her steadily for a moment. No, he would not answer. Let her worry. He lowered his gaze to the revolver, and was half-finished oiling it when she next spoke.

"Where did you learn to take that apart?"

And when he did not speak, "Have you had it all the time? Or did you buy it especially?"

Without looking up he said, "It belonged to my father."

He sensed she was a little relieved at this. An inherited aptitude for violence was obviously preferable, in her eyes, to one that was self-motivated.

Still she was not satisfied. "You wouldn't . . . use it, would you? Today . . . I thought you might."

So she had seen it too. He looked up, met her gaze, "I'd do whatever I had to do, to protect what's mine." She seemed to shrink back a little, a minute movement, perhaps even only an inward shrinking. "But I'd take no joy in it," he continued. "I couldn't kill in cold blood," lowering his gaze to his work, "or walk off and leave a man to die."

He looked up at her again, pointedly, and then she did move back against the cushions, leaving her fear to occupy the space between them. Reliving that struggle in the water made him reconsider his madness, and what had driven him to it.

"I saw your footprints in the sand," he told her, calmly enough. "What made you come back? My lungs were filling with water by the second, another minute or two and I'd have drowned – you'd have been free."

"Stop it! I couldn't do it."

"Why not?"

"I don't know! I ran, and looked back – and you were floating face down, and . . . and I had to come back, that's all." There was bitterness in her voice, a trace of resentment.

"If I hadn't regained consciousness," he asked, thoughtfully, "would you have left me there, on the beach?"

She frowned. "No. The tide would have turned. You were too heavy for me to pull any higher up the sand." When he continued to regard her steadily, she added, "I would have waited . . . to see if you were alright."

He was giving her every chance. She knew him well enough by now, knew the programme well enough to know that what was needed was a lie. But she could not, even now, give him that. Unless it was the truth that she was avoiding. That, somehow, he could more readily believe. For she *had* come back to him, and in the dark of the driveway, with all her defences gone, she had come to him, flown to his wrist without a lure or call.

"Stop it!" she said, nervous beneath the warmth of his gaze, and knowing him too well. "That wasn't it! I didn't come back for you because I love you! I hate you for frightening me! That's why I . . ."

He gave her nothing. She said, finally, in a lower voice, almost accusingly, "You know I hit you."

"*Did* you hit me?"

248

Unsure, "Yes . . . I . . . there was a rock, and . . ."

"Oh, I've got the concussion to prove it – but who were you aiming at?"

It was unfair. Wherever they might go in the world, in all her dealings with him there would be a dark area of confusion, her own dark and silent studio that he had bequeathed her. "I . . . I don't understand."

He had her now. He could see the way. He rose to his feet as he spoke and moved around the settee until he was standing above her. "What were we talking about before you became angry, before you tried to run, before you looked around for a weapon?"

"I don't understand," she repeated. She did not like him standing there at her shoulder, just behind her, and she did not want to twist around and look up into his face for fear of what she might see there. "We were . . . we were talking about Geoff." Her voice faded at the mention of his name, then, "Geoff? You're saying that I was thinking of Geoff when I . . . !" She turned now to gaze up at him, disbelief on her face.

He perched on the low back of the settee and gazed at the exposed length of her throat, white, the blue veins faintly visible. And he had to touch her, to rest his hand there, feeling the suppleness of her neck, the softness of its flesh, the underlying muscle and sinew, and the pulse that beat like the heart of a bird within his grasp, faster for the touch of his fingers.

"All I've done is kept you close to me," he said. "I gave you the love and security you need – that you know you need, or you would never have come to this house with me."

She would like to fly – he could sense it – it was there in the frightened eyes that dared not leave his face. But his fingers remained where they were, stroking the pulse point at her throat.

"Geoff's the one who took your dancing from you, who filled your life with petty trivia and pretty young men, who kept you too busy to notice that the years were passing and your chances to bear a child were growing more and more remote . . ."

"No." She swallowed the word.

"Geoff's turned you into one of the most envied women in Australia – he's given you celebrity, riches, glamour – everything, in short, except himself. And in return? He took your pride, your independence, your sense of who you are . . ."

"He loved me!" She reached up and grabbed his wrist, but her grip was weak and her talons, these days, were blunted and could not tear – but they gripped and held there.

"How often did you and Geoff make love?"

"Stop it!"

"Tell me."

"Let go!"

"Tell me."

"I don't know!" The little claws pulled, harmlessly.

"You do."

She threw her body sideways, out of his grip, but by the time she stood he had moved behind her and had his arm around her, so that to step away from his grip was to step back against him.

"Please, Mark . . ."

"How often?"

"Once a week."

'You're lying."

"It varied! He was never home . . . he was tired . . . " Suddenly she pushed out of his grasp, whirled to face him, "Leave me this! What we had! Leave me that memory of him, if you have to take everything else!"

He stood very still, waited for her emotion to subside a little. Then, "You said you were fond of me." He waited.

"Yes."

"You said that you were in love with me."

Warily, "Yes, in the studio . . ." She stopped, confused. "Yes, I said that . . ."

"Did you mean it?"

There was only one answer, "Yes." And there was no way of knowing where the truth ended and the lies began, for he saw in her eyes that she no longer knew herself.

"You've never reached for me."

What could she say? *I lied – I don't love you at all?* Or, *I only make love to my husband?* Or, *I love you, but I don't want you to touch me?* There was no answer she could give that Mark's twisted logic could not refute. She no longer had the courage to argue with him, to persevere with those long denials that would only lead back to the dark of the studio and the taped message that had begun to engrave itself on her psyche. For the first time, in that veiled demand, she realised the relationship between them as it was at its most elemental – life, that world outside the studio, was to be lived on Mark's terms, ordered by Mark's truth. Now he wanted proof of her commitment to that life.

Those six long weeks had trained her for acquiescence. Repeating the words gave their meaning some reality, no matter how she fought against it. The human mind must make adjustments – either the lie becomes the truth, or the mind will shut down into idiocy. It was one of the main tenets of behavioural modification, and Rosalind, confronted by the terrible choice, withdrew into the safety her mind knew.

"Can I go back to the studio now? I'm awfully tired."

Mark had not expected this. He was still gazing at her when she turned and walked out of the room. He followed her.

I had no thoughts at that moment – I had not thought she could so easily escape me. I would have expected her to fly anywhere but back into the trap.

She paused at the first of the double doors, then turned towards the living room and the bedroom. "I need some clothes," she said, for she was still wearing the satin kimono.

"No," Mark said, making up his mind in that moment.

It goes to show, he reported afterwards, *that you shouldn't try to take short cuts with proven methods. She's submissive enough now – it was the only way to make her admit it. And she won't regard the studio as a place of safety from me, not any more.*

They say rape is an act of hatred, not of love, or even of lust, and I'd agree with that. I don't hate her at all, but if acts of hatred will do it, then I'll do whatever I have to do. There will be time enough for tenderness.

I made her say it. Held myself in check until she said it. I love you, I love you – over and over.

I don't feel any guilt. I should have realised that this was a necessary evil.

Later, she'll believe her own words. Then it will be up to me to make up to her for all this, and she can forget it. And so can I.

The programme resumed its old, earlier pattern. He left her, without tenderness, shut and locked the doors and turned the lights out. He played the tape every three hours, and, perhaps most cruelly of all, he left her alone for thirty-six hours.

He did not phone his mother. After making the tape that described his terrible treatment of Rosalind, he did not record anything more for nearly three days.

Rosalind, locked in her prison, tipped out the contents of the bathroom cabinet drawer. With the corner of it, she smashed the little mirror on the inside of the cabinet door. Searching in the blackness for a shard of the right length, she cut her hand.

The shard was only five inches long, but she got a face washer and wrapped the blunter end of the glass in that, to get a firm grip on it. Then she made her way, confidently now for she had become a creature of the dark, to the wall close to where the door opened. And there she waited for Mark.

When he came, unsuspecting, carrying a plate of food for her, his first reaction was one of concern.

"Rosalind . . . " he began, for she was huddled against the wall, one hand over her eyes, her head down as if in pain or despair. And "Rosalind," was all he was able to say before she rose like a wild thing and flew at him. One hand clawed at his shoulder, groped there, but even as Mark let the plate of food drop and reached over to grab her hand, the shard of glass came round in an arc, and flashing, struck him on the side of the neck, slicing downwards along the length of the muscle to hit the collar bone.

There was only the one blow, for he grasped her wrist and flung her backwards with a twist of such strength that her wrist was badly sprained. The face washer and the shard of mirror flew out of her hand to land halfway across the room.

Mark held her with one hand, felt the gash in his neck with the other, groping slipperily for a hold, for the blood was flowing swiftly, spreading out across his chest.

Rosalind tried to pull back from him – he let go of her wrist, only to take her by the back of the neck and pull her forward. She was too small to resist, and he almost lifted her in his grasp, pressing her face against the bloody wound, almost suffocating her and choking her screams.

"What's it like, Rosalind? Feel it!" He was mad himself with pain and rage. He took her hand then and pressed it to the wound, careless of anything, everything, meaning every terrible thing that he said. She tried to pull back from him, but her hands, her face, were covered in his blood. "Feel it! Touch it! Smell it!" Mark held her body against his and shouted over her cries, "Is it your blood or mine, Rosalind? *Is it yours or mine?*"

Hysterical, mindless, she could not speak. He gripped her face between his bloodied hands and pulled her upwards to face him. "It could be either, couldn't it? *Couldn't it?* And it will be. Yours and mine – flowing like one. If I die, you die. So it's our blood, Rosalind."

He took her shoulders and shook her, hard. "*Whose is it?*"

"No!"

"*Whose is it?*"

"Ours! It's our blood! Ours!" Her voice became a wail, the last wail of a lost creature.

Mark pulled out his handkerchief and pressed it to the wound. Without him to hold her up, Rosalind collapsed slowly to the floor, at the end of her emotional and physical strength. Her whimpering stopped, and Mark, bending to her, discovered that she had fainted.

In the silence, the horror of what had just happened, what *could* have happened, finally penetrated his mind. He leaned back against the wall and gazed down at Rosalind.

Somehow – perhaps I know her better than I ever thought I would – I sensed that the struggle was over. I no longer felt wary of her, nor was I disturbed that she would shrink from me again.

I was right.

It was a flesh wound only. I held the handkerchief to the ragged cut – it looks like a back-to-front seven – and washed the blood from both of us in the shower, holding her close to me. Later, she sat quietly on the bathroom stool and looked slightly green – as she damn well deserves to – while I sewed myself up with Dermalon.

I would have liked to make love to her but couldn't risk the wound opening again. But we slept together and I held her close. She didn't speak, but she clung to me and cried herself to sleep. I didn't question her. She's been through enough.

CHAPTER SIXTEEN

R on Christianson loved his new job. He had
been lonely ever since his wife had died, two
years earlier, and work gave him little consolation
now that most of the investigative work was going
to younger men.

Then his old friend Jack Risley had thrown the
Harcourt job his way. It was an old man's dream –
a third more than his usual fee and all expenses
paid. And for what? For a three-week working
holiday staying at a top motel in Cairns. He had
begun to think that maybe he should hope that he
did *not* find the woman – this job could string out
for six months.

But his professionalism would not allow that. He
took pride in his job, and being an ex-cop he had
the honour of the force to uphold. It might sound
funny, but that was the way it was.

Ron had always seen himself as a kind of hunting
dog, not one of those flashy long-legged ones, but a
harrier, a beagle, made for the long-distance chase.

No one had recognised Rosalind Harcourt at Cairns airport, but one passenger on her flight hesitated over her answer. He shouldn't base his decision on a hesitation, but his instincts were often good.

Miss (she was very definite about that, no *Ms* for her) Ann Scarrett. A librarian at one of Brisbane's exclusive girls' schools, she had flown in to Cairns on the same flight as Rosalind Harcourt. Until that interview back in Brisbane, he'd begun to think that questioning Rosalind's fellow passengers was useless – Rosalind, in her dark glasses and broad-brimmed hat, had not been in the least memorable.

But, knowing that he was looking for a man as well – the man who had called to postpone Rosalind's arrival at Silver Palms – Ron had come armed with as many photographs as he could find of Rosalind's male friends. He had old mates in the Sydney newspaper offices who had helped him with this – the escorts all tended to be up-and-coming men about town who actively courted the social paparazzi. But the exception to this lot was the young cancer specialist, Mark Parrish. The only photograph of him was one taken with Rosalind Harcourt herself. And it was this photograph that Miss Scarrett lingered over.

He didn't like to try to lead his contacts, but the pause had gone on for too long. "You recognise him?" She had already denied recognising the head-and-shoulders shot of Rosalind Harcourt.

"No . . ." she said, slowly.

"Are you sure?"

She did not answer him immediately. Then, "This is a terrible business, isn't it? I take it the young woman has run off from her wealthy husband."

He decided against lying – the suppositions were filling newspapers all over Australia. "Yes," he said.

"And these were all young men of her acquaintance?"

"Yes."

"And she fell in love with one of them – despite the difference in their ages – and the two of them have escaped somewhere, in order to be together."

She seemed to know more about the situation than he did – or perhaps, like most people who spent too much time with books, she had an over-active imagination. "Perhaps," he said.

All this time she had been gazing at the photograph of the couple. They did look attractive, Ron had to admit, looking at the picture, upside down, since it lay in Miss Scarrett's hand. They looked like something out of Hollywood: golden people who had everything.

Miss Scarrett handed the photograph back to him. "I don't recognise them."

"But, you seemed to hesitate when you first saw the young bloke . . ."

She met his gaze. "He's an exceptionally handsome young man," she said.

"Yes, but . . . I thought you may have recognised him."

"He bears a passing resemblance to the father of young Amy Barnes in Grade Four," she smiled. "I'm sorry, I can't help you, Mr Christianson."

Her refusal continued to niggle at Ron, he was convinced that Miss Scarrett may have seen Mark Parrish at the airport. Parrish had been Rosalind's most recent and popular escort until he left for the snow country. And that was a funny business in itself – no phone, no definite address, and a mother with the protective instincts of a tigress.

Ron had told Harcourt that Rosalind may have flown into Cairns then out again on a different flight, under an assumed name, but the more he thought about it – and he thought a great deal about it after talking to Miss Scarrett – the more he believed that Rosalind had remained in Northern Queensland.

If she had wanted to postpone discovery of her elopement for a few days, she had only to cancel her ticket to Cairns – indeed, she need never have bought one – driven to the airport at the time of her 'Cairns' flight and taken a plane going to any city in Australia, using another name. Her lover could have been waiting in Melbourne, Perth, Hobart – any number of places. She could have phoned the resort, and Geoff Harcourt, from any one of these destinations.

But the more he thought about it, about Miss Ann Scarrett's reaction, the more he felt that

Rosalind Harcourt was in Cairns, or its environs. His next task would be to drive north, and when civilisation ran out and only the rainforest wilderness remained, he would drive south. He'd take his photographs to every supermarket and every real estate agent on the Queensland coast. The runaways had to have food and shelter – someone, sooner or later, would recognise them.

He had another hunch – again it came from Miss Scarrett. There were too many photographs of the men. Some people had asked exactly what Ron was looking for – a battalion? So, in future, he planned to use only two photographs – the head-and-shoulders studio portrait of Rosalind Harcourt, and the photograph of her at the Opera House, on the arm of Doctor Mark Parrish.

It really was a first-class job. The Queensland coast was dotted with resorts, and he stayed at establishments on the beaches, because he wanted every chance of catching sight of Rosalind Harcourt, and because – well, why not? There were quiet bars, swimming pools, and lovely young things to look at during his long working days – ten to twelve hours a day, seven days a week.

Ron began to feel sorry for the Harcourt woman. Geoff Harcourt was a hard bloke, never had any time for her – how could she be blamed for wanting to live a little before settling down into middle age? He and Louise should have run off to Cairns years ago. Instead they'd been sensible and had stayed in Lane Cove, where Louise had died. He'd had no idea that Queensland was so beautiful; he wished he could have shown it all to Louise.

When he walked into the little real estate agency in Daintree Bay, south of Cairns, and the tanned extroverted owner recognised Mark Parrish at once, Ron's first reaction was one of disbelief.

"No, no – I'm sure it was him – about six foot three, same height as me. That was unusual in itself, and his speaking voice – educated, almost English. And he was so fussy about the place he was looking for. Parrish – yes, that was his name. I remember because it was on television that night."

"What? On the news?"

"No, that old movie, *Parrish*. Made in the sixties – the actor in it was a bit like this feller." He tapped Mark's photograph. "I said to my girlfriend, 'I had a bloke in the office today that looked like him,' and she said that if I had Troy Donahue looking for real estate in Daintree Bay then I'd better find him something. But he – this bloke – didn't leave a number. Said he was passing through, and he might call back – but he never did."

Ron went back to his motel and sat, musing, in one of the quiet bars. So Miss Ann Scarrett *had* lied, just as he'd thought. And Rosalind *had* stayed close to Cairns – she'd flown straight into the arms of the waiting Mark Parrish. His bloody instincts – how about that?

He was having some difficulty rationalising his feelings. He was quite ready to go home – he'd like to see his new granddaughter again – and he could probably wrap up this case in a week, or less. But he'd begun to feel, in a way, part of the magic that the runaways must be feeling. He could understand them – it wasn't as if these were two maladjusted, self-indulgent idiots with more money than sense. Everyone he had spoken to in Sydney had shown great respect for them. The Harcourt woman worked hard raising money for charities, and Parrish was a devoted and single-minded doctor.

But you can't hide forever, he told them, silently, over his beer. He drained his glass, and went to his room to phone Geoffrey Harcourt.

CHAPTER SEVENTEEN

L inda Parrish rarely entertained, but when she did the evening was always a great success. She had none of that sense of mischief that some hostesses indulge in, mismatching guests at the dinner table in order to delight in the sparks of dissension as conflicting ideals grated against one another. She always chose her guests well and, on that evening, all was harmonious on Castle Crag Road; even the old house looked well by candlelight, and became a warmer place for the soft talk and laughter.

It was at that dinner party that Father Leo Calder first met Geoffrey Harcourt, only a few weeks after he had arrived at her consulting rooms, his arms full of roses.

Everything she had said of him, Leo found to be true. Oh, he could sense the toughness, but he did not believe Geoff Harcourt to be an unfeeling man. Most people presume that millionaires become millionaires mostly through their callousness and their unscrupulousness, but it need not be so. Leo surmised that Geoffrey Harcourt had a nose for money and for market trends, a gambler's impetuosity combined with the prudence of Scottish forebears and, perhaps most importantly, an enthusiasm for his work and his projects that swept others along with him. He had personal charm, yet never seemed to be aware of the weapon he possessed. One would expect him to manipulate people, but he did not. It was at this point that one realised that this man had an inner integrity – and the realisation always came as something of a shock to those assessing him.

The other guests at the dinner party came from a cross-section of wealthy Sydney people – a media personality and his pretty wife, the artistic director of the Australian Opera, a visiting Wagnerian soprano from the United States, two or three urbane medical men and their pleasant wives, a top journalist with an enviable gift for repartee, a woman writer and two ebullient society matrons. It was a wonderful evening, but all through the dinner, Leo watched Linda and wondered what her motivations were in giving the dinner at all.

The conversation was very amusing, very witty; everyone, it seemed, had stories to tell. Gradually it dawned on Leo that Linda, Geoff Harcourt, the American soprano and himself were all listening, rather than speaking. All the stories had, as the central character, someone who was *not in the room*.

Leo almost broached the subject with Linda on the Saturday following the dinner, when he called in to visit. "You brought together some of the most voluble and popular gossips in Sydney to witness the fact that you had Geoffrey Harcourt to dinner," he had planned to say, looking forward to seeing the surprised look on her face. Leo was not normally perspicacious, and this piece of deduction on his part had rather brightened his otherwise dull week.

But, when it came to it, he could not bring himself to speak. He had only just arrived, and was sitting with Linda in the broad conservatory, filled with plants, that opened off the rear garden, when Maria, Linda's housekeeper, announced Geoffrey Harcourt. He looked embarrassed, a little agitated, and it was obvious that he would like to speak to Linda alone. "I'll just go out for a stroll in the garden," Leo said, and made his exit, like the clergyman in an English drawing-room comedy, through the French doors.

They spoke for perhaps half an hour, which was quite long enough to strain the patience of any polite guest, not to mention one as curious as Leo. It seemed that Linda *could not drop* the subject of Rosalind Harcourt, and now, after last Saturday, was actively courting the friendship of her husband.

However, the tentative friendship ended in that half hour. Leo, tired of meandering about the manicured lawns and communing with the fat carp in the pool, made his way back to the house to find it empty. He eventually found Linda standing on the front step, where she had obviously just farewelled Geoffrey Harcourt.

She turned to him, unseeingly, when he spoke her name. "How dare he?" she asked, "*How dare he?*"

Leo was bewildered by her distress. Leading her back into the house, he managed to extract from her the purpose of Geoff Harcourt's visit: "He believes Rosalind is in hiding in Queensland with *my son.*"

Geoff had brought a manila envelope with him. He drew from it the photograph of Mark and Rosalind, taken the night of the *Madame Butterfly* performance. "The real estate agent recognised him from this – he was very certain it was Mark. He was looking for a beach property – to buy – around the Daintree Bay area."

Linda's face was closed, its expression unreadable. She had handed the photograph back to Geoff. "That man is mistaken. Mark is in Thredbo. I've received mail from him."

Geoff had studied her for a moment, then, his voice cool, he said, "I don't think you're telling the truth. But it doesn't matter. Tell him, when he phones – or when you phone him – to bring her back. I'm a reasonable man and I only want Rosalind to be happy. We can work things out. But I want to see Rosalind. Tell him . . . Don't make me come looking for her."

They had both stood at the same time, and Linda had walked him to the door. She had wanted to say something, to convince him that this was a terrible mistake, but she could sense his purpose and it chilled her. He had made up his mind and there could be no more words between them.

Leo felt helpless on hearing her story – he had no idea how he could help her. "So he doesn't have a definite address in Cairns?"

"What difference would that make?"

"I . . . I don't know. I thought, perhaps, if I could get away, I could go up there and . . ."

"*Mark is not in Cairns.*"

Leo stopped speaking as Linda's words cut across his with an icy finality. He hesitated, needing to discuss the matter further, but knowing at the same time that he was pushing her towards a truth she did not wish to confront.

After a moment, he said, "Linda, what proof do you have that Mark is in Thredbo – other than his own word?"

She turned to look at him. Still beautiful, always beautiful, but the face seemed thinner, more strained, and the eyes were hard. "Only that. His word. And that is good enough for me, Leo. It should be good enough for you, also, if you're his friend – and mine."

Leo didn't realise that he'd stopped breathing until he swallowed, and nearly choked. When he had recovered he looked over at Linda, only to find that her expression had not softened or changed in any way.

"He may be a confused young man – he may need our help . . ." Leo ventured.

"He'll get it . . . when he asks us for it. Until then, we owe it to him to have faith in him."

"But, Linda . . ."

"Has he ever lied to you?"

Leo answered, truthfully, "No. Never."

Only then did her voice soften. "No. And Mark has never lied to me, either. Until he tells me that he's in Cairns, I'll continue to believe that he's in Thredbo. I owe it to him."

She was truly amazing. "You mean, you're not even going to *ask* when he calls you again? You could at least mention the rumours . . ."

"And have him think that I'm worried by them? That I'm prying into his affairs?"

"You have a right – "

"He's a grown man. He has his own life, his own rights – including the right to make mistakes, even ghastly mistakes."

"But to run off with a married woman – you *should* say something. It's your duty – he's your son . . . "

"Yes. He's my son.

"I don't want to discuss it anymore, Leo. Come, let's go into the garden, and then we'll have tea."

Leo trailed after her obediently, not daring to broach the subject again. He felt cut to the quick. She could be cruel, sometimes, she did not mean to be, but . . .

It was the way she said the words, with a faint emphasis, "He's *my* son" – only a little thing. But shutting him out. Shutting him off from her, and from Mark. Leo didn't think he deserved that. It spoilt the day for him.

CHAPTER EIGHTEEN

I have a theory, too, that women respond better to behavioural modification programming than men. They're naturally more submissive, more adaptable. Look at the bizarre loyalty of the Manson women, and the length of time it took for Patricia Hearst to overcome her domination by the SLA.

Mark was debating aloud into the small recorder the matter which was uppermost in his mind these days. To what extent was Rosalind truly attached to him? How far could he trust her new-found dependency upon him, her seeming affection for him? That it was not feigned, he was in no doubt, but she was in an extremely fragile state, and he worried about the effect of sudden visitors to the beach house, or how she would react when he introduced her again – as he knew he must – into the world outside.

272

She was subdued and tractable, and, as she had done before that terrible day on the beach when everything had almost been lost, she followed him everywhere, as if afraid of the world that existed beyond the sight of him. She still would not reach for him of her own volition, but this, he considered, might be as much due to a hesitation to intrude upon him as to an insensibility of the affinity between them.

The permanency of Rosalind's conversion would depend, he knew, upon that spark of attraction for him that had made her his friend, that had forgiven his first clumsy declaration to her, that had brought her here to his house and into his arms for that one passionate embrace. Beneath her strength of morality, her affection for Geoff, the long years of habitual matrimony and the fear of society's disapproval of the liaison between a forty year old woman and a twenty-seven year old man, there had been a spark, a flame of true feeling for Mark. And if that was strong enough, then Rosalind was now his. He had gambled everything on this – that if they had met and both been single and the same age – both twenty-seven or both forty – and had not had the glare of celebrity focused upon them, they would have formed a union naturally, permanently, and no one would have been harmed in the process.

If someone should ever ask me why I have done this thing I'll tell them without any

shame whatsoever that there is nothing sacred
about society's conditioning. It was this
synthetic barrier that I swept away. The reality
is one man, one woman, and if there is to be
a struggle, it is between these two – the world
has no place in the argument.

The weeks passed and, gradually, Rosalind was
allowed more and more freedom. He played testing
games at first – left the room when she sat close to
the phone, encouraged her to go for walks along
the beach, yet never allowed her to go out of sight.
But it was becoming increasingly clear to Mark that
Rosalind could not escape – or did not wish to.

"Phone Geoff," he suggested, once. "He'll be
back in Sydney now. Ring him at his office."

She shrank back. He had to place the receiver in
her hand, and then she almost wept. "No . . ."

"Why not?" gently.

"He doesn't want to hear from me. He doesn't
love me, he doesn't care. I don't want him to know
where I am."

How had this happened? Mark gazed at her in
genuine surprise. "You never want to see him again?"

"No! I don't want him coming here. He's angry, I
don't want him to hurt us."

"How could Geoff hurt us? Physically?"

"No. Yes. Maybe. I don't know. He wouldn't have
to do it himself, would be? If he hated me for what I
did, if he felt I had to be punished . . ."

She began to tremble, and he had to comfort her. She clung to him, and when he lowered his face to hers, his mouth to her mouth, she was giving, pliant, as if grateful for his arms about her, as if he were her protection from this world in which they were fugitives.

It became clear that Rosalind believed that she was to blame for all that had happened and that, being guilty, she somehow deserved to be punished. The horrendous logic of those sessions in the studio, the threat of an imminent return to them, was not, now, the major cause of her fear. They lay behind her now. It was Geoffrey Harcourt who had become the cause of her trepidation. Mark recorded her words and they were always in the same vein: "Geoff hates me for what I've done ... Geoff will want to make me pay for hurting him ... "

Mark himself, of course, had put this idea into her head. Part of the training in the studio had been to confront her with her sins – all those smaller and greater crimes since childhood – so she would feel that she somehow deserved to be treated as harshly as she was, even that she did not deserve to know the reasons behind her torture, nor the fate that assuredly awaited her.

At the same time, Mark had been hinting at Geoff Harcourt's darker side – even his business dealings were made to sound suspect. He had no proof at all, but innuendo was enough. Rosalind had often felt shut out of Geoff's life, and she had no rebuttal now, when Mark seemed so sure.

Mark did not need to connect the two arguments – Rosalind's confused brain did this by itself. She had been wicked and deserved to be punished; her husband, who had been the one most wronged, would obviously wish to exact revenge.

And this terror, coming as it did from one who should know Geoffrey Harcourt better than any other, began over the weeks and months to slowly infect Mark also.

For Mark had his own guilt, deeply repressed and excused as it was by his logic and bravado. One cannot overturn a lifetime of religious and moral ideals without some sign of destruction – Mark's conscience might lie buried in the rubble of his old life, but still it existed.

So Mark, too, became afraid of Geoffrey Harcourt. He did not know the man, had no intimate knowledge of the man's character, but he knew that stealing a man's wife was bound to bring out the dark and primitive urges in even the mildest of men. Stealing the wife of a man such as Geoffrey Harcourt could bring God only knew what retribution. And so, for Mark, in the absence of knowledge, fear ruled.

Rosalind seemed to know. "If he finds us, he'll kill me."

"Us."

"No. I'm the one who betrayed him."

"*Us.* If you die, I die. As one. What are we?" his arms around her.

"One."

And she would hold him to her, returning his embrace.

The weeks led into months and summer approached. Storms crackled and crashed overhead and the palms bent over the house, their demonic clatter of leaves sounding like gossip from hell. The weather outside their air-conditioned bubble was heavy, pregnant with the sultry heat and rain that would not come. The trust deepened between them, and she would respond to him in the dank nights, while outraged nature howled outside. Mark was happy, happier than he had ever been in his life. He did not ask himself whether Rosalind was responding to him for his own sake; he presumed this. He did not, or could not, face the possibility that Rosalind – denied all safety except for the strong young arms he offered – lost herself within them, for beyond there was only the night, and chaos.

Linda, when Mark phoned her, made no mention of anything unusual developing. She was a good actress; Mark sensed nothing from her, and seemed unconcerned when she mentioned Geoff Harcourt. But, of course, Linda did not tell the entire truth; she kept postponing it.

"Are you going to wait until that private detective is knocking on Mark's door?" Leo asked her. And she replied, stubbornly, "I'm waiting to hear the truth from him."

But, as the weeks went by, and there were so few calls from her son, she had to face the fact of Mark's duplicity. She phoned the doctor who had taken over Mark's practice and was told that the arrangement was to have been for one month, then two, but now, it seemed to be for an indefinite period, even though Mark had told Linda he would be home in another six weeks.

And there was something else. Geoff Harcourt, just before leaving the house that last time, had said to Linda "If you want to know where your son is, open his bank statements. If he's been using his account from Threbdo, then tell me, and I'll offer you both an apology."

Linda, of course, had refused to do any such thing. Mark's mail was sacrosanct, it remained in a small basket on the desk in his bedroom.

Leo had not known of Geoff Harcourt's suggestion until one of his Saturday visits, when, during tea under the shade of the old elm in the garden, Linda handed him a bank statement. Gazing at it, Leo realised what she had done, and looked at her admiringly – the idea would never have occurred to him.

"It was Geoffrey's idea," she said, grimly. "He began opening Rosalind's statements as soon as he arrived back in the country. She hasn't made a single transaction through her bank accounts or credit cards in months."

"But, Mark has . . ." Leo stared at the pages and pages of figures, "I had no idea that Mark was so wealthy."

"Really, Leo," impatiently, "you're not thinking of the Missions *now*."

He was stung. "Of course not!" And perhaps to irritate her, "But I will."

Linda chose to ignore him, looked out over the garden with a sigh and a scowl. Leo returned to his perusal of the statements – hundreds of thousands of dollars to a real estate agency, thousands more to a large furniture company, to builders, electricians – the list went on. His heart sank. Mark had created a new life, there in the north of Australia. Everything pointed to a desire for permanence. A whole future, built on lies told to those who were closest to him, who loved him.

Leo made up his mind, then. He turned back to the first page, and was searching for the name of the real estate agency, when the statements were jerked out of his hand. "You're not to make any contact with him," Linda said, severely. "I can tell by that zealous look on your face when you're stirring yourself to action, and I don't want you to do anything."

"Then *you* – "

"I will. I promise you. It's gone on long enough."

Leo's housekeeper handed him the message as he came out the door of the church, four days later. Parishioners were beginning to file from the doors after him, smiling, moving towards him for their usual after-Mass chats, but he had to hurry away. "An emergency..." he mumbled, leaving them with concerned, understanding faces, asking each other who could be ill, who could need him.

But none of them knew Linda Parrish. Leo's little smog-stained church lay in a suburb of Sydney's inner west. It had undergone something of a resurgence in popularity over the previous two years or so, and there were many Volvos and BMWs parked against the narrow curbs where once crowds of poorly-dressed children had played. The area was a good twenty minutes from the city if the traffic was bad, and it was, that evening, when Leo had to reach St Vincent's Hospital quickly.

He coped with that night only because it did not seem possible that it was happening. In God's wisdom, Leo thought, He does not give us warning of cataclysms that will shake our lives, and this Sunday had been a pleasant day: an excellent lunch, a rather competent homily knocked up the night before and polished during an early morning walk about his presbytery garden.

And during seven o'clock Mass, perhaps just as he lifted his arm for that first blessing, Linda's heart had betrayed her. All the way through the traffic Leo prayed: for God to leave her with them; for the grace to be able to let her go, if that was His will; and through it all, at the back of his mind, *Mark ... Mark ...* a litany of reproach.

Leo had watched Linda grow thinner, more tense, in the weeks since Geoffrey Harcourt's visit. He had become worried about her, had taken to phoning her three or four times a week, but there had rarely been news of Mark. Even his visits to the house were no longer the comfortable, relaxed communions he had once shared with Linda. They both missed Mark's presence. Even the house missed him. Always oppressive, these days it seemed to be waiting, as if holding its breath for the sound of that familiar footstep on the flagged path, on the broad steps.

Linda told Leo about the rumours with a tight smile. She denied being upset by them, but he later felt that he should have known, should have seen that she was feeling them dreadfully. He doubted that Geoffrey Harcourt himself was responsible for them, but certainly other people – besides Ron Christianson – were deducing that Rosalind Harcourt and Doctor Mark Parrish were together. Few people dared to mention this story to Linda's face, but there were enough pseudo-friends and envious fellow members of her profession to make it clear to her that the rumours were circulating, and it must have been torture for her.

Leo usually called in to visit her on Saturdays, but the day before he had had to officiate at three weddings, not a usual occurrence. So he had phoned her instead. She had been in bed with a virus, but said she was fine, and that Mark had not called. She had seemed drowsy, but Leo put that down to the medication. He had said Mass for her that day, and today, on Sunday, also. It wasn't until Leo saw her face, and the tubes, the wires, the terrifying medical paraphernalia, that he truly believed what had happened. So little time, so little time, his mind kept repeating as he said the prayers for the sick and anointed her. She looked so tiny, there against the pillows. He had never before been able to gaze and gaze upon her. Now he could, and he felt his heart would break.

The doctor came. "I must leave for an hour or so," Leo told her. "I need to go to her house and find an address, someone who may know where her son is."

The young woman doctor seemed very certain: "Father, she will not be with us long. You seem to be her only friend – can't someone else find her son? I'd like you to stay with her."

At that moment, Linda woke. It was difficult for her to speak for a narrow tube was leading down into her lungs. But she *would* speak.

"You are . . . not . . . to contact Mark," were her first words. Leo stared at her, dismayed. "No." She spoke as if she already knew Leo's next words before he had formed them, and perhaps she did.

"Linda, we *must* contact Mark. Have you spoken

to him? Do you have his telephone number?"

"He didn't ... tell me. We ... quarrelled."
Suddenly her eyes filled with tears – they rolled
down the sides of her face into the hair at her
temples. Leo took out his handkerchief and dabbed
at them, ineffectually. This seemed to make her cry
the more. "Darling Leo," she said.

"Linda, Mark should be here."

"I won't ... have him here. I don't want him to
see me ... like this. I'd rather ... he remembers me
the way I was."

Leo stared at her, "You're thinking of your pride
at a time like this?"

In her smile there was a trace of the Linda he
knew. "My ... vanity," she corrected.

"Please, if you'll only let me – I can get the police
to make an announcement on local radio. He must
be close enough to Cairns to – "

"No."

"But, think of how he'll feel. How would *you*
feel, knowing that he was hurt, in hospital?"

"He ... isn't. But if he's hurt ... it's not me that
he needs. Not ... any longer. Do ... as I say, Leo.
If my wishes matter to you ... do as I say. Leave
the boy alone."

Leo wished he was more articulate – there had
to be words to make her change her mind.

"He may never forgive you," he said, bluntly.
"Linda, my dear, you may die – and he'll never
forgive you, or himself."

"He has a new life. I don't want him . . . standing there . . . as you are . . . feeling helpless." Her hand fluttered on the coverlet and Leo took it in his and held it.

She closed her eyes, and her breathing seemed to slow. Then she turned her head and fixed her gaze upon him. At a loss, he said, "Is there someone else you'd like to see? Maria? Or your secretary? I could . . ."

"No," she said, "no one." Then, "Have you given me extreme unction?" she asked, unconsciously using the old-fashioned phrase. Her hand came up to her forehead and touched the dab of holy oil there. "Oh," she said.

"Don't worry." Leo patted her hand, and began to think of further ways to bring up the need for Mark's presence. But Linda had closed her eyes once more. He thought she was sleeping, but, suddenly, she said, "I was never honest with you. Not really. When we . . . first became friends, I didn't know you . . . or how far to trust you . . . and later . . . it was too late.

"When I followed Bill to America . . . I behaved . . . very badly. You don't know. I loved him . . . too much, you see. I was . . . obsessed. I plotted . . . very carefully, managed . . . to destroy him. Made enemies for him, ruined . . . his reputation. He was asked to resign his teaching appointment. And . . . I sent anonymous letters . . . to *her*. I'd follow her, never too close, but she knew

I was there. Let her know . . . I could kill her. Stupid woman . . . believed it. Bill said . . . she lost their child . . . because of me. Tried to kill herself . . . overdose . . .

"But I *lied*. About Bill. Started . . . terrible rumours. Told them he'd been . . . forced to leave Australia . . . big scandal."

She murmured something else and Leo had to ask her to repeat it, had to bend over her to hear. "Child . . . molestation," she said. It was barely audible, but she opened her eyes on these words and looked directly at him. "I think . . ." she said, "in the end . . . even Sandra doubted him."

Leo could not speak. She regarded him quietly for a moment, then said, "I was sorry, afterwards. I went to confession . . . came back to Australia. I'd come to see . . . I'd destroyed myself as much as Bill. And loving Bill . . . I destroyed the only thing . . . that made me want . . . to be alive."

"Mark . . ." Leo began.

"Mark." Her voice was heavy, one of her laboured breaths expended on that one word. "I couldn't forgive him, couldn't love him. Bill and I . . . hadn't needed him. And later . . . he was all . . . I had left. So much like his father . . . but not his father. And, inside, like me. Cold. Like me."

"No, Linda . . ."

"Shut . . . up, Leo. He came . . . to see me . . . just before his final exams, at St Jude's. Very belligerent. So tall . . . a great, handsome *stranger* in the house.

But ... more like his father in his outburst. Looked me in the face and said ... he wanted to ... come home. We were family, he said. I was his mother ... and he wanted ... to know me. He said ... we didn't know each other. And it was true, of course."

"Linda, I know all this."

"We held each other. Of an evening. Just the two of us ... listening to music, or ... watching the television. He would ... place an arm around me, fondly, and ... But ... that's how it began. It was so easy. He seemed ... to need me ... and it was too easy ... to pretend. So like Bill. And he needed so much affection. I'd ... denied him for so long.

"They were ... very happy months. We were so close. I was wrong ... I know. I didn't realise ... knowledge can't help ... when feelings are involved. One night he wanted ... I was afraid. Knew, then, what I'd done. We'd never ... and he couldn't see, when I tried to tell him it was *wrong*. He raged against me, said things ... It was terrible. I tried to convince him that we should live apart ... he should go to college. He saw that as just ... another rejection. He turned against me for a long time. You remember ... when he turned on me ... on everyone ..."

Leo remembered. Mark at nineteen – always a tractable boy – going through his rebellious stage a little late, that was all. The growl when he answered the phone, the surly face that met guests, only to disappear as quickly as possible into his room.

"Poor Leo ..." Linda said, and took a deep breath, so abruptly and violently that a thousand buzzers seemed suddenly to be sounding in sympathy.

The nurses ushered Leo away. When he was allowed back, the tubes were gone, the machinery was silent. Again, he gave her absolution. Finally she was at peace.

The nurses were very kind. Leo had not realised that tears were coursing down his cheeks. When did it begin? He only hoped that Linda had not seen it – it would have upset her.

CHAPTER NINETEEN

Mark had been furious with his mother, but afterwards realised that his anger was directed as much at the news she gave him as at Linda herself.

He had been for an early morning swim, and was still drying his hair with his towel after his shower as he phoned the house in Sydney.

She had sounded distressed at the sound of his voice, "Mark? Oh, Mark, thank God!"

His good humour had fallen from him. "What's wrong, are you alright?"

"I'm ... I've had a virus the last day or so, I'm staying in bed over the weekend, but that's not what I want to speak about. Darling, I know where you are – and I know that Rosalind is with you."

He had felt the blood drain from his face. So it was almost over. A slight movement in the periphery of his vision had made him look up – Rosalind, in one of his t-shirts over her swimsuit, was setting the table on the balcony for their breakfast. Fruit, muesli and a blue ceramic jug of milk.

"Mark? Are you there . . . ?"

"Have you told Geoffrey Harcourt?"

"How can you even think that?" there was hurt and irritation in her voice. "Who do you think told *me*? He doesn't know your exact address, but he's hired a private detective. It's only a matter of time, Mark. Mark?"

Rosalind had chanced to look up and smile at him before disappearing into the living room, heading towards the kitchen once more. "I'm here," Mark had said, trying to make his mind work, trying to plan – and all the while he had gazed at that absurd little blue jug, sky blue against the dark turquoise of the sea, thinking: how long did I expect it to go on?

"Geoffrey Harcourt has a lot of power," Linda had said, "I think he'll be a dangerous enemy." Mark had smiled grimly. "Come home," Linda had said. "Come home, my darling, *please*."

Home, Mark had thought, but this is home.

He hadn't realised that the pause had gone on for too long. He had heard, in Linda's voice, that she was distraught, was struggling to retain her inner calm.

"Mark, don't you see what you've done by running off like that? When the papers get hold of it . . . The woman's always been newsworthy – and now a scandal! The smut, the innuendos could ruin your career. And she won't stay with you – that's the tragedy – she'll become bored, and leave you to be the laughing stock of the country!"

He had held himself in check, said, "I have to go now," in a tone that had made it obvious that he would not discuss this.

"Wait!" For she must have been afraid that he would hang up. In a calmer voice, "All I'm asking is that you think very carefully about your future. I can't sleep for worrying about you. Mark, can't you come back? Let Rosalind go back to her husband, just for a few months, until the scandal dies down."

He had been too angry to speak. The very thought of what she was suggesting made him tremble. As if sensing his reaction, as if she could see his obdurate face, Linda had broken down. "For God's sake," she had almost shrieked at him, "don't allow that promiscuous little ... *tart* to ruin – "

It was at that point that he had replaced the receiver.

Rosalind found me, down on the shore. I don't have any memory of leaving the house. I was trembling, really shaking, so to stop this, I began picking up pebbles and throwing them as hard as I could, as far as I could, into the sea.

I heard her say, "Mark?" softly, behind me, but I didn't turn. I didn't want to look at her, knowing I was going to lose her so soon. Tomorrow, even today.

"Mark?" She moved in front of me, and still I tried to ignore her, would not look at her. Whatever I have done to her, I've never ignored her, and she knew that something was dreadfully wrong.

I saw another stone on the damp sand and went to bend, but she placed her hand on my shoulder, and I gazed down at her, then, and stopped. My God, she's become everything to me. Was my fear written there on my face? She seemed to know, without my words, without her own, for her hand came up about my neck, the other about my body and she drew my head down upon her shoulder. I hadn't reached for her, she reached for me. And I stood there, my face half-buried against her neck, leaning on that fragile frame, and cried like a bloody child, for the first time in my life.

He'd had so many plans. There would be time, he had thought, lulled into complacency by the quietness of their life there. Three months had passed since Rosalind had come with him to the beach house, but it seemed longer, for he could not imagine, now, a time when they had not been together. And a future where they would not be together was unthinkable.

That night, lying in his arms, she finally asked him about the phone call. "It was my mother," he said. "She thinks we should go back to Sydney."

Rosalind was very still in his embrace.

"Do you want to go back to Sydney?" she asked, finally. She did not seem to think it of consequence that Linda Parrish knew Mark was with her.

"I want you to be happy," he said. "If we go back to Sydney we could get an apartment overlooking the harbour."

"But we'd have to see Geoff."

He thought a while, then. "Perhaps," he said, carefully, "it might be better to go back and confront Geoff, rather than waiting for him to find us."

"No," she said, and her voice was strained, her body suddenly stiff. "No, Mark!"

He leaned over and switched on the bedside light, the better to see her face. She turned away from him, but there were tears, the first he had seen for some weeks now.

"It's Geoff, isn't it? Why does the thought of Geoff upset you?"

"It doesn't!" quickly, her eyes afraid. "I just don't want to see him anymore."

"You'll have to, eventually."

"No, I . . ."

"Or maybe your lawyers can handle the divorce

without the two of you having to meet. It's not as if you want anything from him. You don't, do you?"

"I . . . No. A divorce . . . " wonderingly.

"You must have realised that he'd want a divorce. And even if he didn't, you do, don't you?"

She gazed at him, studied his face as if only there, in his eyes, she would be able to find an answer for him.

"Rosalind, I want to marry you. Hadn't you realised that?"

Now she *was* confused. She looked away, her lip trembled and one hand came up to her face – all early signals of her distress. Yet he was puzzled. Could she have possibly not realised . . . ?

"You didn't know, did you?" he said, gently. "I guess I never told you. Or asked you."

He got to his knees on the bed, and pulled her up against him. "Here I am, on bended knee, asking you for your hand in marriage, Miss McGowan."

She stared at him, startled, then began to laugh.

"What's so funny? I'm very serious. Or are you going to be a stickler for etiquette and insist we put our clothes on for this solemn moment?"

"Nobody's called me Miss McGowan for . . . years." Her face clouded, and she began to tremble slightly in his arms. One hand came up towards her face and he imprisoned it, firmly.

"You do want to marry me, don't you?"

She did not answer, gazed at him in the way she

293

used to look at him in the studio, with wariness, with fear. He controlled the urge to shake her.

"Rosalind . . . " warningly, "we have to talk about this. Living here has been wonderful, but it's been one long honeymoon – we'll have to get back to the real world. I can start that general practice in Cairns, but I won't have you locking yourself away here. I want the world to know that we're together . . . Do you understand?" He shook her, gently.

"Yes," she said.

He was unconvinced, then a sudden thought came to him, "It's not just Geoff you're afraid of, is it? It's everything. You'd really prefer not to leave this house, this beach, wouldn't you?" Again, a little shake.

"Yes," she said.

He gazed at her, and murmured, "I've done too good a job." He held her to him.

"What?" she breathed against his neck.

"Made a sparrow from a sparrowhawk," he said. At least this had the effect of making her forget her apprehension and raise her head to look at him, questioningly. He pushed her hair back from her forehead and smiled. "I think we might drive into town tomorrow and do the shopping together."

And as the fear leapt anew into her eyes, "No excuses. I'll be with you all the time. We have to get you used to the world again."

Except for her silence, no one would ever know that anything was wrong. She seemed to enjoy the trip into Tilga, gazing at the passing farms, plantations and rainforest with interest. Only when they reached the outskirts of the town did she seem to become tense, and kept looking at Mark as if for confirmation that this was a good idea.

"Stop worrying," he soothed her, but she remained wary. When he parked the car she stayed in her seat, unmoving until he came to her door and opened it. He held out his hand to her, and she took it, and alighted. She did not let go of his hand until the check-out counter at the supermarket, and even then he had to prise her claw-like little fingers from his, surreptitiously.

There was a small park across from the supermarket; they had crossed it coming from the car. Now, on the way back, Mark stopped suddenly. Both of them were carrying shopping bags, but Mark now handed his to Rosalind, "Damn! I forgot razor blades. There's a seat just there – I won't be a minute."

And he ran back across the road, away from her.

She stood in frozen terror, staring after him. She remained standing thus for some two minutes – he could see her through the windows of the supermarket. He backed away towards the counter, and started when the woman behind it said, "Can I help you?"

He turned to her. "Razor blades," he said.

The woman rolled her eyes towards the dozen or so brands on the counter. Coming to his senses, Mark chose a brand, paid the money and, while waiting for the change, glanced out the window once more.

Rosalind was sitting on the park bench now, and a neatly dressed middle-aged man was speaking with her.

Mark's first impulse was to run out of the shop and hurl himself across the road to her – but no. He made himself remain by the window, gazing out between the signs painted on the glass that announced bargains in electric green and orange.

But the man would not go. Worse, he was standing between Rosalind and Mark, so, although Mark could see the cloud of her hair, her shoulder, and her feet in white sandals planted neatly on the grass, he could not see her face, her expression.

The man turned around and gazed at the windows of the supermarket.

It was all Mark could do to remain still, but Rosalind was, perhaps, less recognisable alone than she would be with him. It could be innocent, he told himself, this needn't be Geoffrey Harcourt's bloodhound.

The man was leaving Rosalind now, turning to face the road, waiting for a break in the traffic. He crossed towards the supermarket.

Mark waited. As soon as the man came through the doors, he slipped out, raced across the road, took hold of Rosalind's arm and drew her to her feet. "Who was he? What did he want with you?" While he was speaking, he gathered up their parcels and almost herded her, with his shoulder, towards the car, looking back at the supermarket as they walked.

Rosalind, terrified at his sudden arrival, found it difficult to speak. "He ... he wanted to know the way to the t ... tourist bureau. I said I didn't know, that I was from Sydney, and he said, so was he and his wife – from French's Forest. And he asked where I came from and I told him Mosman, and he said that was a lovely spot. And I suggested he ask in the supermarket – they might know the way to the tourist office ..."

Mark lowered the shopping down on to the grass, and turned to her. "Oh, God, I'm sorry. I must have scared you out of your wits." He took her in his arms, despite the glances from a mother and young child who passed them, despite his avowal not to do anything in the town that might draw attention to them. He hugged her and almost rocked with laughter, with the madness of relief.

Rosalind had coped very well. Once they'd arrived home, put the shopping away and made coffee, they sat out on the balcony in the dusk. Carefully manoeuvring the question into the conversation, so as not to alarm her, he managed to ask why she had not told the man who she was.

"It didn't come up. Besides, why should I tell him that? If Geoff's looking for me, then I don't want anyone to know who I am."

"But," he persisted gently, "when the two boys in their utility came up the drive, you asked them to drive you to a police station. You admitted that to me."

He wished he had not spoken. It was his own insecurity that drove him to it; he should be thinking of her now, of building her confidence, not making her unsure, nervously wary of him.

"That ... that was then. I'm ... different now. *You're* different now. I was confused then. I wasn't thinking clearly. I thought I should be in Sydney with Geoff. But ... it was too late for that – that was wrong. That was *then*."

Her hand was at her face again, running through her hair. She was looking around her, anywhere but at him, as if for escape. But it was not from him that she wished to escape, for when he rose and came to her, she stood and wound her arms around him. Whatever she wished to escape from was within herself. He would protect her from it, he promised himself. He would never take her down that dark pathway ever again.

Mark made the phone calls early in the morning, before she awoke. Rosalind heard him, speaking quietly on the phone in the study, though the bedroom door was shut.

He returned to bed and seemed surprised that she was awake. "Were you calling your mother?" she asked.

"No," he said, but said no more. She did not question him further.

Two days later, he announced that they were going to leave the house for two days to tour the Atherton Tablelands, stopping overnight at Mareeba. She didn't question him, only noted that he seemed to be in a cheerful mood. The mail that day – he usually walked the two hundred metres or so to their mailbox at the head of their drive – seemed to have brought something with which he was very pleased. He came back with a quarto-sized manila envelope and locked it in his desk, humming to himself.

Mark had never been to the Atherton Tablelands, but Rosalind had. He allowed her to guide him, and was pleased with the way that this innocent power brought her out of herself. She actually chatted to him about some of the history she remembered, and about the old mines in the area. She knew the best rainforest walks, and showed him Barron Falls and the great crater lakes. When they were not in the car, she wore a wide-brimmed hat and her dark sunglasses, and he noticed that she always turned away if anyone chanced to stare at her. He found himself thinking, I'll be glad when it's over. Glad when the whole world knows, when she doesn't need to hide anymore.

Rosalind was quite happy to return to the beach

house, he noted, and they stopped off in Tilga only long enough to buy milk and bread. In the car, approaching their driveway, he said, "There was another reason I wanted us out of the house today. I have a surprise for you." She turned to look at him, her smile, as always, tinged with wariness. It was beginning to bother him more and more that, for the rest of her life, she would look at him with fear at the back of her eyes.

He said, "Actually, there are two surprises." He had thought she would ask him what they were, but here was their mailbox – the green four-gallon drum, on its side, nailed to a post at the edge of their drive. Mark had been so amused by it when he bought the place that he'd never bothered to replace it, even though it leaked a little, these days, and a gecko lived inside.

Mark carried the shopping into the house. The door, as usual these days, was left unlocked. Rosalind seemed to sense Mark's feelings of anticipation, but the living room looked the same.

"Sit down," he said, dumping the bread and milk on the dining table and pausing only to push her gently into a chair before going off into the study. A few moments later he came back with a manila envelope, the same one that had arrived two mornings before. He handed it to Rosalind, silently, smiling.

"It's addressed to me . . . but in my maiden name. How . . . ?" She stopped, looking over at him. He seemed so young, standing there, so pleased with himself. "Open it," he urged her.

Rosalind tore at the envelope and drew out its contents – a booklet and a letter. She was very still, reading, then looked up at Mark, whose face was suddenly serious, intent. She read aloud in a halting voice, for there were tears in her eyes and it was difficult to see, "Dear Miss McGowan, thank you for your interest in the external Law/Economics course here at the University of New England . . . "

Her voice broke, for a long moment she could only gaze at the letter. Two tears freed themselves and plopped onto the paper and she looked up. "You did this? You sent away for this?"

"Yes."

She placed her hand to her mouth, and gazed again at the letter and the handbook. She touched the latter as if she would like to open it, but did not dare.

"You mean . . . enrol next year?" She looked up at him, found him smiling at her. "I . . . I can't . . . "

"Why not?"

"It's . . . it's crazy! Even if I attended full-time classes – just the Economics degree – I'd be forty-four by the time I graduated!"

"I know a lot of forty-four year old economists."

She shook her head, put her head into her hands and laughed and cried.

"I have something else to show you." He pulled her to her feet and led her towards the study.

She stopped in the doorway, and Mark was vastly amused by the look upon her face. He kept silent, however, and watched her as she moved forward to where the door of the studio had been.

He had considered pulling the room down, or having builders fit windows in the place, but had thought that might arouse suspicion so soon after telling them he was a record producer and would be fitting it out as a studio for his company. No, the room had better stay as it was until he decided to sell the house, which would have to be soon. This way, at least, the door of the studio was no longer visible, and any accidental visitor would probably not even notice that the interior space of the house was less than the exterior area.

Rosalind stared at the great ornate mirror, walked forward to touch its gilt frame, then backed to the centre of the room as Mark came to stand behind her. "It's . . . enormous. Where did you get it?"

"I read that they were pulling down an old hotel in Brisbane. I had an idea that they may have a mirror like this, so I phoned the auctioneers. I wanted to buy one, but didn't think I'd get one so soon, or such a beauty."

It was fully six feet wide and eight feet high. Rosalind gazed at it in awe. "How do you . . . ?" she began, then stopped.

"How do I what?"

"How does . . . one . . . get into the studio now?"

And he sensed, rather than felt, the tremor that went through her. "What studio?"

"The studio. The room. The room where you . . . where I stayed."

Only this? In the mirror, he studied her face; no horror, only a kind of perplexity. He placed his arms around her, "I don't see any room."

She was tense in his embrace, her gaze on their reflections.

"Do you see a door to a room?" he asked gently.

"No."

"Then there mustn't be a door. Or a room."

He was smiling at the Mark and Rosalind in the mirror, but only the Mark smiled back. "Who's that woman?" he asked her.

She did not answer, did not relax at all.

He bent his head and whispered in her ear, and then she smiled.

"Say it," he said.

"Rosalind McGowan, undergraduate," and there was laughter contained in the narrow frame within his embrace.

"Who, I take it on good authority, is shacked up with her boyfriend somewhere on the north coast." He rocked her a little, and now she was openly smiling. "Who are those two people?" he asked her, softly.

She was more confident now, "You, me."

"So who do you see in the mirror, Rosalind?"

"Us," she pronounced.

"Us." He kissed her hair. "That's all there is. That's all there is to see."

CHAPTER TWENTY

L eo could not bring himself to tell Maria the news over the telephone. Better in person, he thought – she had been with the family for twenty years, and was devoted to both Linda and Mark.

She knew the truth, of course, as soon as she opened the door and saw his face. Leo had attempted a reassuring smile, for Linda was with the Lord now, and He would have them rejoice for her. But his acting ability was poor, and Maria simply looked at him and dissolved into tears, leaning her head against the door frame, still clutching the doorknob in one hand.

It was Leo who poured her a brandy, and then sat with her for an hour and a half. He had to intrude upon her grief to explain that he had to find Mark, and she understood, but had no idea where he might be. If Linda had known, she had not confided in her.

So he had to find the bank statements. With the name of the real estate agency through which Mark had purchased his house, Leo was sure he would find Mark.

But there were no bank statements. Maria stood watching as Leo searched through the mail on Mark's desk. There was no communication whatsoever from any bank, and there should have been three statements, for the one Leo had seen had been a monthly account.

"Could she have them in her own desk?" he asked, but Maria did not know. She led the way to the delicate little cedar escritoire in a corner of the library, where Linda had made up her household accounts.

The library. Leo walked past the now-empty hearth. His mind acknowledged, *we will never sit here together again*, but the words meant nothing. Since becoming a priest he had become accustomed to death. He knew that Linda was dead, but part of him had not acknowledged that she was gone. There had been no time.

The statements were not in Linda's desk.

He cursed his lack of forethought. He had held the statement in his hand, long enough to memorise the agent's name if he had considered. He should have known that Linda would not want him to contact Mark, to interfere in any way. He had had precious seconds with the key to Mark's whereabouts and had wasted them. The name had started with W . . . Watkins, Wilson, Williams, Williamson . . . ?

He had to phone Linda's secretary to tell her the news. She was very upset, of course, but very helpful. She met him at the North Sydney consulting rooms that evening and helped him to go through the papers in Linda's desk, the filing cabinet, they even tried the computer, but found nothing.

Leo began to suspect that Linda had burnt the bank statements.

The secretary, like Maria, wanted to know what they should do, but he had no answers for them. He notified Linda's lawyer, but the decisions needed to be made by Mark – the funeral, for a start. He had to find him – and find him in order to tell him the news, so he would not hear it from some awkward young policeman who knew neither Linda nor Mark, who would not know how Mark would receive this news. Leo did not know himself. But he was afraid.

He phoned Bishop Rye that night and received permission to fly to Cairns. Once there, he planned to contact the police and ask for their help in finding the boy.

Late that night, while Leo was giving final instructions to Father John, his young curate, the Archbishop called. He had been disturbed to hear from Bishop Rye that evening that Linda Parrish had passed away. Being a friend of the family he would be honoured to conduct the service at St Mary's – he asked Leo to pass on this suggestion to young Mark. And how was Mark, he continued. He had been disturbed to hear from his mother only a few weeks before that he had been having some sort of career crisis.

"I do hope he remains in oncology – he's done so much in his field already – everyone speaks so highly of him. After the funeral I'll have a talk with him. And you, Father, use your influence upon the boy, won't you?"

"Yes, Your Grace," Leo murmured, before he had quite realised that these last words of the Archbishop's were rather carefully spoken. And he had rung off before the thought finally dawned on Leo that this clever old gentleman might know more of Mark's present circumstances than he could have believed. He was a man who kept close to his flock, and he was a good friend to his friends. Suddenly Leo's responsibility seemed heavier than before.

The following morning, with his suitcase packed, Leo left early for his flight and drove once more to the house on Castle Crag Road, to bid farewell to Maria and to see how she had coped through that first night. He also hoped she may have found something – she had said that she would continue looking – that may give a clue to Mark's whereabouts.

That something came from a most unexpected quarter. As Leo turned his car into the driveway, he saw a man coming down the steps from the house.

Maria was standing at the door, her handkerchief dabbing at her eyes. For a moment she, Geoffrey Harcourt and Leo gazed at each other, then Maria invited them inside.

Ron Christianson had succeeded, the previous Friday, in locating Mark's address. He had found the real estate agent – the name had been Wilkinson – and, by pretending to represent Mark's wealthy and estranged grandfather, had obtained the address of the coastal property Mark had purchased.

They sat in the spacious and spotless kitchen. Maria, on finding that neither Geoff nor Leo had eaten breakfast, insisted on making them eggs and toast and, sensitive to the fact that she gained comfort from this task, they accepted.

That Geoff was shaken by Linda's sudden death, Leo had no doubt; he had that look of shocked bewilderment about him that forward-thrusting men possess when confronted with mortality, the sudden reminder that not everything around them is controllable. But more than this, though he had not known her well, there was some distress in his own feelings, and a genuine empathy with Maria and Leo that they both felt, and to which they responded.

Leo said to Geoff, "So you'd have a telephone number – have you phoned Mark?"

He shook his head. "The agent didn't know the number, and when I tried the phone company they said it was unlisted. I'm not going to announce my arrival anyway."

Something of Leo's dismay must have shown on his face. "Of course I'm going up there," Geoff said, although Leo had not said a word. "What do you expect me to do?"

Leo considered. "Why have you waited so long? You heard the news on Friday. Could it be that you hesitate to intrude upon them, after all?"

"Why?" bluntly. "Did they hesitate to intrude on me when they turned my life upside down? No, as a matter of fact, it was Linda." He looked down, absently tracing the grain of the table mat with one fingernail. "I knew I'd upset her. I felt bad about it because she'd been honest with me, and we'd . . . we'd almost become friends. The last time I saw her – when she was faced with the truth and wouldn't believe me – I just saw red, that's all. And she saw my anger as some kind of threat to her son. She closed up on me, refused to even consider that my facts were correct."

"And . . . if she'd been alive, this morning? Did you think she'd be grateful to be faced with further proof that Mark had committed adultery with your wife, and had lied to his mother so blatantly?"

"Well . . ." a growl, "at least she could have done something then, couldn't she?"

Maria placed the breakfast plates before the two men, and took a seat at the table herself. Her plump little hands shook as she poured herself a coffee.

Geoff was watching her. "I'm sorry," he said, addressing the words to her and to Leo, "I shouldn't be intruding any further, but I really thought she should know. I even wondered if she'd come with me – I'm driving up today. I just had no idea that the pressures on her had been so great. Did she have a weak heart?"

Leo shook his head. "There was no history of heart problems. She may have been weakened by this virus . . . "

"I caused her a lot of grief – I really worried her. Until I told her that he was somewhere in Queensland she would never have doubted Mark. He was her world, wasn't he? And I destroyed an illusion for her."

Leo said, quietly, "The destruction of an illusion is not a bad thing."

Maria was looking at him. He smiled a little, but her dark eyes were solemn and regarded him for a long moment. But, when she finally spoke, it was to Geoff that she turned, "You must not feel bad. She knew, I think, for a long time, inside her heart, that things were not . . . *right*. The truth – it is cruel sometimes, but what you call illusion is more cruel. Doctor Mark – he was very wrong. Wrong to lie to his mother and wrong to do what he did. But these things happen. He loved your wife very much. I could tell; I knew. He would be happy, the days he would see her – he would come through the door, take the stairs two, three, at a time. He would smile, he was happy. And he was not a happy young man. His feelings were very strong – I had never seen him like this. I knew something would happen." She spoke with a mournful simplicity, her capable hands clasped about her coffee cup.

"I'm flying to Cairns," Leo told Geoff. "I want to be the one to tell Mark about his mother. You'd save me a lot of trouble if you could let me have his address."

Geoff scowled. "I want to talk to Rosalind. If you go up there first they might do a midnight flit to avoid me. For some reason they must be scared stiff of me, or they'd have let me know themselves where they are."

"He'll come home for his mother's funeral," Leo said, "he won't run."

"He's left his patients *and* his mother for three months, and lied through his teeth to her. I think he's capable of anything."

Into this impasse, Maria spoke, surprising them. "Mr Harcourt is right. Doctor Mark is not himself, he was not himself before he left Sydney. He was ... strange. He ..." she chose her words carefully, "... he is not like normal young men." She blushed, confused now. "I mean, he was too much ... in here." Two fingers tapped her forehead. "Always. Even as a little boy, when he came from school to visit. Always in his own mind. It is not good."

She looked from one man to the other. "You should find him together," she said, as if making up her mind. "*Si*. You should go to this place and find him together."

CHAPTER TWENTY-ONE

A nd so Leo came to know a good deal about Geoffrey Harcourt; about his life, his love for Rosalind, his view of the past ten months that had led to this journey they were making. That he insisted on Leo cancelling his ticket and driving with him surprised Leo – it seemed Geoff flew only when he had to go overseas. But they would never have had those long discussions and come to know each other, had they spent only two and a half hours together in a crowded plane. And there was, for Leo, an added pleasure – how many parish priests get to drive three thousand kilometres in a Rolls Royce?

"I'm very surprised," he admitted, as the great car glided up the Pacific Highway. "You don't appear to me like a man who would be afraid of anything."

Geoff scowled over the wheel. "There are only three things in my life I've ever been afraid of – losing Rosalind, being broke, and flying in bloody aeroplanes."

They decided not to stop, except for meals and bathroom visits, and drove in shifts throughout that day and the night.

Leo was at the wheel during that grey and indistinct time of the morning, when one is aware that dawn is at hand but it seems the world is holding its breath for the sun to appear. All the happenings of the previous day suddenly weighed so heavily upon him, as if the weight of his sorrow had broken through the final barrier of his mind. Geoff was sleeping, but Leo almost wished that he would wake up, that he could hear his sensible voice. In that moment, it all seemed too much for him – not just Linda's death, and Mark, whom he had thought of as a son, suddenly becoming such a stranger to him. No, it had been Leo himself as well. Mark had been correct – Leo had never wanted to give up his teaching. He had missed the classroom terribly, his work that had been no work at all, just the sharing of his love for literature and language. Mark had practically accused him of cowardice, of not standing up for his own needs and desires in the face of the Archbishop's request. Who'd have thought that Mark would know, even before Leo himself knew, that he had left his heart somewhere in the chalk-smelling, draughty corridors of St Jude's? Mark had sensed his unhappiness before he had admitted it to himself. Mark, Leo thought, with something almost like a physical pain within his heart, knew me better than I had known him.

"Tell me about Mark." The voice from the seat beside him made Leo start. Geoff had been sleeping with his head crooked in the seat belt, his face turned away. He must have been gazing out at the dark shapes of black hills on grey sky for some time. Now he turned to Leo, "Tell me from the beginning."

And as the big car rolled north Leo told him Mark's story – as much as he needed to know – and the sun was high and the air conditioning was switched on by the time he had finished. They stopped for lunch and, again, Geoff insisted on paying – perhaps fortunately, as his choice of restaurant was invariably of the type that was far beyond Leo's means and natural predilection.

They were two of only six people dining, and the others were at a table on the terrace overlooking the water. So it was very quiet, and no one overheard Geoff say, "I knew she was falling in love with him."

Leo's hand paused with a forkful of lobster halfway to his mouth. Later, it seemed difficult for him to believe there had been a time when he was ignorant of what had happened at that beach house at Tilga, but then, of course, at lunch, he knew no more than Geoffrey Harcourt. That his wife had run off to be with Mark was no longer in any doubt, but Leo had come to see Rosalind, not as a stunning *femme fatale* as Linda had insisted on viewing her, but – through her husband's eyes over those last twenty-four hours – as a woman still attractive in early middle age, who had never had the opportunity, or perhaps the self-discipline, to find her happiness as something apart from her husband. And when Geoff had become too busy, she had become lost. Even her work for charity, extensive as it was, had not given her any sense of fulfillment. Leo was beginning to see some similarities between himself and Rosalind Harcourt. Perhaps, in loving Rosalind, Mark had come to see them also. Perhaps that was why he had seen through Leo so easily that evening before he left Sydney. Rosalind and Leo had both made service to others their lives; Mark had seemed to think this was not enough. Rosalind had obviously thought so, too.

And Leo? Now?

It was something he could not think about. He was still staring at Geoff, "But . . . you never seemed to doubt her before . . ."

"Doubt her? I don't. I think she's with the boy out of pity – there's such a strong maternal instinct in Rosalind. Why do you think she had all those blokes buzzing around her? She attracts lost souls like a magnet, and there wasn't one of them – no, not *one* – " after a quick scowl of calculation – "who was content with himself, who really *liked* himself. They had looks, money, family background, and a kind of inner self-loathing. I've had a lot of time to think about these things, and that's one thing I'm sure of."

317

"And Mark? If he felt this . . . inner self-loathing, that still doesn't explain why she chose him, from all the others."

Geoff did not hesitate. "He was a good person. I knew that even before I met Linda, and you. He might not have liked himself, but it didn't stop him from doing the best he could to help other people, I mean, Jesus – sorry, Father – I've never been able to bring myself to visit the kids' cancer ward, but that man has given his life – with nothing much left over – to healing those children. Rosalind admired him for that. And something else, she was a woman easily moved – tears, laughter, whatever – she couldn't hide her feelings. Mark did though, she often used to speak of it. He was an enigma. She even said, once, that she'd like to be an enigma." He smiled a little at the memory, his gaze on the view of the Pacific through the plate glass windows.

"She wanted to understand Mark? To see what lay beyond his reticence?"

"No need for that. That happened fairly quickly – he simply seemed to trust her almost immediately and really opened up to her. No, it was more as if by spending time with him she could somehow learn from him."

"Learn what?"

"How to . . ." He frowned in thought, toying with his food as he searched for the right words, "how to be self-contained, like Mark. When I said 'falling in love' – maybe that's too strong a phrase.

She was interested in him, she cared about him more than any of the others. I was beginning to get worried, but I trusted her – both her loyalty and her common sense. All the same, I was glad when she told me he was going off to Thredbo. She was a bit subdued that day. I had a feeling something might have been said between them. I was sure the friendship was over, that's why I didn't immediately suspect Mark – and maybe I didn't want to. I pushed all the signs of Rosalind's interest in him to the back of my mind. But still . . ." He grimaced, stabbing at the poor carcass of his lobster, "I wouldn't have thought it was an interest strong enough to break up our marriage, or even to make her forget her sense of right and wrong and to sleep with him. Like I said, it was mostly a fascination with his ability to keep so cool, so remote – to exist without really *needing* anybody."

Leo said, quietly, "If she thought that of Mark, she was wrong."

"Maybe," he conceded. "I have to hope that, whatever the feelings were that led her to go off with him, they've cooled a bit. Everyone makes mistakes, but Rosalind's got a lot of pride. She'd never ask to come back to me after doing something like this. She could be miserable – I can't help but feel that she *is* – and yet she might feel committed to Mark. If he's become dependent on her, then she'd feel trapped. I want to let her know that nothing's changed . . . Shit – sorry – it's all my fault, anyway. If I hadn't been such a money-hungry power-drunk turd, none of this would have happened. I can't blame Rosalind for running off with this guy who looks like a Greek god, who seems to adore her and gives her the attention I didn't. And I can't blame Mark – she's a wonderful, beautiful woman. He's got great taste." He grinned, wryly, "That's what I tell myself, when I find myself wishing I could kill them."

Leo said, and meant it, "You're a remarkable man."

Geoff had taken a mouthful of lobster, and looked up in genuine surprise. "Why?" he said, and swallowed. "Because I worked all that out about Roz? That's no big deal. I love the woman – I love her more than my own life. No matter how bad things get, that's the bottom line. That makes everything easy."

They were looking for a green mailbox, "shaped like a drum," Geoff added.

Leo looked at him. Geoff was driving now, needing to be in control at the end of the long search, just as Leo was glad to merely be a passenger. His hands were trembling a little, and he could feel the slow leak of adrenalin that felt less like butterflies in the stomach than vultures. Why were they here, he asked himself. They were intruding. They should have left this to the police, or at least used their influence to gain the telephone number first . . .

"Ron and his stupid handwriting!" Geoff exclaimed.

"Sorry?"

He scowled and jerked his head forwards, indicating the makeshift mailbox that was just coming into view behind a clump of the wild tropical vegetation.

"The instructions said, 'Ten kilometres down Tilga Road, green mailbox, drum-shaped'."

He slowed the car, and Leo had an opportunity to take in the four-gallon drum, set on its side atop a short post. The slit was a two-cornered tear pulled upwards to form a flap. Within the drum he could see the white shape of a letter.

"Should we stop and check the name on the letter in the box? How do we know this is the right place?"

But Geoff was too close to his quarry now. They were driving, a little too fast for Leo's liking, between what seemed like jungle that met overhead in a tangle of vines. The road sloped away slightly to either side of the drive, where the trees and huge ferns faded into blackness, repeating themselves time and time again, away into the shadows.

"Hadn't we better slow down? If we meet someone coming the other way on these bends . . ."

But they had just turned the last bend, and there

the house lay – and beyond it, palm trees, white sand and the blue of the sea.

It was a lovely house, a little modern, a little stark, but its architecture was softened by its riotous garden, ablaze with tropical plants and shrubs in full bloom. Leo was still wondering at the effect of all that colour against the surrounding blue of the sea, when the Rolls came to a halt and Geoff climbed out. Leo followed, taking in the fact that the house seemed silent, and the large garage doors were open but no car was within.

Geoff knocked on the door, then opened it.

"Geoff!" Leo was appalled. "We have no right to – "

But Geoff had disappeared into the house. Leo ran to catch up, worried now. What if they simply did not have a car? What if they were spending the afternoon lying down together . . .

"Geoff!" Leo was cross with him – the man of discipline seemed to have disappeared.

"Rosalind?" By the time Leo found his way to the living room, with its rather eclectic mixture of cane furniture, Persian rugs upon the highly polished floors and scattered valuable antique pieces, Geoff's voice was issuing from some other part of the house. "Rosalind?" Leo could hear the wistfulness in it, the pain, as he tried to find him. "Geoff . . . ?"

The house was tastefully but sparsely furnished. In the room leading off the living room there was only a couch, a coffee table and a large oak desk and swivel chair, both similar in style and antiquity to those in Mark's bedroom at Castle Crag.

Leo saw Geoff, then, in what appeared to be the main bedroom. He almost called to him once more, for he was embarrassed, felt they had no right to be here, to walk in like this, but Geoff had forgotten him. He stood for a moment, just inside the doorway, then moved, slowly, to the left-hand side of the large bed. Almost fearfully, he lifted the pillow. Leo did not consciously pry, but he had only to move his head a little to see the small folded garment – some kind of silk and lace feminine thing – that Geoff picked up in his hand with a terrible tenderness. He sat down, almost like an old man in pain, on the edge of the bed. His back was to Leo now, and Leo was glad of it. He moved away just as Geoff lowered his head and those great broad shoulders over the garment in his hands. Leo turned away, and started violently, confronted by a pale dark-haired man who gazed hollow-eyed at him as if with great reproach. Then he let out his breath in a heavy sigh of relief, finding himself gazing at his own reflection in a mirror of such size and gilt-edged festoons that it could have done justice to the Vatican.

Leo moved closer, examining it. Of course, he thought, this was for Rosalind, for her ballet exercises. But there was no *barre* which was odd . . .

323

He felt very ill at ease in that house. Of course it was empty, but at any time they might return, and how could the two men explain breaking in like this?

Mark and Rosalind should have locked the door, Leo told himself severely, as he went to the sliding glass doors that led to a balcony. But even if the couple had absorbed Queenslanders' openess and hospitality and left their doors unlocked for any neighbour to make themselves welcome, how welcome would they be, Geoff and himself?

Leo stood on the broad timber deck and took deep breaths of the sea air. Up and down the beach, he looked, but there was only sand and surf – no two figures, arms entwined, making their way homeward through the dusk.

He prayed again then, for the strength to face whatever was to come, to be strong for the sake of what was right, and for what must best be done to cause as little pain as possible to these people for whom he had, somehow, come to care very much.

There was another room to the house.

Leo blinked, taking in the extra length of the outside wall, and the fact that the house, from the inside, seemed to end with that large mirror that glowed a little, beyond the reflection of fading sky, in the plate glass windows.

Yes, he could see it now – the places in the white outer wall where the windows had been bricked up. He gazed at the flat expanse of wall, then went back into the house. Going up to the mirror, he tried to pull it out a little, to see what was behind it.

"What are you doing?" Geoff's voice, behind him, was flat, almost disinterested. Leo turned to look at him. He seemed older and very tired. He realised with a shock that until he had found the familiar nightdress of his wife's, he had hoped, with part of his mind, that there had been some mistake, that there would be some other explanation.

"There's a room behind this mirror," Leo said, and turned back to it, pulling a little at the heavy frame . . .

Leo could hear someone calling his name, and as he realised it was Geoff, had the absurd feeling that he was hitting him, striking him with his fists about the body, and he could not shout, could not protest in any way.

But Geoff was trying to help. Thank God he was as strong as he was, for he somehow held the mirror up from where it had fallen on Leo, and managed to pull him free. Neither of them had any idea of the damage it had caused – Leo only knew that he could take in only the tiniest sips of air, and even those brought agony. His face was sticky with blood, and his trousers were torn and bloodstained where Geoff had had to drag him a little to free him from the crushing weight.

"Are you alright?" he said. As Leo responded, "Yes, I think so . . .", there was a slight sound. The men turned to see Rosalind standing in the open door leading to the balcony. She was wearing a pale cotton dress and sandals. Leo could barely see for the blood in his eyes, but he did see the flowers fall from her hands and the look of terror upon her face. Her hair was very long – he was surprised to see that it was loose and very curly, and he wondered if it truly was Rosalind. But Geoff called her name, loudly, wildly, and then she was gone, down the stairs that led to the beach.

Geoff helped Leo to the nearest chair, but once he had pulled his handkerchief from his pocket and found the place upon his forehead where the cut poured forth blood, he waved Geoff away. "Go after her – she looked terrified. Don't frighten her more . . ."

Leo was conscious that he did not quite make sense, but Geoff was already gone. His neck was stiff from leaning awkwardly upon Mark's desk, and he found he had left smears of blood upon its surface. When he stood, and made himself walk to the glass doors and out onto the deck, all he could see were footprints in the sand, leading away from the house.

Then he heard the car.

Mark came through the door like a madman. Leo, even seated as he was by that stage, trying to look as calm and normal as possible, almost recoiled. Keeping the sodden handkerchief pressed to his forehead, he made himself stand to confront him.

Mark came to a halt on seeing him, almost as if he had run into an invisible wall. It would have been comic, in any other circumstances, to see the veneer of the man, the lover, the doctor, stripped away in that second, the guilt changing him to *Leo's* Mark, suddenly caught running along the cloisters.

"He's here, isn't he? *You* brought him!"

"No, Mark . . ."

But he would not wait, ran into the study. As Leo stumbled after him, he heard the sound of a key in a lock and a drawer opening. He reached the doorway in time to see Mark checking the chamber of a small, deadly looking revolver. "No, Mark – no!"

But Mark was gone, out the glass doors and down the stairs, vaulting over the handrail to drop out of sight into the sand below. Even if Leo had been uninjured he would never have caught him. Mark's physical fitness gave him a speed and agility that the older man could never have matched. And Leo was giddy and faint – he had to hold on to the metal edge of the glass doors for support. The last thing he knew was the light-grained timber floor, cool under his cheek, then darkness.

When Leo woke, it was dark, and he was still alone. Had he heard a shot, or just imagined it, in his feverish state? He listened for the last of the echoes, but concluded he had been wrong. He must have been wrong.

He called an ambulance, for he had no idea how long the others would be, or even where they were. He also called the police, and tried to explain as matter of factly as he could that there was the possibility of a domestic problem and that one of the parties was armed. The fact that he was a priest, and the calm way in which he explained the situation seemed to be effective. He was told a police car would be despatched immediately.

There would be a scandal, but how had they thought to avoid that? It would wash over Geoff, and he would bob up once more as ebullient as ever – if he could keep his beloved Rosalind, he may even thrive on it. Mark may be ruined socially, but Leo did not care a fig for that. As far as he was concerned, the young fool should consider the social stigma to be a lenient punishment indeed.

And Rosalind? Linda's descriptions, Geoff's descriptions – both were wiped away by the rather theatrical apparition that had materialised briefly in the doorway, smaller than he had expected, with a cloud of dark hair and terrified eyes, the flowers falling from her hands. She had looked, somehow, so vulnerable, that Leo no longer wished to form any judgement about her.

Let them sort it out amongst themselves, he told his Lord and himself, sitting on the settee with his bloody head in his hands. Only don't let them hurt each other . . .

Rosalind was almost out of her mind with terror. The unthinkable had happened – Geoff had come for her, and she was alone.

She made for the Tilga Road that followed the border of Mark's property. The road was not far from the sea, but was hidden by the dense tropical vegetation. Rosalind, however, knew exactly where it lay and, not far from the beach house, she cut up into the bush. She knew that if she kept following the slight rise in the land, she would come to the road and may meet Mark, on his return from Tilga, or find another car and a means of escape. She was scrambling up the last incline, the sight of the road there above her, when she heard the first shot.

It could only be Mark. She turned around, called his name, realising that she had to retrace her steps, back through the tangled green forest where Geoff might be searching for her, in order to find Mark.

It occurred to her then that perhaps Mark was not the only one who possessed a gun, and she screamed his name again in her terror and ran back the way she had come.

Rosalind was running blindly, calling his name, when she heard Mark's voice, calm, quite close, "I'm over here!"

She found them, facing each other in a narrow clearing, and even in the fast-descending dusk she could sense the animosity, the danger, that lay between them. She tripped a little, exhausted, in making her way to Mark, and placed a hand on his arm, as if to convince herself that he was still there, safe. Mark's other hand held the short-barrelled revolver. She tried not to look at it.

"I heard a shot . . ." almost questioningly, and she turned to Geoff. He had no gun in his hand, but he was tense. She recognised the signs of his contained rage, and was afraid.

"Geoff was trying to be heroic," Mark said, almost mildly. He was very calm now. The worst had happened, what he had feared most had happened, and it was as if he were much better prepared than he had thought possible.

"Put that thing away," Geoff growled.

"When you leave. The road is just up there . . ." He gestured with the gun in the direction of the higher ground. "Give me your car keys and I'll drive Father Leo to pick you up."

"Can't we go back to the house and discuss this like reasonable adults?"

"No!" Mark's rage broke through his calm, "That's *our* house! You had no right to be there!"

"I wanted to see my wife," Geoff said. Both men seemed to become aware of her then, standing there, holding lightly on to Mark's arm. Under their scrutiny she looked from one to the other, apprehensively.

"Rosalind," Mark said, gently, "do you want to talk to him?"

"No." But her eyes were on Mark, not Geoff.

"Tell him."

330

She continued to gaze at him – it was almost as if she had not heard his words, despite their proximity to each other. Then she turned her head, quite slowly, and looked directly at her husband. "Go away, Geoff. Leave us alone."

Her face was so cold, it seemed she looked through him rather than at him, and it was so unlike her that he took a step forward, the better to see her in the gloom. He stopped when Mark raised the gun, and tensed. Their faces were a blur in the dim light, and so close together, maddeningly close. He wanted to scream, *she's my wife. My wife!* But his feelings, his needs, meant nothing to them. They had found each other and had their own needs now. Geoff looked at the small, pale ghost that was Rosalind, and tried to place upon that vague shape in the tropical wilderness the image of the woman with whom he had shared half his life.

"Roz? Just . . . just tell me why you felt you had to do things this way. We always talked to each other – about the good things, the bad things – we never held anything back. When Jamey died, you said, 'Now we've known the worst'. But . . . but this is the worst, Roz. When Jamey died, we had each other. Without you . . . there's nothing."

"There's no point in going over all this," Mark began, but Geoff kept speaking to Rosalind, and he could tell, even with only the blurred outline of her ghost-shape visible in the dark, that she was listening.

"Why couldn't you tell me you were unhappy? Why haven't you contacted me in all these months? I went mad, not knowing where you were. Only that one conversation – and you lied to me. You never needed . . ."

"That's enough." The deep and final voice came from above Rosalind's head.

"Shut up!" Geoff roared. "This is between me and my wife, so just *shut up*!"

Mark said, tightly, "Give me your car keys. Now."

Geoff took them from his pocket and threw them hard at Mark's face, "Take the fucking car keys!"

Mark just caught them, but before he could turn on Geoff, the man was once more addressing Rosalind. "Roz? Say you don't love me. Say it. Say, 'I don't love you', and I'll walk up that slope and you never need see me again."

There was a silence that stretched on, into hope for Geoff, and a terrible waiting for Mark, who held the woman's gaze but could no longer control her, no longer force his will upon her.

She made a strange little sound, and both men, who knew her so well by then, knew she was weeping but trying not to. She said to her husband, "I . . . don't love you."

Mark placed his left arm about her shoulders as they jerked slightly with her sobs. "Now go," he said, "*now*, Geoff."

It was not Rosalind. Geoff knew that she would never dismiss him like this. It was not ego, it was not. She showed no pity for him. Her tears were for herself. And this was not Rosalind. He looked at the intangible shade of the woman, the larger blur of the man who stood over her, barring her from her husband's reach, and he found he was careless, suddenly, of what would happen to him. It took only an instant, but the words poured out, "You've destroyed three lives, you selfish young shit, do you realise that? You can blame yourself for what happened to your mother – "

The shape that was Mark seemed to rear up, and the tension, the danger, the very size of the man, seemed to be magnified in that one dreadful moment.

"What about my mother?"

Leo could not have told him, Geoff realised. He did not know. Oh, God – he did not know . . .

"Come back to the house and – "

Even Geoff's sudden conciliatory tone gave him away. Mark was as alert as a dark jungle cat, and his warning growl cut through Geoff's words, "*What about my mother?*"

"She's . . ." It was hard. There was nothing for it but the truth, but . . . "She's had a heart attack."

"I don't believe you!"

"She's . . . very ill. Father Leo will you tell you."

Mark started to turn back, drawing Rosalind with him, in what Geoff hoped was the direction of the house, and some reminder of civilisation and sanity. He took one step to follow the man and woman, when Mark stopped and turned once more, and paused.

In the silence, there were sounds all around them – chirpings, chatterings, rustlings that Geoff had not noticed before, but that, he realised now, had been going on all around them, all this time – all those small beasts devouring each other in the moist dark ...

Mark spoke in a flat voice, devoid of any expression, frighteningly devoid of feeling, "Father Leo would never leave my mother while she needed him."

No one spoke to refute him. He looked down at the woman next to him, and moved away from her. He had both his hands on the revolver now. "Father Leo would never leave my mother while she needed him," he repeated, blankly, as if it were a lesson learnt by rote. Then, "She's dead. My mother's dead."

It was too dark to see the gun. Geoff saw the man's hands, as grey and indistinct as the fact above them, but did not know if they held the weapon steadily or were trembling – nor even which would have been worse.

"*She's dead, isn't she*?!"

Geoff took a breath, then, unwillingly, "Yes. I'm sorry."

"You're ... sorry."

Rosalind, puzzled at his withdrawal from her, moved a little closer to Mark. Geoff wanted to scream to Rosalind, *get away from him. He's going to kill me! Don't move, don't try to stop him or he'll turn on you.*

"Mark?" Rosalind spoke softly, but he did not hear her. All his attention was upon Geoff, and his voice shook with his effort to control it.

"*You're* sorry? You hounded her to death! Asking questions, demanding to know where we were, making her doubt me! She told me you were dangerous. It was practically the last thing she said to me – warning me about you. She never had a heart condition – *you* killed her! And you're sorry . . . ?"

There was no real warning – or perhaps a sharp inhalation of breath, a further tensing of his body next to hers – but Rosalind knew, threw herself towards him and looped her arms about his, pulling them down and towards her. "No, Mark!"

The three of them struggled there, in the dark, for to Geoff it seemed as if the gun had been turned on Rosalind, or pulled by her own volition towards her and away from himself. He had Mark's hand in his, was forcing the gun upwards, or trying to, when it discharged.

It was difficult to know what had happened. The roar at such close quarters made Geoff's head ring. There were one or two seconds of shock before he realised that he had not been shot. *Rosalind . . .*

She stumbled backwards, her cream-coloured dress was splashed with black. She teetered and would have fallen, had not Geoff reached out an arm for her.

But it was Mark who fell.

How did she find the gun? Had it fallen into her hand as Mark felt the bullet rip through him? She had it now. Geoff was on his knees beside her – he was close enough to see that she had it.

"Rosalind?"

She crawled to Mark, murmuring his name, and they were all, then, on the forest floor, the thick vines cushioning their hands and feet. There was a dreadful pause as he saw her cradling Mark's head, and he could only watch as she brought the gun up towards her face.

"*Rosalind*." He dared not shout, dared not reach out to her, for the gun – that small black deadly thing in her grasp – seemed to have a life of its own. It moved between them, and watching her colourless little oval of a face he thought his heart would stop in his terror for her.

Sobbing, she placed the muzzle in her mouth.

"*Oh, God Rosalind, no . . .*"

He put out one hand, pleadingly, and almost reached her.

"Anything, Roz – anything you want . . ."

Mark. Even Mark.

"Rosalind – he might not be dead. Roz, don't do it. Mark might only be hurt, he might not be dead."

The little grey shape did not move. But she listened.

"Give me the gun, love." Gently, "We have to go for help, get him to a hospital."

The gun came away from her mouth, slowly.

"Give me the gun, love."

She moved Mark's fair head from her lap, as carefully as if he were a sleeping child, and when he was resting quietly, so quietly, on the earth, she stood up.

Geoff, in his relief, moved towards her quickly, and she screamed then, suddenly, held the gun out towards him with both hands and fired.

CHAPTER TWENTY-TWO

Rosalind ran blindly up the slope and onto the road, back towards the only safety that she knew – the drive that led to the beach house. When the police car came around the heavily wooded bend, they almost did not see her in time. Slewing across the road, they came close to colliding with the car travelling behind them. Both cars skidded, came to a halt at strange angles across the road, and a truck coming from the opposite direction saw them only just in time. Caught in the cross lights of the vehicles, Rosalind stood still. Her arms were wrapped about her head, as if blocking out the sights and sounds of a world that had become too insane for her to bear.

Geoff was not badly hurt, though he would always bear a deep scar across his forehead where the bullet ploughed through his flesh and scraped his skull, taking away a narrow strip of his hair at the temple.

"She ducked her head as she fired," the

policeman told Leo. "Women do that. Scared of the noise. Lucky for her husband."

Lucky for everyone, Leo thought. Lucky they were driving so slowly, looking for a break in the vegetation that might take them down into the bush where the three were, the windows wound down for any sounds of more shots.

Lucky that Mark was still alive when they found him. Geoff, a pad of dressing from the police first aid box pressed to his head, guided Constable Cameron and Leo down through the jungle-like growth to where Mark lay. The young police-woman stayed with Rosalind.

Rosalind did not speak. Not at all. And did not seem to hear any words that were addressed to her. Grief over her young lover being shot – that's what everyone believed – everyone except Mark, of course.

When Leo and the young police constable found him, they tried to make him as comfortable as possible. He regained consciousness to hear their voices, to hear Geoffrey Harcourt's voice, telling of the events.

Leo sat close to Mark, and in the dim light of the police torch, aimed away from their eyes towards that part of the rainforest through which their rescuers would come, he saw him watching Geoff, quietly. He was in shock, and must have been in great pain, but he seemed lucid. After Geoff had given his account, he murmured something, barely intelligible.

Leo bent closer to hear, and the young officer, his notebook still clutched in his hand, came to Mark's side as well. "Did you say something, sir?"

It was hard for him to speak, but, "He's . . . right," Mark said. "Everything . . . he said . . . is right."

"You mean, you *were* going to shoot him, before Mrs Harcourt deflected the gun and the three of you struggled?"

Again a long pause while he battled for breath, and the strength, "He said . . . he *thought* . . . I was going . . . to shoot him. Don't . . . lead the witness . . . Constable."

The young officer blushed and looked discomfited. He did not know Mark, didn't recognise the humour in his eyes, fighting with the pain.

Mark said, "Geoff . . . could . . . have thought . . . I was. It . . . was an accident. I tripped a little . . . I pulled the trigger." His eyes rolled upwards a little and his lids closed.

"Oh, God," the constable muttered.

"Yes, indeed," Leo murmured, feeling Mark's pulse at his neck, still beating, faintly, evenly. "He's just unconscious."

There were sirens soon after, and lights appeared around the bend in the distant hillside, travelling down towards them. The pale gold of headlights and scarlet and blue flashes glinted through the trees, and Leo almost wept with relief, so welcome was the sight.

340

"I'm going back to Rosalind," Geoff said. Leo sensed, rather than saw, the policeman glance at him speculatively. The woman had shot him, and he wanted to be with her?

Geoff went off, up the slope, towards the lights that were now coming down from the roadway towards them.

"How could I blame her for what she did?" he told Leo later. "She almost blew her own brains out – is *that* sane? And I went to grab her – I really was going to rush her – and I knew she was hysterical and deathly afraid of me. I'm only glad I'm still alive. I don't believe she wanted to *kill* me, she just wanted to *stop* me."

Geoff saw Rosalind only briefly before the ambulance officers led him away to have his head wound attended to. She did not shrink from him when he appeared before her. The policewoman watched them, warily, but there was no need to worry. Geoff took Rosalind by the hand, and she turned unseeing eyes to him, made no objection when he drew her to her feet.

This, perhaps, was the most frightening thing of all for Geoff. He looked into her face, but she looked past him, through him. Down there in the rainforest, she had looked like a ghost; now she felt like one, as if she was not there, in his arms, at all. He held her to him, but there was no response. His tears fell on her hair, and she looked over his shoulder into the night.

"I'll be whatever you want me to be. As near, or as far, as you like. It'll be alright."

But he knew she could not hear him.

As Leo accompanied Mark's stretcher up the slope towards the waiting ambulances, Mark told him about the tapes.

"There are fifty or more . . . in a cardboard box in the second drawer of the desk. And diaries. Key . . ." His hand fumbled at his trouser pocket, Leo removed the keys for him. "Smallest . . ." he managed, "second drawer of desk . . ."

"Yes, I understand, but what . . ."

"You take them." Firmly. "*All* of them."

What had he done? Leo looked down at him, feeling so helpless. There was so little time. "Mark, will you make a confession now? I don't want details – you know what to say – if you mean it. Mark . . . quickly, boy."

But by then they had reached the road, and Mark had turned his head and seen Rosalind.

She did not see him. Or if she *did* see the stretcher and its burden she made no sign. She was sitting in the front seat of the police car, with the door open, leaning sideways against the seat. Her feet were still resting on the roadway. The young policewoman offered her a cup of tea from a thermos, but Rosalind made no move to take it.

"Mark?" Leo reminded him gently.

Mark turned. His face had a ghastly pallor, and Leo was desperately afraid for him.

"Alright," he said. "Only because . . . of what . . . she'll have to go through now."

Leo thought he meant the scandal. Then, of course, even though he had seen the door behind the mirror, he had no idea of the whole terrible truth.

"Mark," Leo said, patiently, as he was rushed towards the open doors of the ambulance, "I can't absolve you if your only regret is that you didn't succeed."

Mark turned towards him and made an effort to smile, "Poor Leo. It's alright. You have . . . to follow . . . orders."

Leo was stricken. Was that what Mark thought of him? Was that what he still thought?

Was it the truth?

Leo thought quickly. "Mark, do you *know* what wrong you've done?"

The blue eyes looked up at him with genuine puzzlement. And, even after reading the diaries, listening to the tapes, Leo still believed that he spoke the truth in that moment. "*Wrong?*" he said. "No."

The ambulance officers lifted him into the vehicle. The stretcher slid forward, away from Leo.

"I absolve you, in the name of the Father, the Son and the Holy Spirit . . ." And he blessed him.

It was the last thing Mark saw before the doors closed upon him.

By the time they had all been questioned at the hospital, and each of them had settled into their various rooms, it was very late and the news of the shooting was being sent out all over Australia, all over the world. There would be Harcourt friends and Harcourt enemies in London, New York, Los Angeles, Tokyo who would have their days brightened or ruined by the headlines: *HARCOURT LOVE TRIANGLE ENDS IN TRAGEDY*. There were others, too, all sensational.

Leo tiptoed down the corridor in his hospital pyjamas to phone the Archbishop in Sydney. How had he, Father Leo Calder, one of his most unimaginative, most *reliable* priests, got caught up in this? His name, and the Church he represented, was being bandied about television, radio and newspaper offices everywhere. It was dreadful.

All Leo's agonised rehearsing, while his head was being stitched, his two broken ribs were being examined and he was being dosed with pain killers, was unnecessary. His Grace was not in Sydney, his assistant said. He had left that evening for his yearly leave. He was spending a month with his brother and his family and would be back on the third of December. Leaving, so close to Advent? Leo thought. He knew where His Grace's brother lived.

"Doubtless he'll be in touch with you himself, Father," the calm voice went on. "I expect you'll be in Brisbane too?"

"Well, I ..."

"His Grace tells me you have a fellow seminarian, Father Tom Hunt, who's at St Ann's in Toowong ..." Leo could hear the papers rustling – he was trying to find the names.

"Yes," Leo murmured, "I'm good friends with Father Hunt, though it's been many years."

"He'll be delighted to have you to stay," the voice continued complacently. "Just let him know when you're arriving, and he'll meet you at the airport."

"And ... His Grace?"

A reassuring smile sounded in the officious young voice, "His Grace will be in touch."

LEO

I t may be that His Grace will say, "You have
been too lenient upon the man. How much is
conjecture? In telling his story you seem to be
struggling to find reasons for everything he did. You
have not once mentioned the word 'evil', Father."

No, Your Grace.

But His Grace has not been to the hospital. If he
does go – and perhaps he will – and sees the face
of that young man, who is so very far from us and
so close to God, he may hesitate to use that word.
What Mark *did* was evil, but that does not make
Mark an evil man. He is too far from me now, and
too close to God. I must leave him to his Father in
heaven.

Geoff comes to the hospital every day. We stand
there and look at Mark, and we say very little.
Geoff blames himself for the shooting. Rosalind, I
do not doubt, blames herself, while Mark, before
he lost consciousness, claimed it was his doing. I,
too, have my demons. If I had moved faster across

the study towards the boy, if I had found the words to stop him . . .

I returned to the beach house early the next morning, and found the tapes and the diaries, just as he had told me. I brought them away with me, to this modern little brick presbytery in Brisbane. We are all now, after one night in hospital in Cairns, in Brisbane. Mark lies fighting for his life. Neither Geoff nor I wish to leave Mark, and as for Rosalind . . .

My friend, Tom Hunt, is a sensible and kindly man. It was he who suggested Villa Maria. Originally housing a closed order that did not mingle with the world, the world of later years has come to Villa Maria, and many lay folk have been on retreats there and found peace amongst the gentle sisters, their well-tended gardens, their peaceful house. Rosalind attends prayers and every Mass. She moves her lips during the responses, but so far she has not spoken. The police want to move her to a psychiatric centre. They want her cured and speaking as soon as possible, it will tidy up the ends of the matter – so much easier for them. Geoff, however, trusts me, and I feel that Rosalind is safer where she is. Safer, and happier.

Geoff visits her, but she does not recognise him. I can see that it breaks his heart. I do not dare tell him that the only response I have elicited is when I have mentioned Mark's name. She turns and looks at me, but what feelings lie beneath her cool gaze, I cannot tell.

I left her today, seated in the shade in a corner of the garden. One of the young novices, who has had a few years of nursing training, has been assigned to look after her. The girl was brushing Rosalind's hair. "We don't have to cut our hair any more," she told me, "but I keep mine very short under my veil anyway, or it's too hot." She gazed down at Rosalind's hair, "Isn't hers lovely?" And she added, quite loudly, to Rosalind, "Your hair is lovely!"

I thought of reminding the lass that Rosalind is not deaf, but then I thought, no. If Rosalind becomes too irritated, she may feel driven to speak for herself.

I hate to think of her leaving this place. There are wonderful hospitals in Sydney, but I fear for her there. The best psychiatrists in the world, with the best of intentions, will only perpetuate the nightmare of the studio for her. I wish I could save her from it. I am praying that a solution will come to me.

Mark looks so young. A machine keeps his heart pumping and another breathes for him. In the midst of all the technology and equipment, his fair head lies on the pillow, all dark thoughts and all pain gone from his face. It is the face of a small boy, asleep on a narrow bed in a dormitory. A boy with hope and life and love before him. Here, at the end, he is my Mark once more.

The doctor said today, "There's almost no chance, Father," but I knew that already. It's a matter of waiting, and praying, now.

As I was leaving, the doctor said, "If he does wake, we'll call you straight away."

I looked back at him. If Mark woke, it would not be me he called for.

The doctor said, "Try to stay by the phone, won't you?" He added, "But he may go at any time, without warning."

I leave Mark's side only to sleep, or to visit Rosalind.

If he wakes . . .

He may wake. He may live.

If he wakes, he will want to see her. Only then will he decide if he wants to live.

If he wakes, and he wants to see Rosalind, do I go to her and tell her? Do I go to Geoff, as Rosalind is *his* wife, is in *his* care? What if Geoff says no?

If Geoff knew about the tapes, about the room behind the mirror – a harmless store room now, filled with boxes, newspapers, exercise equipment and spare furniture, a bed, a table, a chair – if Geoff knew the truth, he would not let Rosalind go to Mark.

And if Mark awoke, and called for Rosalind, and she did not come – would he *want* to live?

And if Mark did live? The Archbishop would not – and could my conscience disagree – allow him to go free.

Mark might go to prison. Or to a hospital for the criminally insane. They will lock the boy away with thieves and killers . . .

I cannot still the small voice that whispers at the edge of my mind. *It would be better for Mark if he should die. He would, given the choices, want to die.*

If he wakes, if he calls for her, I will go to Rosalind.

It's late. I have sat here, in front of His Grace's letter, for five hours. He brought his stationery on holiday with him; I wish he hadn't. A simple note would have sufficed. The official note paper looks so intimidating. The telephone is ringing.

The telephone is ringing.

Other books by Veronica Sweeney

The Emancipist

0–7322–5742–5
$14.95

From his earliest days in Ireland, Aidan O'Brien was only too aware of the insurmountable social gulf separating his family from that of the wealthy Devlin Kelly. This gulf forms the basis of their lifelong feud.

While Devlin inherits the privileged position of landlord, Aidan, like so many Irish tenant farmers, finds his life devastated by the successive failures of the potato crops in the 1840s. Through his participation in the ensuing unrest, Aidan is sentenced to twelve years in Australia.

Eventually Aidan joins an exclusive breed of wealthy and powerful colonials, and looks set to carve a new destiny for himself – one that nevertheless holds a final confrontation with Devlin Kelly.

"*The Emancipist* tells a galloping tale arising in Ireland in the potato famine years of the nineteenth century . . . a tale of triumph against all odds." – *The Age*

"Impressively researched and detailed account of Ireland's sufferings under the English and the pioneering days of Australia . . . a gripping story . . . " – *The New York Times Book Review*

South Lies the Valley

0-7322-5743-3
$14.95

The mannered drawing rooms
of Victorian colonial society
hold little appeal for a woman
such as Katherine Carron. Her
intelligence, perception and
ambition make her all too aware
of the hypocrisy, the hidden lusts
and the cruelties of her time.
They make her aware, too, of
how little freedom she possesses.

After the Fenian rebellion of 1866, Katherine is
released from a loveless marriage and, fleeing from the
one man she finds herself drawn to, both intellectually
and physically, she returns to her homeland, Australia.
But here the laws of society are equally strict, and
Katherine must fight even her own beloved family for
her right to independence.

Australia, newly emerging towards nationhood, is a
rough and sometimes savage place, more bloody and
more violent than the turbulent Ireland Katherine left
behind.

"Fiery-spirited, credible, compelling . . . Sweeney's grasp
of social history is as authentic as her portrayal of
human passion." – *Publishers Weekly*

A Turn of the Blade

0–7322–5698–4
$14.95

Angry and grieving over the break-up of her marriage, book editor Sarah Stanforth dreams of vengeance against Erica Tudor, the young and beautiful author her husband Keir has come to love.

Driving north from New York with a confused idea of confronting Erica in her country home, Sarah is careless of her fate and her ultimate destination. Eventually, in the Canadian town of St Claude, through her interactions and growing friendships with the caring, sometimes eccentric locals, Sarah begins to heal herself.

She is at last contemplating a future without Keir when, out of the blue, Erica drives up to her isolated farmhouse and Sarah's past thoughts of revenge turn into a dark nightmare . . .

"... a gripping story of revenge that switches between New York's fast-paced publishing world and the backblocks of Canada ... an inspired change of direction for Veronica Sweeney ... one of our biggest-selling writers ... " – *Australian Women's Weekly*